Swede On You
Love in Larkspur Series Book 2

Katie Stearns

Chapter One

Lee

My stomach grumbles as I step inside, met immediately with the delicious aroma of coffee, sugar, and butter. Laughter and familiar voices drift from the kitchen. I kick off my shoes and head through the living room of my parents' house, feeling the stares of the many *tomten* statues watching me from all over the room. Mamma swears those tiny gnomes protect the house and everyone inside it. Regardless of whether that's true or not, the sight of them is just as comforting and familiar to me as the well-loved couches and family pictures on the walls.

Fika is a staple of my life, going back as long as I can remember. It's a Swedish tradition from Mamma's side of the family, where you intentionally set aside the time to catch up with friends and family over coffee and baked goods. Mamma takes it very seriously.

I head into the dining room where Pappa is sitting at the head of the table.

"*Hej*," he says, lifting his white coffee mug to me with a weathered smile.

I dip my chin in greeting.

Looking at Pappa is like a glimpse of my future. Tall and broad with brown eyes and dirty blonde hair, though his is streaked silver now. I wish I had gotten his warm personality too, but somehow it skipped me and went to Will instead.

Will waves tiredly, slumped in his chair. His green eyes, which he inherited from Mamma, quickly return to his girlfriend Lacey, following wherever she flits to in the kitchen.

"Hey, stranger," I say to him, because even though he moved in with me in January after he left Larkspur Inn to open his restaurant, I probably see him less now than I did when we didn't sleep under the same roof. He wouldn't be here if it wasn't a Monday when The Swedish Chef is closed.

"There he is!" Lacey calls cheerfully.

I side-eye her like she might be a rabid racoon. When she first moved here from Minneapolis this winter, I thought she was trying to butter me up by always greeting me with so much enthusiasm. Turns out she's just really happy to see the people she cares about. I'm glad I'm one of them, even if I envy how easily she shows her emotions.

"Come bring this," Mamma says, bypassing a greeting. She holds out a plate of *kanelbullar*, or Swedish cinnamon buns, from the other side of the kitchen island. She's wearing her favorite faded blue apron with yellow flowers, her graying light brown hair pulled back into a neat French braid.

I take the plate as Lacey passes me with the coffee, patting my arm as she goes by.

"No Lars today," Mamma says with disapproval, her eyebrows lifted like it's somehow my fault.

I sigh. *Definitely not my fault.* Since my best friend Lars started dating his girlfriend Amber back in December, I've seen a lot less of him—and he's been showing up to *fika* less, too.

Mamma follows me to the table with a plate of *drömmar* cookies. I put down the plate next to the coffee, and then sit across from Lacey. Mamma sits next to me and reaches for the coffeepot.

"I saw Mark at coffee the other day," Pappa says, referring to Lars's dad. "He said Lars hasn't been himself lately." His brown eyes find mine. "Have you seen him much, Lee?"

I hold out my coffee cup so Mamma can fill it. "Not much. Cancelled on me the last three times." We usually go to the Drunken Mallard for a beer and a burger every Friday. *Before Amber, that is.*

"Amber came into the shop last week," Lacey adds, snagging a cookie. "I asked how things were going with Lars, and she complained about how he always smells like motor oil."

I roll my eyes. "He can't exactly help that," I grit out between my teeth. "He's a mechanic, for Pete's sake."

Mamma makes a disgruntled sound and mutters something in Swedish I don't catch.

Lars is an honorary Christiansen kid. Growing up, he was always here—probably ate dinner with us three times a week during the summer. He gravitated toward me over my two younger siblings, despite them being more friendly and outgoing than me. He's family, so seeing him less lately seems strange and unlike him. *I'm his best friend—I shouldn't have to make an appointment at the shop just to see him.*

"Svea says she's on her way," Lacey says from her place next to Will, looking at her phone.

"She's not bringing that boyfriend, is she?" Mamma asks, scowling.

"Hope not," I out roughly. She's been seeing Clay Cox since the Holly Ball, and we all hate him. Honestly, I don't even think Svea likes him that much. They've "taken a break" at least three times in as many months.

"I think they're off again," Lacey says, then lowers her voice with a wince. "It's hard to keep track, honestly."

Will's nose wrinkles up as he leans forward with his coffee cup. Mamma fills it as he says, "I would never try to convince Svea to do literally anything, because she wouldn't listen anyway, but there has to be some way we can get her to break up with him for good."

Lifting a cinnamon bun to my mouth, I take a bite and chew thoughtfully. He's right about Svea. There's no telling her anything she doesn't want to hear. Mamma gave up years ago, and if she won't listen to *Mamma*, then I don't know who she would listen to. Definitely not her overprotective older brothers.

"She'll figure it out," Pappa assures us.

There's only a slight pause before Lacey pipes up. "Soooo...anything exciting happen this week?"

I don't have to look up to know she's talking to me. She asks me this almost every time I see her. Just to be a pain, I take another bite of cinnamon goodness to delay answering.

Being a police officer makes me privy to a lot of the events which become the basis of town gossip. Just a couple of weeks ago, a colleague pulled over Sandy Leeland for rolling a stop sign. Two days later at the grocery store I overheard Sandy got out of a ticket by flashing him her boobs. So naturally, Lacey wants all the details. Unfortunately for her, most of what happens at my job involves reports and paperwork.

"Nothing crazy," I say in a bored tone.

Disappointment deflates her face for a moment but then her eyes brighten.

"What's the craziest thing you've ever seen as a police officer?" she blurts out expectantly, like I might have some wild story about a drug bust or double homicide. Drug busts are few in our community, and thankfully there hasn't been a murder in Larkspur since before I was born.

My annoyed look does nothing to wither her bright expression. With a sigh, I sit back and decide to have a little fun.

"I do have one story," I say slowly, putting on a hesitant, begrudging expression which makes Lacey bounce in her chair with excitement.

"I won't tell a soul, Lee, I swear!"

I narrow my eyes. "Swear?" I repeat, and she thrusts her pinky finger at me.

Will chuckles and pulls her hand back.

"What is it?" Pappa asks, his curiosity piqued as well.

I clear my throat. "There was this one winter storm," I start, inflating my usual stern, surly way of speaking with something a little more mysterious. "I was on the highway, making sure no one was in the ditch needing help, and I came across this car stopped. So I slow down and get out to make sure everything is alright. The woman in the car didn't seem hurt, but as soon as she opened the door, I realized this lady was completely losing her mind. I was afraid for my safety." Lacey's brown eyes are wide, hanging on every word. The table is quiet, everyone's attention glued to me, probably because I never talk about the things I encounter at work. "When I asked her what happened, she kept going on and on about what she swore she hit."

"What did she hit?" Lacey breathes out in a rush, hands clutched beneath her chin.

A faint smile crosses my lips as I take a sip of coffee. "She swore it was a Yeti, but it was just an albino deer."

Pappa barks out a laugh and Mamma snickers too.

Lacey's previously uplifted eyebrows fall instantly, but then she smirks at me in good humor. "It was an accident!" she exclaims, just how she always does whenever anyone brings up Albie, the famed albino deer she hit this winter.

"It ended up being the best thing that could've happened, though," Will says with a dopey smile. Lacey returns it and kisses his freckled cheek.

"Agree to disagree," I mutter.

Lacey throws a napkin at me, laughing. "You love me, Lee. Don't pretend."

"I'd love you to quiet down, yes."

Will snorts while Mamma shakes her head.

The front door swings open and shut. Svea traipses in, sweeping her light brown hair over her shoulder as she sits down at the foot of the table.

"Hello family," she chirps happily. She helps herself to a cookie as everyone says hello.

Out of the corner of her mouth, Lacey mutters what sounds like, "definitely off again."

My shoulders tense. A happy Svea is a pranking Svea.

I quickly scan her—searching for any indication she's concealed something in the pockets of the handmade dress she's wearing. I drag my mug closer, scraping across the tabletop, because she's been known to salt people's coffee when they aren't looking.

The last prank she played on me was at Holly Ball right before Christmas, where she stuck a Post-It note on my back which read, "kick me." I thought for sure she would get me on April Fools' Day—which is her favorite day of the year—but the day came and went without incident. She targeted Will instead by setting off a glitter bomb in his truck. Took him an entire week to get it all out, and sometimes I swear I still see a shimmering speck on his clothes when he gets home.

I'm definitely due for a prank, and being in the same room as her has me on edge.

"Sorry I'm late," she says, chewing. "I got totally in the zone with a dress I'm working on."

Lacey gasps. "The wedding dress?"

Svea grins back at her business partner. "Yup. I should be able to start the beading tomorrow."

"The shop is doing well, then?" Mamma asks before Lacey can squeal out her delight. The amount of squealing she and Svea do when they talk about clothing is unreal. On occasion, I go over to hang out with them and Will at their apartment above Svea's shop. After the first time I bought some earplugs. Their friendship is *loud*.

"I'd say so," Svea replies proudly.

"And the restaurant is too?" Pappa asks Will, who nods with a tired smile.

"It's only been about a month, but yeah, I think it's doing alright."

Lacey scoffs with a big smile. "It's packed every night, Will. The restaurant is doing *great*."

He smiles softly and brings her hand to his mouth.

Mamma lets out a quiet sigh. "So nice to hear everyone is doing well." She eyes Will with a measure of guilt pinching her expression, because for the first time Will is doing what he wants to be doing career-wise. She pushes the plate of cookies toward him. "Especially you."

"It's been a whirlwind," he says with a sigh, dragging his hand through his hair. "I couldn't have done any of it without you guys." He glances around at everyone else. "Thank you."

Pappa pats him on the shoulder with a proud smile. "Say, did you hear the Gustafsons bought a cabin in Ely?"

The conversation moves on without me.

My mind stays on what Mamma said. Sure, I'm happy being a police officer, but there was a time when I wanted something else. Apparently, Kindergarten teachers require a softer, friendlier personality. Police officer suits me better.

Svea leans over, squinting at me. "What's that face for, Grumpy Goose?"

I scowl at her. "Nothing."

She raises one eyebrow expectantly, looking very much like our all-knowing mother. No one is paying attention to us and I'd like that to continue. I lower my voice.

"This is just how my face looks."

Svea snorts but lowers her voice too. "You think I can't tell when something is bothering you? Spill, dude."

"There's nothing to spill," I growl. "Drop it."

She sighs and rolls her eyes.

I turn back to the rest of the table.

"They said we could come up and visit as soon as they put in a new deck," Pappa says with a grin.

Svea kicks my shin and leans closer. "You know you can tell me things. You don't have to be so private about everything."

I kick her back and finish my cinnamon roll. When I say nothing, my nosy little sister finally sits back with a huff.

There's no use in telling anyone what I'm upset about. So I'm too intimidating to be a Kindergarten teacher. That can't be changed. It is what it is. Thankfully, I'm good at my job and I have a good reason for doing it. That's really all I need.

I don't say anything else for the remainder of *fika*, and no one seems to notice.

The late June prairie wind pummels me as I get out of my truck and stride across the street to my favorite building in Larkspur. The library has seen better days. The white paint is peeling in places and the cement sidewalk is cracked and crumbling at the edges. But the flower beds flanking the wheelchair accessible ramp give the whole thing a friendly boost.

Library book in hand, I eye the daisies in particular before I go inside.

The dry, sweet scent of aging books meets my nose like an old friend. Everything relaxes as I take in the well-worn dark green carpet spread out beneath my feet and the off-white ceiling tiles hanging above. To the left is the kid's area, with shorter wooden bookshelves, a few kid's toys, a round rug and a green velvet chair used for storytime. Beyond, beige metal bookshelves stand tall in neat rows, and to the right are a few tables set up, some with computers.

My stupid heart beats so hard it hurts when I spot Emma Mackenzie standing behind the library checkout counter. She's wearing a maroon sundress with a gray cable knit cardigan, her glossy black hair laying gently on her small shoulders. Her attention focuses on the computer slightly to her right, one hand on the mouse, the other holding a book. The computer screen reflects a little white square in each lens of her black framed glasses.

Her little shy smiles have haunted me since high school. I'm at the library once a week, sometimes twice, not just because I like to read, but because it gives me a reason to see her. Because the library is the only link I have to her. The only way I can be in her orbit.

I squeeze the book in my hand as I move toward the counter. She looks up with the kind of pleasant smile no one else would think twice about. But to me it's everything.

A nervous lump forms in my throat. She's the only person I get nervous around because I care what she thinks of me. *So much.*

"Hey, Emma," I say and set down the book on the counter next to a handful of flyers for various things like Book Club and story time.

"Hi," she answers sweetly, quiet as usual.

Her eyes are a color I've never seen on anyone else. From a distance, they look like a deep, dark brown. But up close, they're only dark brown around the edges, and the inner ring surrounding her pupil is an iridescent sort of dark green. Like gasoline mixed with honey.

I glance down at the book of poetry and try to think of something to say about it, but not one single thing comes to mind.

My heart just beats harder, as if it's chanting *Emma! Emma! Emma!*

She smiles softly at *Walden* by Henry David Thoreau and reaches for it so she can add it to her stack of books to return. Her trimmed fingernails are painted a summery peachy pink.

"We just received a new Emily Dickinson book," she says with a bright expression, her creamy complexion just slightly rosy at her cheeks. "*The Gorgeous Nothings.* I just shelved it this morning."

My eyebrows raise slightly.

You just shelved it this morning...and thought of me?

I give her my friendliest smile, which really just comes out as a broad, close-lipped smile.

"Thanks, I'll check it out."

She smiles a little bigger, hopefully because she's pleased I'm taking her recommendation.

My head swimming a little from her smiling at me, I quickly find the D's and locate the book she mentioned.

I flip through it, realizing it's all poetry written on scraps of paper and used envelopes.

Huh.

That's really interesting.

My chest warms realizing some part of her knows exactly what I like reading.

I shouldn't be surprised. Books are the only thing we've ever talked about, and besides my occupation, my preferred genre is the only personal thing she knows about me. The sappy part of me wants to read into it because I've been in love with her for years. But the logical part of me says it's much more likely she's just a fantastic librarian who loves her job.

I take the book back to the checkout counter.

"Found it," I say unnecessarily, and dig out my library card from my wallet.

Emma beams and scans my card and then the book. "I hope you like it."

"Sure I will."

She hands me back my library card, and her warm fingers brush mine, sending a zing all the way up my arm.

"Due back July 15th," she informs me softly, even though we both know I'll be back next week. It's nice of her to pretend that I don't know I could check out all the books I want and only show up once a month to return them.

"Thanks," I say, and the familiar stab of wanting to talk to her more but not knowing what to say hits me in the chest.

"Have a good day." Her smile is genuine, and so is her tone.

"You too."

Resigning myself that I'll be reliving this interaction for the next week until I see her again, I casually rap my knuckles three times on the counter and turn for the door.

My shoulders sag and my smile fades as I move away from her. But just when I reach for the door handle, Emma speaks again.

"Oh—Lee, wait," she calls out, and my head whips to look over my shoulder.

She's coming around the counter with a sheet of paper in her hands. The excitement on her sweet face has butterflies exploding in my stomach.

"I forgot to tell you—on Sunday we're having an Author Event," she says, handing me the flyer. I look down at it unseeingly, too happy she's

SWEDE ON YOU 11

talking to me to even read it. "Garrett Waterstone is coming to talk about his new book, and he'll be doing a signing too. We're so excited to have such a big name come to our little library!"

I smile, enamored by her excitement. "Sounds cool, Emma."

"We're expecting a big turnout, so make sure you get here early if you want a seat. It starts at 2."

Warmth fills me up.

"I'll be there," I tell her, grateful that I have Sunday off.

"Can't wait." She steps back; the combination of her grin and the blush on her face has my chest buzzing.

Mostly though, I'm surprised.

She can't wait to see me there?

She fidgets with the leg of her glasses as she smiles one more time, and then she heads back to the counter.

I turn back to the door and push it open, the warm summer air smacking me in the face. I let the door close, standing there on the stoop like one of those damn cartoons with hearts coming out of their eyes.

She went out of her way to invite me.

Huh.

No one really invites me to things. I can't say I blame anybody. I know how people see me. Being a police officer keeps people from wanting to get too close. Even walking through the grocery store without my uniform on, I still see the way people straighten up and speak to me in an overly polite way. I've lost count of how many times people have been talking about a funny story and then suddenly clamp their mouth shut because they were about to admit they did something less than legal. That factor wasn't something I considered when I became a police officer, and it can be alienating, even in my hometown.

So no, I'm not used to people including me. Even beyond my profession, I come off intimidating. It's not intentional, though I sometimes use my gruff personality to my advantage in my job when I need to. My get-to-the-point tendencies aren't exactly warm and fuzzy, so people don't really enjoy my company.

That's how I know my chances with someone like Emma are nil. She's shy and soft-spoken with people she doesn't feel comfortable around, and that definitely includes me. Which is why asking her out is something I repeatedly talk myself out of.

I know Emma. Her shyness is almost as impenetrable as my intimidating personality. She's *never* initiated seeing me outside of the library, and I doubt she ever would. There's no interest there, even if Will thinks otherwise.

But what did she mean? *Can't wait?*

Did she mean she can't wait for the event because it's such a big deal to have whatever his name is, coming to our library?

Or...did she mean she can't wait for me to be there too?

Did she tell me to come early so that I could get a seat next to *her*?

I scoff at myself, but then I look down at the book in my hand. It's proof that at least I'm on her radar—even if it's a work-related radar. It's more than I could hope for at this point.

I fold the flyer in half and stick it inside the book. Sunday is four long days from now, and I already feel myself leaning forward in anticipation because I'll get to see her again.

I head for my truck but don't get far. The flowers wave at me in the wind, and I don't hesitate to go over and pick one single daisy.

Inside my truck, I set the book on the passenger seat and reach for the glove compartment. I take out my sketchbook from beneath the user's manual and small first-aid kit. The pages are all wrinkled and rippled from use, strewn with smears of dirt and ink. I open it to the next blank page and put the daisy there. Then, I carefully close the book so it stays in place.

I put it back under the manual and first aid kit so that the weight will keep the book closed tightly as the flower dries.

Closing the compartment with a slam, I let out a sigh.

It's useful to be stubborn sometimes. I'm too stubborn to stop running, but that keeps me in good shape. I'm too stubborn about following the rules, probably, but that just keeps me in good standing as a citizen and as a police officer. I'm too stubborn about the company I keep, but that just means that I can truly trust the people closest to me.

Stubbornness can be good in some situations.

Being stubbornly in love with Emma Mackenzie is not one of them.

Chapter Two

Emma

T he front door opens and slams shut. It startles me so violently my book drops from my hands, landing face down with a loud *plop*. I gasp and quickly stoop to pick it up off the kitchen linoleum as my sister barges into the house.

I frown at my book in dismay.

There goes my page.

I can't keep my eyes away from the newest Elinor Riverside book. Even at work, I kept sneaking pages here and there between library patrons. Her love stories are masterpieces of human rawness and visceral emotions. If I could write, I would write books like hers. Instead, I purposely lose myself in them, because at the end there's always a happily ever after.

"Hey," Caitlin says distractedly, her attention down on her phone as she slides onto one of the two stools on the other side of the kitchen peninsula.

"Hey Cait."

Setting the book down reluctantly on the counter, I go over and lift the lid off the crockpot. My glasses momentarily fog up, oregano and lemon perfuming the kitchen from Dad's favorite meal simmering inside.

Mom's laughter drifting from the living room makes me smile. She's watching her favorite show, *The Bachelorette*, her wheelchair pulled up alongside the couch with a glass of white wine in her hand. It's the simple things she enjoys the most, especially since the car accident that paralyzed her from the waist down and we lost Dad twelve years ago.

We've long gotten accustomed to the changes made to the house for Mom to stay living here. Widened hallways and doorways, low-clearance carpeting in the living room, an accessible shower. All of it had to be done while she was recovering in the hospital. Caitlin and I were teenagers dealing with the death of one parent and the marked change in the other. A daily home health nurse now required to help her do the things she didn't want us to have to do.

It seems like forever ago, and even though Mom, Caitlin, and I found a new routine, I still think of Dad often. I still wish I could tell him about every book I finish. He was a reader too. His books are still here, sitting on the shelves in the den like little pieces of everything he loved.

Caitlin snorts as I replace the lid. She's rolling her eyes in response to whoever she's texting with, her thumbs flying over her screen.

She's wearing a flowery, boho-chic dress with a lower neckline than I would wear myself. Her blonde hair is perfectly styled in loose waves, as it should be because she's a hair stylist. The frustrated expression on her perfect face has me instantly bracing myself.

Adjusting my glasses on the bridge of my nose, I glance at my book on the counter. Before I can decide if it would be rude to pick it up again—she dives right into it.

"You know," she breathes out with a tense sigh, "sometimes I feel bad for you because the only relationships you've been in are fictional," she snarls, glaring at her phone.

"*Hey*," I respond defensively, but she continues, her irritated blue eyes meeting mine.

"But then I realize you haven't had to deal with how stupid men are in real life, and I can only envy you." She tosses her phone on the counter and folds her arms with a scowl.

My defenses melt away, because what she's saying has nothing to do with me. It's true we're pretty much total opposites. Caitlin has always been the pretty, extroverted, popular one. In high school she was on the dance team, which performed at the football games Gavin played in. She was voted Prom Queen and always had hordes of friends.

And me? I had mostly acquaintances, zero boyfriends, and spent all my spare time between the pages of a book. Nothing has changed since then. Mostly by choice. Working at the library, where I have unlimited access to books, is my dream job, but my shyness doesn't help in the boyfriend, or even friend, department.

It's clear as day that we couldn't be more different. Even after Dad died, Caitlin stayed very much the same—and possibly became even more popular in our community. I shied further away from people and the world, delving headfirst into every book Dad owned. Then, into any book I could get my hands on at the school library.

Years later, I'm still deeply invested in reading and books, both as a career and in my free time. While Caitlin is the most sought-after hair stylist for fifty miles around...and still chasing Gavin.

I narrow my eyes, realizing who she was texting with.

"What did he do this time?" I ask, because it's almost every week he gets on my sister's nerves.

She rolls her eyes again and huffs. "He doesn't want to go to the Street Dance next week. It's the first year they're having one, and it sounds so fun."

Oh yeah, I remember hearing about that. Usually Larkspur only has one dance, the Holly Ball, at the community center right before Christmas. Even though I'm way too shy and self-conscious to dance, I still like to go and watch everyone else dancing the night away.

This year the Chamber decided to close Main Street on the Fourth of July before the fireworks to have a Street Dance. Everyone is excited about it. Except Gavin, apparently.

"Why doesn't he want to go?"

"Because he's lame?" she answers immediately, and I chuckle. She lets out a big sigh, deflating a little on her stool. "All he wants to do is play video games with his friends," she mutters. "Why is it so hard to convince him to do things with me?"

"Because he's *lame*," I echo back, earning a little smirk. I come closer, leaning my elbows on the counter across from her. "You're right that I don't have much experience with relationships, but I *have* read many, many romance books that can be summed up like this..." I pause, reaching across to put my hand on hers. "If he *wanted* to, he *would*."

My sister's irritation melts into something sadder, because we both know Gavin has repeatedly shown her he isn't willing to go the extra mile, or even a few extra steps, for her. There's a reason they've broken up and gotten back together so many times over the years, and it pretty much always comes down to the fact that Caitlin puts more effort into their relationship than he does.

I give her a sympathetic expression, and she gives me a resigned one in response.

"You'll still have fun if you go to the Street Dance without him," I point out, letting go of her hand and reaching over to lift the crockpot lid so I can add the olives and grape tomatoes. All that's left to do is add a handful of feta cheese, and then we can eat.

"Romance is dead, isn't it?" Her question is rhetorical, more of an indication of her state of mind than anything.

I put the lid back on the crockpot. Her dramatics make me want to laugh, but I hold it back because I know she's hurting. "I think you just chose a very unromantic boyfriend."

Caitlin says nothing for a long moment, staring sadly at the white countertop in front of her. "Maybe I should just do what you do," she tosses out. "Read romance books and give up on men."

"Who says I've given up on men?" I blurt out with a laugh.

She gives me a look, one perfectly shaped eyebrow raised. "Uh, because you don't date."

"Not on principle," I argue, then shrug. "I'm just picky." And shy. Really shy. It's almost impossible for me to speak to anybody outside of my family, much less a man, without blushing.

Caitlin narrows her eyes, squinting. "Right," she drags the word out.

I stick my tongue out at her and turn away to grab the feta and tzatziki out of the fridge.

"You know the picky ones die alone," she says matter-of-factly.

Shaking my head, I bring the glass bowl to the peninsula. "I'm not going to die alone."

"You will if you don't date, Emma. I know more than anyone that the dating pool is shallower in a small town, but come on. You need to get out there. Tell me your dream guy requirements. Maybe I know someone I could set you up with."

My shoulders tense slightly as I glance at my Elinor Riverside book sitting on the counter next to me.

My stomach sinks as I think about her main characters. They're brave and take control of their lives. They step out of their comfort zones to be with their true loves in the end. But me? I'm not main-character material.

I'm barely even side-character material.

I'm not brave enough to step out of my comfort zone. I'll just keep my nose in a book because it's where the action is in my life, and I can live vicariously through these brave characters who get what they want because they dare to go after it.

I've made my peace with the fact that the hero never goes for the shy, quiet, nerdy girl. Historically, that has been true for me, especially when, by comparison, my beautiful blond sister is the epitome of a romance novel heroine. I've always just been an unchanging background character who no one is interested in because they don't do anything interesting.

But I can't really explain that to my sister, or anyone really.

So, even though I know my dream guy probably doesn't exist and even if he did, he wouldn't be interested in me...I entertain Caitlin's request. At best, it will take her mind off of Gavin; at worst, she'll just laugh.

I cross my arms and let my eyes drift up toward the ceiling.

Dream guy requirements. Hmm.

An amalgamation of every male hero I've ever read comes together in my mind's eye. A tall, brawny man who oozes charisma and warmth, with muscles, dimples, and grand gestures.

"Well," I say as I move around the kitchen, "he should be kind. Thoughtful, with a job he cares about or at least a passion that fuels him." I stir the feta into the chicken. "He should be intelligent, and like to read in some capacity. He knows how to take care of himself and his body."

Warmth spreads up my neck as I imagine his *body.* "Handsome in his own way, with a nice smile and a good laugh." I grab the package of pita bread from the counter and bring it over. "He's charming and sweet. Knows how to be vulnerable. Trustworthy. Humble."

For some reason, the word "humble" has my mind turning away from this imaginary man toward someone who actually exists. Instead of the dreamy, perfect man I've been describing, I see Lee Christiansen standing next to me at the Holly Ball back in December, looking so incredibly handsome in his suit and yet seeming completely unaware of it.

Lee doesn't do small talk. He doesn't talk much at *all.* Not that I talk much either, but it isn't because he's shy like me. He's just...not much of a talker. So that night, with Christmas music swirling around us, I was surprised when he asked me a few questions about the book I was reading.

Not only is he a man of few words, but he has a voracious appetite for reading poetry. It's why I'm constantly curious about what's going on behind his perfectly flecked brown eyes. There's no way a man can read poetry regularly without having some deep well of beautiful thoughts inside of him.

There's really no use in thinking about him, though. He barely knows I exist. I see him every week at the library, and each interaction is simple and to the point. He's never given me any inkling that he sees me as anything more than the friendly local librarian. I have certainly never given him any inkling I've had a secret crush on him since high school. When I invited him to the Author Event yesterday, I'm almost positive he said he would come just because he was trying to be nice. All of the Christiansens are nice.

I shake my head slightly to get Lee out of my mind's eye and give my sister a tight smile. "Someone like that."

Caitlin's eyebrows are raised in an amused sort of way, because she and I both know there's no way all the qualities I described exist in one person.

"You read too many romance books."

I just sigh. "I know."

"You're never going to find your dream guy with your nose stuck in a book all the time." She sneers at the book on the counter, as if to make her point. "Mr. Right isn't in there," she says, pointing, "he's out *there*." She hooks her thumb toward the front door.

Her words make my palms sweat, and I hurry to deflect from the idea that finding Mr. Right would require me to put myself out there.

"Well, you let me know if you see him and send him my way," I toss out, pushing the tzatziki and pita toward her so she can bring them into the dining room.

Caitlin laughs softly and shakes her head. "What, you expect the universe to just drop Prince Charming on our doorstep?"

I shrug, turning off the crockpot. "Yes, that would be nice." With oven mitts, I pull the crock out and carry it into the dining room across the hall.

Caitlin follows me, placing her items on the table. I'm about to go back into the kitchen for the dishes, but pause when my sister gently grabs my wrist. She holds my gaze with slightly narrowed eyes.

I brace myself, biting my lip, because that's her Tough Love Face.

"You can't just *not live*, Emma. You'll never be happy if you don't take action."

I scrunch my nose, not liking how sludgy those words make my insides feel.

"I'm serious." She eyes me, hesitating. "You know Dad would say the same thing."

Tough Love Face *and* the Dad card? Oh, she means business.

And it makes my stomach drop, because my sister is saying she notices how I'm opting out of my own life. I'm not fooling anyone, apparently.

"Do *something*. One thing. All you need is twenty seconds of blind courage, and you can do it. Trust me."

I frown at her, but nod.

She releases my wrist, but then points at me.

"And for Pete's sake, if the universe really *does* drop Mr. Right at the door, *answer it*."

Chapter Three

Lee

It's my last patrol loop around the outer edges of Larkspur, then I'm in the home stretch. Because of my rotating work schedule, I'll have the next two days off. Thankfully that means I can attend the Author Event tomorrow Emma invited me to. I've been looking forward to it, not because I've ever read a single book by Garrett Waterstone, but because it's an excuse to see Emma.

I pull onto the highway, my eyes peeled for traffic violations, but my mind is still stuck back at the library on Wednesday. I finished the book she recommended last night, and every page I turned caused a low-level hum of excitement in my stomach because—*she thought of me*.

Relationships aren't something I've really pursued, not since high school at least, mostly because I don't think there's any point in dating someone I couldn't want as much as I want Emma. That kind of dishonesty could only result in heartache, and it wouldn't be mine...because my heart only belongs to her. Not that she has any idea.

Mamma raised us not to play with people's emotions. We were raised to be honest and loyal and never to be unkind. So, being with someone else when my heart is constantly whispering Emma's name would be impossible and pointless.

Unfortunately, that means I've resigned myself to being alone, because every time I consider asking her out and acting on my feelings, I remember who I am. *How* I am. There's nothing warm or inviting about me. I'm all growls and scowls. No one can see past them into the soft, gooey part inside. Not even Emma.

It's why, every once in a while, I jolt awake, drenched in sweat in the middle of the night. Usually, from the same dream where I'm watching from the back of a church as Emma walks down the aisle in a beautiful wedding dress toward some faceless man. I shout and scream for her, but no sound comes out and I'm dragged away from her by some unseen force.

My attention snags on a car up ahead, a couple miles into Larkspur city limits, pulled over on the shoulder. I slow, leaning forward a bit more. The right front side of the classic car is sitting lower than the rest of it. Probably a flat.

Thoughts of Emma retreat as I pull over behind the dark red 1967 Ford Mustang. I wish Lars were here—he's the only reason I know anything about cars. I almost snap a picture of it to send him, but push the thought aside. I put the squad car in Park as the driver gets out with his cell phone pressed to his ear.

I glance over my shoulder for any passing cars, then get out as well. The driver angrily throws his arm out to the side as he speaks into his phone. I catch a few words, "catastrophe" and "your fault" standing out the most.

There isn't anything dangerous about his behavior, but the temper on him still has my hackles rising. I walk slowly, assessing him. The sun beats down on us, interrupted only by the circling shadow of a magpie overhead.

"Everything alright, sir?" I ask.

I'd peg him to be early thirties or late twenties. Strong arms and a trim waist, dressed in gray chinos and a burnt orange polo. Behind horn-rimmed glasses, his face is flushed from both irritation and the heat. He rakes a hand through his styled brown hair as he swings his attention toward me.

Blue eyes quickly flick over my uniform, and I watch him closely, stopping with about five feet between us. A person's reaction to a police officer can say a lot about them. Some clam up, afraid of getting in trouble, while others wipe their expression purposely clean in an attempt to hide something. This man looks at me impatiently, with no intimidation of being approached by an officer.

"It's a flat," he spits at me in exasperation, holding his phone to his chest. From his tone alone I can tell he isn't used to being inconvenienced. Or he's in a hurry to get somewhere.

I move around to the shoulder to look at the front right tire, completely deflated.

"Do you have a spare tire?" I ask, gesturing to the back of his car where I assume there's a mount beneath the car for a spare. The trunk is too small to hold one.

"How the hell should I know?" he mutters to himself and moves his phone back to his ear. "For the love of God, Ben, please tell me there's a spare."

I squint at him slightly, my brain whirring. Maybe this isn't his car. Maybe it's Ben's, and this guy is just borrowing it.

"Yes, under there." He points toward the back of the car, still using the same impatient voice.

I take in his expensive-looking clothing and shiny wristwatch. I don't like to assume things about people when I'm on the job, because even put-together people like this can be criminals, but it's a pretty safe bet he has no interest in changing his tire. Whether because he doesn't know how or he just doesn't want to, I can't tell.

"Turn on your hazards and let's get it out," I demand quickly. The sooner we get him on the road again, the sooner I can get back into my air-conditioned squad car.

The man says something else into the phone I don't catch and reaches into the car to get the keys out of the ignition. The hazard lights flick on.

"Yes, right outside town," he says into the phone. "I swear to God if you're not here in two minutes, I'm deducting your paycheck."

I frown at him. *Harsh.*

"This *is* your car, right, sir?" I ask as he meets me at the back of his car.

He scoffs and points knitted eyebrows at me, the phone still tucked against his ear. "Of course it's my car. I just rarely drive it this far, and *my useless assistant* said he checked it over before I left to make sure I wouldn't have any problems."

I assume the useless assistant is who's on the phone with him.

"Let me see your license and registration." I need to validate what he's saying.

With an annoyed huff, the man digs out his information from a thick leather wallet. "This is the last thing I need," he growls into the phone as he hands two cards to me.

His license says his name is Todd Weiner; his address is in Minneapolis. The name on the car insurance matches his license. I hand them back.

I glance at the small trunk of his classic car, wondering if he has a car jack and the right wrench in there to change the tire.

"It's bad enough I'm going to be holed up in some rinky-dink bed-and-breakfast. Now *this*?"

There's only one bed-and-breakfast nearby, but I bite my tongue. I remind myself not to make assumptions. It might not be Larkspur Inn he's referring to.

"Next time I want a rental car and a driver—we can ship the car or have it towed to events," Todd barks out like a petulant child, like he's used to getting whatever he wants and can afford it.

"Where are you headed, sir?" I interrupt, trying not to grit my teeth at his attitude.

He frowns. "Not far," he replies. "Only a few miles."

I frown back. He was definitely talking about Larkspur Inn.

"This is *your* mistake," Todd says into the phone, his face twisted in anger. "So *you're* going to fix it." He hangs up and only then seems to realize I could hear his side of the phone conversation.

Todd slips his phone into pocket and unnecessarily smooths the front of his shirt. He arranges his ugly expression into something perfectly friendly, and the speed at which he does it makes the hair on the back of my neck stand up.

"Assistants, right? Can't live with them, can't live without them," he says with a soft laugh, his tone lighter and teasing, like he's trying to find camaraderie with me.

I don't return his smile or acknowledge the easy, practiced way he switched his personality from a whiny baby to a cool, nice guy.

He's a good actor with a bad attitude. *Strike one.* And he thinks Larkspur Inn is rinky-dinky. *Strike two.*

"I appreciate you stopping, Officer," he adds, smiling like I didn't just overhear him berate and threaten someone else. "Ben will be here in a minute and will have it all fixed up."

I stay where I am, not intending to let him shoo me away. "Let's get the flat off," I tell him, nodding toward the trunk.

Todd blinks at me, probably not used to anyone disagreeing with him. "I said Ben will do it."

"It will go faster if we start now. Open the trunk."

The scowl returns, and for a second he doesn't move. He glances at the badge on my uniform and rolls his eyes with a sigh. Dropping the friendly act, he unlocks the trunk like it's costing him ten years of his life.

There's nothing in the trunk but the Allen wrench we'll need to get the lug nuts off, so I leave Todd standing there to get a jack out of the road kit in the cruiser. The heat beats down on me as I bring the jack back to where Todd is waiting.

"Ever changed a flat, Todd?" I ask, the question coming out as a growl, and I'm not even slightly sorry for it.

His blue eyes go wide behind his glasses, like he can't believe I'm going to make him do the job. He doesn't give me a verbal answer, but he looks at the flat tire with disgust. I hand him the jack, not giving him the chance to refuse, and instruct him where to put it and how it works.

After pushing down on the lever just twice, pumping the body of the car up a few inches, he lets out an aggravated, guttural sort of wheeze. I press my lips together to keep from scowling. If he thinks *this* is the hard part, he'd better hope his assistant gets here before we get to the lug nuts.

Thankfully for Todd, a moment later, a car in the oncoming lane slows down and turns around to park behind my squad car. A man gets out and runs toward us on the shoulder. He looks a lot like Todd, with a similar build, brown hair and blue eyes, though not as brightly blue as his boss's. Ben skids to a stop, his face shocked as he realizes his boss was kneeling in the dirt and working a jack.

"Thank God," Todd mutters, getting up and abandoning the jack. "Get the spare," he barks, pointing at the back of the car.

Ben does so without a word, bending down and reaching underneath the car to undo the clasp keeping the spare in place. He quickly brings the spare and sets it down next to me while I jack the car up the rest of the way.

Todd stands there with his arms crossed, as impatient and pissy as ever. He fires off questions at Ben that have nothing to do with the car.

"Did you get my things put away?"

"Did you get a table for my room?"

"Did you get a breakfast menu?"

Ben answers in the affirmative to each question and isn't given any gratitude from his boss.

Sweat dripping down my back, I side-eye Todd once I get the car high enough that the flat tire is off the ground and can be removed.

There's a panicked, frazzled air about Ben as he grabs the wrench and does his best to loosen the lug nuts. After the third one, I pat his shoulder and gesture for the wrench.

"I'll do the other two," I offer, surprising the hell out of him. He glances at his boss, who goes silent, but gives me the wrench. With some difficulty and elbow grease, I get the last two lug nuts loosened then I alternate, loosening them the rest of the way.

The silence is uncomfortable, which is saying something because I'd much rather work in silence. But I can tell Todd is biting his tongue and will probably give Ben another verbal lashing once I'm back on the road.

I get the flat off and Ben takes over, fitting the spare into place and tightening the lug nuts in the same alternating way I removed them.

Intending to be a pain, because Todd deserves it, I hand him the flat tire to put back beneath the car. "Make yourself useful and put this where the spare was."

He blinks at me in astonishment and indignation. Ben makes a surprised, choking sound.

When Todd remains frozen with the flat in his hands, staring at me, I raise my eyebrows impatiently.

With the same disgusted look from before, Todd takes a step back, looking down at the flat. Ben drops the wrench and gets up.

"I got it," he blurts out almost desperately, taking the flat tire from his boss. Todd smiles, smug and ugly, as Ben gets down on the ground and secures the tire beneath the car.

Withholding my grumble only because I'm on the job, I pick up the wrench and get the lug nuts tightened the rest of the way. When I'm finished, Ben puts the wrench in the trunk and closes it as I turn the handle of the jack counterclockwise to release the jack. The car eases down onto the spare and seems to hold air.

I wipe my sweaty forehead with the back of my hand and get to my feet. "The spare won't get you very far," I tell Todd. "Be careful and don't drive it more than you have to until you can get a new tire."

He nods, looking me over with an uncomfortable, almost put-out expression.

"What do I owe you?"

"What?"

Todd nods at the tire and takes his wallet out of his back pocket. "You didn't have to stop. How much?"

I stare at him like he's an idiot, because he must be. Ben stares at him too.

"I'm a police officer," I tell him needlessly. "It's part of my job to help people like this."

He blinks, like he can't comprehend what it means to help someone without a price tag attached to it. "You didn't have to help," he tries again. "I want to pay you."

"No," I growl out, glaring at him.

"I can afford it," he assures me with an insulted snort.

"Good for you." I reach down to grab the jack. "Kindness is free. Get in your car and be on your way." I stalk past him to put the jack away.

When I'm finished, I'm eager to get out of the heat and head straight for the driver's side door. The yuppie is pulling his car back onto the road, and I sincerely hope it's the last I see of him. Hopefully, his stay at Larkspur Inn is brief, and he doesn't give Patty a hard time.

I give Ben a nod as he slumps past on the shoulder to get to his car. He pulls onto the road, pointing a grim smile at me through the windshield as I wait to open my car door until he's gone past. Hopefully poor Ben gets a break.

I get into the cruiser and slam the door shut, immediately sighing with relief at the air conditioning. I blast it and am about to reach for the seatbelt when I see it.

A twenty-dollar bill tucked under the windshield wiper.

I grit my teeth.

"What a schmuck," I grumble.

I throw open the door and retrieve it, already brainstorming which charity I could send it to that would piss off Todd Weiner the most. I wish I could send it to his assistant, actually, because there's no doubt poor Ben needs a free drink or three.

Grumpy as hell, I drive through town back to the police station. It'll be at least another hour of work to do my reports, then I can go home. I do my best to push the out-of-towner from my mind, but the interaction stays with me like I've walked through a spiderweb. Part of me really wants to follow him over to the inn and throw his damn twenty-dollar bill right in his snooty face.

Then I think of my little sister, who lives to prank people, and consider recruiting her to pull something on him. Would serve him right for treating people like hired help and not human beings.

I became a police officer because I wanted to help people. I wanted to protect my community. It's all I know how to do—that protective instinct has always been strong in me. Sometimes I forget other people don't have that kind of instinct about people, strangers or otherwise. Some people are only out to help themselves. I won't ever understand it.

I've seen a lot of things on the job. Mostly stupid, thoughtless things usually because of bored teenagers growing up in a small town. But sometimes horrible, traumatic things happen, and despite how much those situations tear me up, I'd still rather be there trying to help than hide from it. I'd rather be the one to carry someone out of harm's way than just avert my eyes. Even if I can't save someone, at least I can sleep at night knowing I tried. Because people matter. Helping matters.

And I have a sneaking suspicion Todd Weiner doesn't think this way at all.

I shake my head as I park at the station, trying to Etch-a-Sketch the feeling of his gross, sticky arrogance out of my brain. Hopefully, he'll be on his way soon enough, gone back to whatever suburban metropolis hell he came from.

My phone rings as I get out and see Pappa's name on the screen. I answer.

"Hey, Pa," I greet in a low voice.

"Lee, are you going to the Author Event at the library tomorrow? Garrett Waterstone! In Larkspur! Can you believe it?" he gushes excitedly. It makes me smile.

"Heard of him, huh?"

"He's one of my favorite authors," he tells me, and I realize the only reason I've heard of him is because of Pappa talking about his books. "I have all of his books—I'm bringing them so he can sign them. Are you going?"

"Yeah, I'm going," I say, heading into the station. I nod at Sherry, the dispatch officer, as I walk by the front desk. "I'd offer to pick you up, but I was planning on getting there extra early in case they need help with set up. Emma said they're expecting a big crowd."

I follow the hallway to the right, into the main room with four desks set up for each of the officers. I sink into my desk chair and shake the mouse to wake up my computer.

"Oh, that's fine, Son. I'll probably drag Mamma along too. I'll see you there."

"See you there."

We hang up, and I get to work filling out my reports. I punch the keys extra hard when I get to the unfortunate encounter I had with Todd, but because of the conversation with Pappa, my mind is back in the library again with Emma.

Chapter Four

Emma

E ven though the library isn't usually open on Sundays, Regina and I happily set up for the Author Event. The excitement of having such a big-name author in our little library is more than enough to make up for all the work on our usual day off.

She sweeps past me with her arms full of plastic cups and napkins, excitement radiating from her bright smile, as I help our boss Henry bring chairs in from the back of his ancient pickup truck. The library only has about two dozen chairs, so thankfully we borrowed some from the community center. We might still have people standing in the back, and it just amps me up even more.

The library is hands down my favorite place in the world. The sweet, dry smell of the books, the resources we provide to our community, the book clubs and storytimes... There's nowhere else I'd rather come to work every day.

I set down a stack of four chairs and huff out a few breaths, adjusting my glasses. Regina and I have already cleared the area, so we can set up the chairs across the front of the library.

Henry puffs in with two chairs, walking slowly so he doesn't hurt himself. He has no business doing any kind of manual labor at his age, but he's stubborn and would consider himself useless if he didn't help. And there's nothing he hates more than feeling useless.

"Ginny will never forgive me if you hurt yourself," I tell him, narrowing my eyes at him as he takes a white handkerchief out of his pocket and mops his forehead with it.

"She's spiteful enough to haunt us, Henry, you know that," Regina joins in from where she's scooting the snack table a little closer to the door.

I grin at her, and she winks back, her friendly crow's feet on display.

Henry grimaces just slightly, waving a wrinkled hand at us. In his early eighties, his white hair is thinning at the temples, his face marked with smile and laugh lines. He's stubborn, sure, and desperately trying to keep his independence, but at his core he's a hard worker, devoted husband, loving father, and doting grandfather. He's a good boss, too, and every year that he refuses to retire just makes me fonder of him.

I follow him back out to where he's parked his truck on the street and loop my arm through his as we go down the sidewalk.

Summer is in full swing, which means the heat of the afternoon is climbing to its peak. I glance at Henry's weathered face, seeing how pink it is. We need to get the rest of these chairs into the library and close the door so the air conditioning can keep up.

I hop up into the bed of the truck, holding the skirt of my burgundy sundress down behind my legs as I do. I push a stack of six chairs toward the tailgate, then take one off the top.

"Take this one and then go in and get some water," I tell him.

Henry frowns as I hand it to him, not impressed.

"I'm serious," I say, pointing to the library. "You know if you hurt yourself, that'll be it for running this place."

"I know," he grumbles back and takes his chair.

Turning back to push the two other stacks of chairs, I wish I had thought to do my hair differently today. It's half up, tied with a ribbon, but the rest of my hair is down like a blanket on my shoulders. Looks like I'm going to be a sweaty mess while meeting a famous author.

Yay.

It isn't often we get big names to come all the way out here. Tourism in Larkspur ticks up in the summer, but it's usually people who camp or fish. There isn't much to tempt people from the cities, and obviously we're a small community, so Henry had no expectation that Garrett Waterstone would accept his request to speak at our library. Regina had to help Henry scramble to get the grant approved to pay for his speaking fee, but it was approved and now the day is finally here.

I lug in four more chairs, my arms tired as I plunk them down.

Henry's sitting in a chair near the table Regina is putting the cookies out on. He's sipping from a cup, glaring at me from beneath bushy white eyebrows. I don't take it personally because I know him. He's not mad at me; he's mad he can't do as much as he could in his younger years.

I'm moving back toward the door to get more chairs when someone comes through it, a full stack of six chairs blocking the person carrying them.

My first thought is that Garrett Waterstone is early and graciously lending a helping hand, but once the man comes inside, I easily recognize the strong, muscly build of Lee Christiansen.

My stomach swoops at the way his olive-green shirt strains at the seams. His dirty blonde hair makes his brown eyes pop by comparison, and I always find myself studying his stoic features whenever I see him...because he isn't supermodel handsome or romance novel handsome. He's...some other kind of handsome that I can never seem to find the right word for. There's something rugged about his high cheekbones and dark eyebrows I've never seen on anyone else.

I check the clock over the door, confused why he's here so early. The event doesn't start for over an hour, and yet here he is.

"Well, hi, Lee," Regina greets warmly. "That's nice of you."

He brings the chairs over to the others and sets them down. "Thought you might need some help," he says with his quiet, deep voice. He nods at Henry and then looks around until he sees me standing there. A blush rushes into my cheeks.

"Emma."

"Hi," I squeak out, because I was staring at him.

I don't usually stare at him. Not out in the open like this, anyway. I've become a pro at sneaking my stares so no one notices. It works in my favor that I can usually shrink into the background wherever I am. No one really pays me much attention, which usually means I can observe as much as I want.

Except with Lee, apparently, because he just looked around expectantly, purposely, for me. Something warm curls up in my chest.

That's nice.

And it's nice that he came early in case we needed help. Though that doesn't surprise me at all. The Christiansens are a helpful bunch.

One side of his mouth pulls back in a small smile, and then he's off to get more chairs. I follow him back into the summer heart with butterflies in my stomach, fully aware that I'm a hot, sweaty mess. He lifts a stack of four chairs down and then reaches for the last full stack, moving them like they weigh nothing.

I take the four chairs, he closes the tailgate, and then follows me inside with the last of them. I put mine down quickly then go move the doorstop so the door shuts tight, keeping the heat out.

Henry directs Lee on the spacing he wants between each row. Regina weaves through them with two empty plastic pitchers so she can fill them up in the small breakroom and make lemonade. I help unstack the chairs with Henry, then Lee and I put them all in neat rows.

Even with the door closed and the air conditioning going full tilt, I still feel flushed, and most of it is from working alongside Lee. He works quietly, efficiently. He radiates his usual no-nonsense attitude.

"Pretty exciting, huh, Lee?" Regina says when she comes back into the room with her pitchers filled.

He glances up at her as she walks by. "Yeah. Pappa's a big fan."

I smile as we line up chairs in front of the checkout counter now. His dad is the best. Every Christmas he does storytime dressed up as Santa.

"Who *isn't* a fan?" she answers back from the snack table, mixing lemonade powder into the pitchers. "Every book he publishes goes straight to number one on every bestseller list. I heard he's got a movie in the works based on *Fire in the Night* and it might be filmed in Minnesota. Can you imagine?"

Henry lets out a loud scoff from where he's needlessly straightening the first row of chairs. "What is it with everyone wanting to turn books into movies?" He shakes a fist. "So much is lost."

"I agree, Henry," I tell him affectionately. "The book is always better."

Lee shoots me a tiny smile that floods my cheeks with heat.

"I can't believe we got him to come here," Regina continues a little dreamily, ignoring us.

If Lee wasn't next to me, I would tease her about having a crush on Garrett Waterstone, even though she's been married for fifteen years.

When Lee and I get the last row in place, I hold my breath and say, "thanks, Lee."

I don't know why saying his name feels so personal, but I immediately wish I could cram it back into my mouth.

He just nods in response, his expression cool and even like always. Not unkind, but...remote. Like he keeps himself back from his edges. I think it gives him a mysterious sort of air, but anyone being arrested by him would find it off-putting.

"What else can I do?"

My brain fritzes out a little with his flecked brown eyes fixed on me so steadily. Thankfully, Regina answers.

"The banner," she says, pointing toward the window across the room.

Lee follows me over to the counter, where I left the banner we print-ed. It isn't anything special—just "Bestselling Author Grant Waterstone Author Talk" printed in bold letters spanning about four printer pages. I taped them together already, so it just needs to be hung up.

I hand him the tape roller with a shy smile, and we head over to the front. It only takes a couple of tries of me holding it up and Henry saying "higher!" to realize I'm not tall enough for where it would look best.

"Here," Lee says, taking the sign and handing me the tape instead. He reaches up, my eyes snagging shamelessly on the curves of his biceps and the lines of his back.

"Right there," Henry says in approval, and I hand Lee pieces of tape, my fingertips tingling whenever they touch his.

Even though he said would be here, I'm still a little surprised he showed up. Poetry is his main genre, not thriller or mystery. Though to be honest, thriller isn't my genre either. I have read a couple of Garrett

Waterstone's books, and they were good, but I'd say I'm most excited to meet a successful author and hear about his story. I like the idea of getting a peek into the other side of a book, into the author's mind.

So, I wonder what Lee's purpose is for attending. Is he interested in the author side of things too? Or is he just here to support the library?

There's a lot of things about Lee Christiansen that I've accepted I'll never know. He's incredibly private, says very little, and keeps to himself. He always has, even back in high school. I've never been brave enough to ask him why he likes poetry or if he's ever tried to write poetry himself. I'll never know what his favorite color is or whether he has a bucket list. I couldn't even guess whether he's been in love before or if he wants to have kids someday.

None of it is my business, and I don't have the audacity to ask. But I want to know *so much.*

Lee steps back to inspect his work and I stuff down my stupid crush.

He barely knows you exist, I remind myself.

I have my shyness to thank, and there isn't anything I can do about it.

The conversation with my sister comes back to my mind. Hiding in my books lets me escape and pretend I'm living more of a life than I actually am. There's comfort in that, sure. But part of me wonders—if the universe really did drop the perfect guy on my doorstep, would I even open the door? If my soulmate walked right up to me, would I be too scared to say hello? If the kind of romance I read about was suddenly in the palm of my hand, would I let it slip through my fingers?

In the back of my mind, I know that real love can change everything. The kind of love my parents had is possible—if I'm open to it. If I say yes when it shows up.

The library door opens, startling me slightly from my thoughts. We all look over, even Lee, and in walks the guest of honor.

Regina gasps loudly enough for me to hear from across the room.

His photo is on the back of his books, but I can confidently say that it doesn't do him justice. His style is overwhelmingly professorial. Walnut-colored horn-rimmed glasses draw all the focus to his sparkling blue eyes, while his easy smile points at his straight, white teeth out on full display. The mustard-colored shirt he's wearing complements his tan skin perfectly, giving him a sort of golden glow to his whole persona, immediately drawing me in. There's something magnetic about him, like a romance hero in the flesh.

"Well, hello," he greets warmly, glancing around at each of us. His handsome smile widens when he gets to me and falters almost imperceptibly when his gaze lands on Lee. Someone less observant wouldn't have noticed.

Before I can swivel my head to look at Lee and confirm my suspicion that he absolutely did not return Garrett Waterstone's friendly smile, Henry shuffles forward with a shaky hand outstretched.

"Welcome, Mr. Waterstone. It's a pleasure to have you here."

Garrett shakes Henry's hand enthusiastically, making my boss beam. "Oh, please call me Garrett," he says with his gorgeous smile pointed at Henry. "It's a pleasure to be here. Thank you for inviting me out to your charming little town."

My heart beats a little faster hearing him speak. His voice is all honey—sweet, almost tenor in pitch, with all the cheeriness of someone who loves getting to meet his readers.

Lee lets out a tiny little sound, something akin to a scoff or a disbelieving huff. I glance at him, and yep...there's not a smile to be found on his rough face. He doesn't look even slightly happy to see Garrett Waterstone and I couldn't begin to guess why.

"You must be Henry?"

"Yes, that's me." My boss moons at the idea of being on a first-name basis with such a big author. "I have to say, your new book is fantastic. I love how Tom struggled with whether to turn himself in and how you made the reader question whether it was actually murder not to wake up his abusive father to get to shelter from the storm."

I grin wide, not used to seeing Henry starstruck. He isn't as much of a grumpy goose as Lee is, but he definitely plays things cool and doesn't get riled up about much.

Lee mutters, "isn't that a Carrie Underwood song?"

Before I can entertain his question, Garrett's attention turns to me.

"And who do we have here?" he asks politely, looking at me with eyes so blue they almost don't look real.

My stomach does a weird sort of swoop like I'm about to fall backwards out of a desk chair.

"I'm Emma," I say, my voice betraying me by coming out almost at a whisper.

Garrett comes closer, his smile going more tender as he outstretches his hand for me to shake as well.

Time slows down, my heart beating hard.

My sister's voice echoes and ricochets in my head as I lift my hand.

What, you expect the universe to just drop Prince Charming on our doorstep?

Tall, handsome, friendly, kind...

The man standing in front of me, reaching for me, looks every bit the man I described to her just a couple of days ago. I get the wild notion somehow I manifested him.

That's not possible though, right?

His warm hand slips into mine, squeezing gently and looking down at me like I'm the most precious thing he's ever seen. No one has ever looked at me like this. No one has ever looked at me at all.

"It's lovely to meet you, Emma."

Chapter Five

Lee

T ension locked up my shoulders when Todd Weiner stepped into the library with all the charisma and friendliness that he didn't show me when I so unfortunately met him on the side of the road yesterday.

It's not unusual to encounter the worst side of people in my job, especially in emergencies. I can give him that. It was a stressful moment, obviously, but the stark difference between his demeanor then and his well-practiced manners now only has red alerts going in my head. He's an actor, all right.

I fight to keep my breathing even as he puts his attention on Emma and moves closer to shake her hand. She lifts her hand and puts it in his, her beautiful eyes looking at him in astonishment and awe from behind her glasses.

"It's lovely to meet you, Emma," he tells her, and I want to die.

Regina murmurs an "aww" from where she's still hovering by the snack table. Bile rises in my throat, and I know the dislike shows on my face, but I'm powerless to move my features into something polite.

"You too," Emma replies just above a whisper.

He holds onto her hand just a beat too long and then releases her. His attention stays on her even as he takes a step to the side, toward me, like he's used to meeting multiple people one after the other. But then he turns his stupid head, and I watch him pretend as if the ordeal with his flat tire never happened.

Oh, how he's mastered the art of being convincing.

Todd smiles pleasantly, offering his hand. "And you are?"

My deep frown does nothing to deter him from oozing the kind of friendliness that I've never been able to master.

Half a dozen questions zip through my mind.

How's your stay at the rinky-dinky inn?

Why don't you want to admit you've already met me? Ashamed of your behavior?

Where can I send your twenty dollars?

With difficulty, I keep my questions to myself.

"Lee," I half-growl, and shake his hand with more force than necessary. The only indication of his wince is a centimeter lift of his left eyebrow.

"Lee," he repeats with a smile that to me looks very shark-like. "I'm Garrett. Nice to meet you."

No, it's really not.

And it occurs to me that I'm probably the only one in the room who knows his real name. I don't blame him for using a pen name, because Weiner is such an unfortunate last name, but right now it just feels disingenuous.

He releases my hand and is about to go over to Regina, but stops, looking thoughtfully at Emma and then back at me.

"Are you two, uh...?" He gestures between us with his pointer finger.

The room spins just once.

It isn't his goddamn business what we are.

"Oh, no. No, we're—we're not," Emma stammers, her face bright red.

I've never been stabbed, but it must feel like this. Like a hard, sharp punch to the stomach.

And he can tell, because even though he smiles innocently as he passes me to greet Regina, I don't miss the way he smugly side-eyes me. He asked on purpose—to make Emma drive the knife.

I glare at the back of his head as Regina not only shakes his hand, but hugs him too. Garrett just chuckles good-naturedly, like he's used to being fawned over.

The tension in my shoulders migrates up my neck and into my head.

Emma is still blushing furiously, but her eyes are glued to Garrett.

I get what she sees. Handsome, successful, friendly, warm, congenial.

Everything I'm not.

It stings knowing where I stand. She hurried to tell him we're not together. Like she was *embarrassed*. She wanted to assure him that she's single, even though he's just here for a short time and nothing could happen between them.

Everything inside starts to shut down. A strange sense of quiet spreads through me as I move away from the others and slump into a chair.

Bending over to rest my elbows on my knees, I try to get myself together. Deep breaths. Picturing myself somewhere else. Punching Todd Weiner in the face. None of it eases the pain of my heart splintering into pieces.

The door opens, and Ben steps inside holding a heavy box.

"Ah, and here's my assistant," Garrett exclaims brightly. "Ben, come meet these lovely people." He introduces Ben to the library staff and then grins around at everyone. "This is going to be a great event; I can just feel it. Thank you all so much for having me."

My stomach rolls at how warmly he introduced his assistant when just yesterday I saw how he *really* treats Ben.

Ben goes back outside to bring in more books, and I get up to help him. I fall in beside him as we go back out into the heat.

"Thanks for helping," he says, and I just nod.

He looks tired and stressed, and I can't help wondering how much of an earful he got from his boss once they got back to Larkspur Inn. He gives me a quick, apologetic glance.

"And thanks for helping with the flat, too," Ben adds, putting a box of books in my hands.

"No problem." I nod toward the boxes, indicating I can take another. "He always like that?"

He huffs a sarcastic laugh and adds a second box to my load. "He can be difficult when things don't go to plan."

Somehow I feel like there's much more to it than that, but I don't ask. Ben grabs two boxes, and we head inside.

It takes one more trip between Ben and I to get all the boxes. Garrett must've brought a hundred books for this event, which to me seems overly optimistic.

Regina takes the books out of the boxes. Emma helps him put them on the table. Garrett eats up the attention and is perfectly gracious about their help.

Not long after, people start filtering in, grabbing snacks and lemonade. The seats fill quickly while Garrett chats up a few of them in the front. I find a spot to sit about halfway back, unable to shake the way Emma was so quick to set Garrett straight about us being together.

Regina's voice calls out for everyone to scoot in toward the middle so more people can find seats. The library is full, voices on top of voices, all excited and laughing, buzzing to see Garrett Waterstone.

A familiar shape drops into the chair next to me, patting my shoulder. Pappa's excitement is written all over the lines of his face.

"Wow, that's really him!" He leans to the left to get a better look at Garrett.

I say nothing.

Mamma sits next to Pappa and reaches over to pat my knee.

"*Vad är fel?*" she asks me. *What's wrong?*

I raise my eyes to Mamma's concerned expression. I can't explain it now, or maybe ever. My spoken vocabulary is small to begin with, even more so with emotions.

All I can think is *förtvivlad.*

Heartbroken.

I sigh and just shake my head.

Henry appears in front of the table with all of Garrett's books and spreads his arms out wide to welcome everyone. Thankfully, Mamma sits back and her attention shifts away from me.

"Hello, hello!" he calls out, and the crowd hushes. Garrett stands off to the side, arms folded casually, looking completely at ease with speaking in front of so many people. "We couldn't be more excited to have Garrett Waterstone here today to talk about his new book, *Thunder In The Night*. He has books for sale and will be signing as well. This is the last stop on his Minnesota book tour, and we're so humbled to have him. Let's give him a big Larkspur welcome." He claps and everyone else riotously applauds too.

But I can't move, because I see Emma sitting up toward the front, the little white bow in her hair standing out against her black hair.

Garrett comes forward, shaking Henry's hand with a dazzling smile, and then waves at everyone. Pappa waves back like a little kid. Regina whistles from her seat next to Emma. I disappear into myself.

"Thank you," Garrett says, beaming. "Thank you so much for taking some time out of your day to be here with little ol' me."

The applause is loud as he concludes the speaking portion of the event. I scowl at his attempt at humility. Everything he talked about was veiled in some kind of boastfulness.

"I'll be here to sign books until Henry kicks me out," he teases, winking at Henry, in the front row. Everyone titters and chuckles. "Libraries have always had a special place in my heart, so I'd love to shout out your fantastic librarians." He gestures for them to stand up and my heart aches when Emma gets to her feet. She nervously folds her little hands in front of her, blushing from being thrust into the spotlight. "Henry, Regina, and Emma, thank you for having me. It's been an absolute pleasure to share my love of books with you." He turns back to the crowd. "Please, if you would, let's give them a much-deserved round of applause." Garrett claps, and everyone else joins in. Henry and Regina grin wide at being recognized. Emma looks like she'd rather hide. "Thanks again, folks!"

Half of the crowd gets to their feet and a long line forms along the right side of the chairs, including Pappa. Most of them have brought books for Garrett to sign. Others have their wallets already out, ready to purchase one.

Mamma scoots over into the chair Pappa vacated. She says nothing.

After at least five minutes, Mamma leans over, touching the side of her arm to mine. "En *påfågel har för lite i huvudet och för mycket i svansen*," she says to me. It's a Swedish saying. "A peacock has too little in its head and too much in its tail."

I blink at the disgruntled expression she's pointing at Garrett Waterstone.

"You didn't like him?"

She turns her green eyes to me and lifts one eyebrow. "Not as much as he likes himself."

For the first time since Garrett walked in, my face softens. Mamma smiles teasingly, looking so much like Svea that I'm half wondering if she has a prank in mind to play on him.

I shouldn't be surprised. Nothing gets past Mamma. All the rest of the attendees might have been eating out of his hand as he spoke about his Minnesota upbringing, claiming humble beginnings, and how writing was just an extension of his love of reading. All I could think was he knew his audience, and maybe he would've changed some details of his story if he had been speaking to a packed auditorium in Minneapolis instead.

A bit of relief seeps in through my heartache.

"I knew a man like that once," she says, looking back at Garrett. "I admired his confidence at first, but I quickly realized it was just another name for his inflated ego."

"Who?"

She eyes me. "The man I dated before your father."

I've never heard her speak about any man but Pappa. I had sort of assumed maybe there weren't any.

"It took me too long to realize he was more in love with himself than with me." She snorts. "But, *skenet bedrar*."

Appearances deceive. And she couldn't be more dead on. I'm grateful someone else sees it.

"With your father, what you see is what you get. He hides nothing, pretends nothing." A sweet smile crosses her face, the creases bracketing her mouth deepening, as she finds Pappa near the front of the line. She nudges me. "You're very much the same. But the difference is that he loves outward, and you love inward."

"What does that mean?"

She gives me a sympathetic, soft look. "He gives his love. You hold it back."

I barely keep myself from glancing Emma's way, even though I'm aware Mamma's referring to me expressing love even to our family, not just romantic love. Mamma smiles gently, pats my arm, and says nothing more, waiting for me to admit she's right.

The book in my glove compartment comes to mind. All the flowers I've picked but never given her. All the strings of vulnerable sentences I've thought of but never said to her.

At length, I let out a long sigh. "I know," I mutter.

"Tell me what's bothering you." Her tone is demanding, expectant. But I still hesitate for an entire minute to find a sentence that encompasses how I feel.

"I can't give my love to someone who doesn't want it."

Mamma studies my face, digesting what I said. She's a human lie detector. I found that out as a kid, but I swear she's half-witch too. She can always figure me out, even when I wish she wouldn't. "How do you know she doesn't want your love if you haven't given it?"

My heart beats hard.

"I'm not what she wants, Mamma." I have no doubt she knows exactly who I'm referring to, but I can't get myself to say Emma's name.

"Did she tell you what she wants? Since you're so sure?"

I give her a flat look in response.

"You can't know that for sure unless you ask her what she wants."

My shoulders tense.

"I don't need to *ask her* if I'm what she wants," I blurt out breathlessly, her embarrassed face coming back to mind. "I'm cold and short with people and not friendly. I intimidate people. Why would she want someone like me—someone who you just said holds back their love?"

The blood rushes in my ears as the words tumble out.

She shakes her head, narrowing her eyes. "Who told you that you're intimidating?"

I scoff and cross my arms.

I'll never forget what it was like hearing an adult tell me so bluntly how other people viewed me. Until my junior year in high school, I had assumed people could tell there was softness and warmth in me, even though I'm introverted and hard to get to know. I looked at everything differently after that. Paid attention to what people said about me and how they acted. I noticed people *were* intimidated by me, even when I was just standing there minding my own business.

"Guidance counselor," I toss out angrily. "She said I couldn't be a Kindergarten teacher because I'm too intimidating."

Mamma leans away from me, staring at me incredulously. "Is *that* why you said you changed your mind? It was because that old bat Mrs. Hellman said you couldn't?" She shakes her head with obvious disappointment. "I taught you better than to let anyone talk you out of something you want to do."

My head drops back, and I grimace at the ceiling. Mamma sighs. She swats the back of my head so I'll meet her eyes.

"Forget what she said," she says dismissively. "You're not intimidating."

"Well, I'm not exactly warm and fuzzy."

She glares and I clamp my mouth shut. "That has nothing to do with anything. You're not unlovable just because you aren't a smiling peacock like Garrett Waterstone." There's so much fire in her voice that her face flushes. "You're *lagom*, Lee. Not too much or too little."

I still as she fans her face. I didn't think I would ever need a pep talk from Mamma, but apparently I do. Even though it makes me feel pathetic. I guess no matter how old I get, I still need her to help me get things straight.

Lagom. That's what she thinks I am. Just the right amount. Not too intimidating, not too friendly. When she puts it like that, it's easier for me to swallow.

She takes a deep breath and lets it out slowly, collecting herself. The color has receded from her face. I haven't seen her that fired up in a long time, and it has me willing to toss her a bone.

"You're right," I murmur, dropping my arms.

"Of course I am," she says matter-of-factly. "Any woman with good sense would choose *lagom.* Including Emma."

I cringe. Mamma knows exactly who I've been referring to.

"She can't choose you if she doesn't know you're a choice."

I frown. I wish what she was saying didn't make sense, but it does. Doesn't mean I like it. What she's saying is I have to stick my neck out. Despite Emma's reaction earlier, I can't know for sure if she could want me, unless I'm upfront with her.

Her eyes crinkle with amusement. "You two are very funny," she says. "You're always looking at her, and she's always looking at you, but your eyes never meet."

This time I do glance at Emma, where she's holding up Pappa's phone as he poses with Garrett for a picture.

Is that true?

Do I miss all the times she's looking at me? Am I too nervous she'll catch me staring? Am I creating the very distance I want so desperately to defeat? Are we too good at holding back that we're constantly missing each other's interest?

...was her embarrassment just because she was shy and not because she was disgusted?

I can't know for sure unless I ask. I can't have her unless I ask. She can't say *yes* until I ask. But if I ask, she could also say no.

"Let your walls down a bit, *min son.*" She reaches over and squeezes my hand three times, one squeeze for each word of "I love you."

She gets up to intercept Pappa by the snack table. He's looking at the signature on the front page of his book with childlike glee. Despite the truths Mamma just laid on me, I huff out a laugh.

My eyes move automatically back to Emma, still taking pictures for the last few people in line. Most of the crowd has dispersed, with just a handful of people hanging around chatting. Mamma and Pappa wave at me as they head for the door, and I nod back, not missing Mamma's discreet eye movements toward Emma.

I get to my feet and head to the last row of chairs. I start stacking them, the repetition calming my mind enough so I can make a tentative plan.

I'll ask her to dance at the Street Dance on Saturday. If she says yes and it goes okay, then I can ask if she wants to go to the fireworks together afterward too. I can tell her how I feel and ask if she feels the same way. And if she says no, then I can disappear into the crowd and go home alone.

It'll either be the beginning of everything I've hoped for or it'll be the end of my hopes.

No pressure at all.

Chapter Six

Emma

"That couldn't have gone any better," Garrett Waterstone says happily, packing the few remaining books he brought along into a box. He signed so many books his fountain pen ran out of ink and he had to borrow a Bic from us. "A smashing success if I've ever seen one."

I smile at his use of *smashing*.

It was packed in here. I've never seen such a turnout for a library event. And Garrett was clearly in his element—speaking so easily, with no nerves or discomfort. Making jokes, answering questions, and talking so proudly about his work I couldn't help but think he loves public speaking just as much as he loves writing his books.

Everyone has left now besides me, Regina, Henry, and Garrett. His assistant, Ben, packed up the books that were left and then Garrett sent him back to Larkspur Inn, telling him to take the night off. It was nice to see that he treats his assistant well. Regina is vacuuming; then I'll help her move furniture. Henry's polishing off the last couple of cookies while he cleans up.

Lee hung around hauled the chairs onto the bed of Henry's truck, but I noticed he steered clear of everyone. Lee's expressions are usually some variation of serious, but he seemed distracted. Probably because Garrett thought we were...

Gulp.

I can't believe that happened. It says a lot about Garrett that he would think I'm even in the same league of human being as Lee. But I barely *exist* to him in the first place, so Garrett thinking we were together was so humiliating I wanted to disappear into the floor. I don't know how I'll ever be able to look Lee in the eye again.

"You know, Ben told me it wouldn't be worth my time to come so far for such a potentially small crowd, but he was wrong." Garrett scoffs, but there's still a smile on his handsome face, like he's delightfully exasperated by his assistant. "He's usually wrong."

"Larkspur is small," Henry concedes, gathering the empty pitchers. "But we're the salt of the earth. Wouldn't live anywhere else." He carries them past me and disappears into the breakroom as I pull one of the kids' bookshelves back into its place.

"It's absolutely charming," Garrett agrees.

"Too bad you're not staying longer," I tell him, scooting the shelf. "There's a bunch of fun things going on this week for the Fourth."

He straightens up, pointing those unreal blue eyes at me with interest. "Is that so?"

The vacuuming ceases, and the quiet of the library finally returns after so much noise. I breathe a little sigh. The presence and volume of so many people here drained the life right out of my little introverted soul.

"Mhm. Fireworks and the parade this weekend of course, but we're doing kid's storytime in the park on Tuesday and then there's the 5k, movie night at the community center, and the fire department water fight..."

Garrett smiles warmly, adjusting his horn-rimmed glasses on the bridge of his straight nose. The action makes my insides glow a little, because it's something I constantly do. Not because I can't keep them on my face, but because it's a nervous habit. Garrett doesn't strike me as the nervous type at all, so that little adjustment just makes him seem relatable to me.

He glances across the room at Regina, who's busy winding the cord up, and then back to me.

"Well, you're in luck, Emma," he says softly. "I'll be here for all of it, and more."

My hands slip on the bookshelf. "What?"

Garrett smiles and moves closer, coming to stand directly in front of me. "Can I let you in on a little secret?" he asks, his honeyed voice quieter than I've yet heard him speak. The back of my neck tingles.

I nod.

"I'm thinking about moving here."

"*Here*? To Larkspur?"

He bounces his eyebrows excitedly. "My next book takes place in a small town," he explains, his voice going even quieter, letting me know he's sharing a legitimate secret with me. "I grew up in Minneapolis and I've visited small towns many times, but never long enough to get the genuine feel of what it's like to live in one, you know?"

"Sure," I agree.

"I want to do it justice, and Larkspur feels like just the right place. So, I'm going to need all the intel. I want to know all about what it's like to live in a small town—the good, the bad, the ugly." He looks me up and down quickly and then winks good-naturedly. "Though I certainly haven't seen much in the way of ugly so far."

My pulse bangs against my temples. My face goes hot. He—?

I manifested him.

It's the only explanation for the perfect guy dropping out of the sky and putting down roots in my hometown. What are the odds?

Caitlin is going to freak out.

"There's no better way to get to know a town than from one of its residents. But the amazing thing about *you*, Emma, is that you're also a librarian and a reader. You'll be so much help to me. So, what do you say, hmm?" He slips his hands into the pockets of his khaki chinos, that friendly, warm smile pointed at me. "Care to have dinner with me, and you can tell me all about Larkspur?"

I just barely keep the squeak of surprise and excitement from exiting my mouth.

Dinner?

With *me*?

I blink at him, stunned.

I can count on one hand how many times a man has asked me out. If there was a subtle way to pinch myself, I would right now.

Wait, wait, wait...

I quickly replay what he said in my head, realizing he said nothing about getting to know me specifically. There was no mention of the word "date." He wants to talk about Larkspur. For his next book.

A little of the nerves evaporate. Just book talk. There's no pressure.

Maybe he'll put me in the Acknowledgments. *Eek!*

Swallowing hard, I return his welcoming smile. "Okay."

Garrett beams. "Fantastic. We can finish up here, and then we can go wherever you suggest for dinner."

I nod, taking an absent step back toward the bookshelves. "There's a new restaurant in town, actually. It just opened last month."

"Perfect."

My excitement simmers through my veins as my coworkers and I finish putting everything back. I try to keep my head about having dinner with Garrett Waterstone. More than anything, I wish I could call my sister right now. Undoubtedly she'd tell me to open the door—let in Mr. Right.

But it's not a date—he made that clear. This is for his work.

I shouldn't assume he's interested in me just because he insinuated that I'm easy on the eyes. No one has ever flirted with me, which just means I'm not used to it. He's a charismatic man, that's all. He meant nothing by it.

Caitlin's whole point, though, was to encourage me to make something happen—to act, and not just hide away in my romance books.

Could Garrett Waterstone be my real-life romance hero?

He definitely fits all the criteria. Handsome, funny, sweet, friendly, intelligent. But most importantly, he loves books. Could there honestly be anyone better for me to end up with than an author? It sounds too perfect to be a coincidence.

Twenty seconds of blind courage...

I glance over to find him already looking at me, smiling. He doesn't look away, and I smile back.

"I'd offer to drive, but I got a flat on the way into town yesterday, so I'm trying to drive it as little as possible until I can get a new tire this week," Garrett says as we step outside. He mentioned in his speech it's the same make and model of the car in his book, which is fun.

The summer sun is bright overhead, beaming down on my shoulders.

"Oh, I didn't drive to work," I tell him quickly. "I like to walk."

Garrett's dark eyebrows raise slightly, just the start of a negative emotion crossing them, but then he smiles sweetly. "A walk sounds lovely. Is it far?"

"Just a few blocks down to Main Street and then a couple over from there."

"Perfect." He pockets his keys and gestures for me to lead the way.

He falls in next to me, his gait casual and at ease. The wind pushes at his shirt, highlighting his trim body and strong arms. I do my best to keep my eyes forward and not imagine him wearing one of those tweed jackets with leather patches on the elbows.

"Oh, I should let my mom know I won't be home," I say, reaching into my purse. I take a second to type out a text explaining not to expect me home for dinner and then stash my phone back in my purse.

"You...live with your mom, then?" he asks, sounding a bit puzzled.

"Yes. My sister too. My mom is—um, she's—" I falter, glancing at him. It isn't that I don't want to tell him my mom is in a wheelchair. I just don't want to talk about how it happened or explain my dad is gone. It's too much to say to someone I don't know, or even someone I do know. I clear my throat. "She's a paraplegic."

For the first time, Garrett's signature smile is absent. "Oh, I see."

I nod, looking down at my tan sandals as we walk.

Out of nowhere, Garrett snorts.

My head whips toward him. I find an amused expression on his face.

"When you said you had to let your mom know where you were—" He snorts again. "For a second I thought I had misjudged your age and asked a teenager out to dinner."

A smile curls on one side of my mouth. He smiles back with so much affection my heart skips a beat.

"Not a teenager," I confirm.

He nods with a chuckle. "Good. And it's good that you and your sister are there with her. That says a lot about you, Emma."

I blush, but can't figure out what to say.

We walk the rest of the way to The Swedish Chef, with Garrett doing most of the talking. He's definitely an external processor. His enthusiasm for my little town makes me feel warm inside. He points out everything like he's never seen a brick building or antique shop before. He even had something to say about the light posts, something I've never given any thought to.

When we get to The Swedish Chef, Garrett opens the door for me like a true gentleman. I smile at him and duck inside. We're met with Larkspur's newest hotspot. The walls are painted a rich navy blue, with cream accents. On the far wall hang a dozen frames filled with family pictures. Beautifully restored hardwood floors ground the space. Most of the tables are filled, even though it's not quite five o'clock.

I know nothing about Swedish food, but the aromas coming from the kitchen—onions, garlic, meat, and yeasty bread—instantly make my stomach grumble. I wonder if Lee's parents' house smells just like this. Does Lee's house smell like this too?

I shake my head slightly, because thinking of him just brings me back to the horrible moment in the library. I don't want to think about it ever again if I can help it. I feel so bad I wonder if I should apologize to Lee, but I shake that away too.

We pause at the wait stand before a hostess bustles over. I glance at Garrett, as if to say *that* is a teenager. But he's too busy smiling around at all the people eating and taking in the space.

"How many?" she asks, understandably eyeing Garrett because his level of handsomeness doesn't exist in our town, only in Hollywood.

"Two, please," Garrett answers cheerfully, and we follow the hostess to an open table by the window.

She sets down the menus and says our server will be with us shortly.

Garrett pulls out a chair and looks at me expectantly.

Oh.

He pulled out my chair for me. *That's very sweet.*

I smile shyly and sit. He scoots the chair in for me and then takes his seat.

I fidget with the hem of my sundress.

When we were walking, I didn't feel as shy, but now I have to sit across from this handsome man and try to think clearly. And speak like I don't have a stutter or lava for skin.

I remind myself again it isn't a date, and make myself busy with perusing the menu.

"What a cozy little café," Garrett says, peering around. "It's a far cry from Demi in Minneapolis, but that's the point, right?" He meets my eyes. "This is what I'm here to experience."

Oh, dear.

Would it be the rudest thing in the world if I disappeared to the bathroom where I could text Caitlin?

I resist the urge to fan my face with my menu.

Garrett just smiles and then looks down to take in the menu. He sees what I do—most of the menu items have a Swedish name and then a description beneath, for us non-Swedish people to read.

Mom, Caitlin, and I came for the grand opening last month. We waited in line for more than an hour, but it was so, so worth it. I had the Swedish meatballs, and they were delicious. I'm happy to be back here to try more of Lee's family cuisine.

"Hello there," says the waitress. Her name is Diana, and she's one of Caitlin's friends from high school. She smiles at me in recognition and then does a double take when she sees Garrett. He just grins at her. "What would you two like to drink?"

"Water is fine," I tell her.

"And for you?"

"Is there a wine list?"

"No, I'm afraid not. Will hasn't gotten a liquor license yet," Diana explains with a slight wince.

"Not a problem at all," Garret assures her. "An iced tea would suffice."

"Great. I'll be right back."

Diana's eyes linger on him before she glances at me in a confused sort of way, like she's wondering how the heck I ended up on what looks like a date with someone like Garrett. That's fair, honestly, because I'm sort of still wondering the same thing. She turns and heads toward the kitchen, another waitress exiting through the kitchen doors.

I instantly recognize her and am pleased when her gaze sweeps over the room and lands on me with a bright smile.

"Emma," Lacey Murdock exclaims as she makes her way over to say hello. Even though she works at Svea's Boutique, she's here a lot on the weekends to help. There's even a menu item named after her, which she shamelessly tells everyone is the best thing on the menu.

I return her smile quickly, feeling special like I always do when she singles me out.

"Hi, Lacey," I say when she stops in front of our table.

"I was just telling Will the other day I wished I had more time to read so I could join Book Club," she says, beaming.

"Oh, I love a good book club," Garrett chimes in, not afraid of inserting himself into the conversation Lacey started with me.

Lacey turns to say something to him and then stops, her brown eyes going round. Even though she's madly in love with Lee's brother Will, she's not blind.

"Uh, Lacey, this is Garrett Waterstone. He did an author talk and book signing at the library today," I introduce awkwardly.

"A pleasure to meet you, Lacey," Garrett says warmly.

She blinks and slides her eyes to me. "Oh, that's nice," she says slowly, her usual bright smile noticeably absent for two beats before it reappears.

"Well, welcome to Larkspur," she tells him happily, studying him closely even as she reaches out to shake his hand.

Garrett flashes those pearly whites at her and releases her hand. "Thank you. Emma here doesn't know it yet, but I'm basically recruiting her to be my tour guide for the next couple of weeks."

Lacey's eyebrows raise in surprise, and she looks over at me, as if trying to gauge the accuracy of what he said.

"Librarian by day, tour guide by night, I guess," I joke nervously.

Garrett lets out a beautiful, deep laugh, drawing the attention of every table near ours. Grandma Janssen perks up from two tables down, which means it's only a matter of time before the whole town knows I'm having dinner with Garrett Waterstone.

I blush, not used to anyone thinking I'm funny. Lacey gives me an indulgent, sweet smile that lessens just slightly when she looks back at Garrett.

"So, you're staying for a while, then—that's great."

"I'll be here for a couple of weeks to do some research for my next novel. If all goes well, I'll be buying a house here before the end of the month," he explains to her, even though his blue eyes stay on me.

My heart pounds. He's totally serious about moving here. *Here.*

Lacey mutters something that sounds like, "bobbins." Garrett continues, not having heard her.

"What better way to write a story about a small town than to live in a small town, right? For now, I'm staying at that adorable little inn and fully immersing myself into the local community, with Emma's direction, of course." He winks at me, and my stomach dips.

"Wow," Lacey says, her smile slowly fading into a serious expression I don't understand. "Um, so you're going to move here...permanently?"

Garret shrugs, finally removing his gaze from me to look at her. "It takes me a full year to write a novel," he tells her. "So at least that long, maybe longer if I like it better than Minneapolis."

Lacey nods once and then keeps nodding, her brown eyes darting between me and Garrett.

"Lacey is actually a transplant from Minneapolis," I tell him, leaving out the story about how she ended up stranded here last Christmas because she hit the legendary albino deer, Albie. "She knows firsthand what it's like to move out of the big city."

His blue eyes light up with excitement. "Is that so?"

"Yes, that's right," she says almost absently, rocking back on her heels. Her hands fidget with the hem of her navy-blue half-apron.

I frown slightly. Is *she...okay?* I don't think I've ever seen her so anxious.

She clears her throat. "Well, I'd like to stay and chat some more but—uh, I have to get back to work. Yeah. Work. So...I'm gonna go."

"Of course," Garrett tells her graciously. "We have a date to get back to."

My head snaps from Lacey to Garrett.

He said it.

He said *date.*

Lacey squawks in surprise, and then immediately dissolves into nervous laughter. She takes a step back, casting an almost panicked look at Garrett. "It was nice meeting you. Okay, bye!" She immediately spins on her heel and hightails it back through the door to the kitchen.

I blink after her, confused by her strange behavior.

Garrett's eyebrows lift in amusement. "She seems nice."

My throat is dry, and I look around for Diana, hoping she brings our drinks soon.

I'm on a date with Garrett Waterstone.

I could insist it's not a date. I could remind him about what he said at the library.

Or...

This is my chance to prove that I *can* act. I can prove to Caitlin, and myself, that I'm capable of taking the reins of my own destiny.

I take a deep breath, making my choice.

My face flames as I smile shyly at Garrett.

Like I told Caitlin the other day, *if he wanted to, he would.* And this man very much would.

Chapter Seven

Lee

Everything Mamma said at the library has been swirling around in my brain since I got home. Sometimes her words bolster me and sometimes I'm left feeling just as hopeless as before. I thought mowing the lawn would be a good distraction from it, but all it's gotten me is a sweat-soaked shirt and a low-level headache.

My phone vibrates in my pocket for the second time in five minutes as I finish the last pass. I kill the engine and grab my phone.

Two missed calls from Lacey.

Hmm.

It's not unusual for her to call or text me, but twice in a row? It's excessive even for her. If it were Svea, I wouldn't think anything of it. Sometimes she'll unknowingly call me five times in a row because she's sitting on her phone while she sews at work.

Anxiety spreads through my stomach. I'm wondering what in the world she would need to call me twice in five minutes for when it rings again, Lacey's name coming on the screen.

With a sense of foreboding, I accept the call.

"Lacey? What's going on?"

"Finally, you picked up! Lee, we're at DEF CON one here, buddy!" she exclaims in the most panicked voice I've ever heard come from her. "This literally couldn't be worse."

"What? What happened?" I leave the lawnmower and hurry across my backyard toward the house, ready to grab my keys and get in the truck, not even sure where I need to be going. My mind instantly races to the worst possible scenarios. Svea's Boutique flooding from a burst pipe. The Swedish Chef is on fire. "Where are you?"

"At the restaurant, and she's *here*! On a *date*!"

I clutch my chest, relieved there's no catastrophe. I should know better. Lacey errs on the side of the dramatic.

"Who, Lacey?" I growl out impatiently.

"*Emma*," she screeches, like I should've already figured that out.

My steps falter. Emma's on a date?

The brief rush of relief I had goes up in smoke, replaced by a downpour of dread.

"She's sitting there by the window and he's smiling at her like she's the most adorable thing on the planet—"

A door opening in the background cuts her off and the volume of the call lessens, like she's holding the phone away from her face. "What should we do, Will? I could drop a drink on him or—"

"We're not doing that," Will answers her.

"Lacey, focus," I snap, my heart beating fast and painfully in my chest. "Who is Emma on a date with?"

She scoffs loudly. "I don't know, some fancy guy named Ferrett Waterslide or something," she answers distractedly.

Ferrett—?

The breath goes out of me completely.

No.

I squeeze the bridge of my nose, hurt and anger slamming into me from all sides. "Åh nej..."

"He's a real charmer, too, Lee—he has her eating out of the palm of his hand."

My chest tightens as I struggle to get in a full breath.

She's...she's on a date with *Todd*.

"Honestly though," Lacey keeps right on blabbing, "when he said they needed to get back to their date, Emma looked just as surprised as I did to find out they were on a date. It was weird."

I sit down heavily on the top step of the deck and rest my pounding forehead in my palm.

"We can't let him make a move on your girl, buddy. Can you get here?"

"No," I say, resigned. "I'm not coming."

"*What?* Lee, this is *Emma. Your* Emma," Lacey blurts out.

"She's *not* my Emma," I mutter painfully. "She can go on a date with anyone she wants to."

"But, Lee!"

"It's just one date," I tell her wearily, dropping my hand away from my face. "He'll probably be on his way back to Minneapolis tomorrow. Nothing serious can happen between them in that short amount of time."

Saying it aloud comforts me. There isn't time for her to fall in love with him. He's not from here. He's going back to Minneapolis, and hopefully he'll never return.

I'm relieved she won't end up with him, but the relief is nearly obliterated by the fact that she won't end up with me either. Because her going on a date with him is proof that she couldn't be interested in me like that.

"Lee," Lacey wails out. "He's *not* going back to Minneapolis."

Goosebumps rise over my skin.

"He's in Larkspur for the next couple of weeks, basically house hunting so he can move here."

My ears ring, and I pull the phone away. Lacey keeps talking, but I can't hear a thing.

My chest squeezes tighter, and I drop my head between my knees to keep from hyperventilating.

"Lee!" Lacey yells through the phone.

"I'm...here," I say with difficulty, switching the phone with a shaky thumb to speakerphone.

"Did you pass out? What the hell?"

"He's *moving* here? You're sure that's what he said?" I ask, my voice coming out all breathy and weak and strangled.

"Yes. He said *moving*. And he said Emma's going to be his tour guide—meaning they're going to be spending a lot of time together."

No...

My mind goes back to the library, when Emma introduced herself and he said it was lovely to meet her. How he asked if she and I were together. I thought he was just being a jerk, but he was actually asking...because he's interested in her.

And why wouldn't he be? She's a sweetheart. She's everything good and pure and...he's definitely not. He showed me his true character on the side of the road yesterday. And he might fool Emma or Pappa, but he can't fool me. Emma deserves to be with a good man, and *Todd Weiner* is no good man.

"I...I'll call you back."

"Lee—" Lacey says, but I hang up and toss my phone on the deck next to me.

I stare out at the freshly mowed lawn, blood pulsing loud in my ears.

The future rearranges in front of me. Deep down I knew that if I didn't shoot my shot with Emma, one day she would probably end up with someone else—some faceless guy at the end of the aisle from my recurring dream. And now I can picture *Todd* there instead.

It would hurt to see her love someone else, but it would be agony to see her love *him*.

She has every right to choose him. But I can't let her choose him without her knowing exactly who he really is. I can't let him fool her into thinking she's getting a happily ever after with the man of her dreams when he's really just a conceited con artist.

He doesn't know how to love anyone but himself.

A dog could show her truer love than he could.

And deep down, I know I could love her better than he could.

If I don't show her I'm capable of the kind of love she deserves, then I'll be forced to watch her spend the rest of her life with someone else. If I take the chance and tell her how I feel—show her how I feel—and she says no, then at least I know I tried. Because if I don't try at all, I'll lose her anyway. Possibly to *Todd*.

I might not be her first choice or any choice at all when it comes to the kind of man she wants. Despite Mamma's insistence that I'm *lagom*, and not intimidating, it's still up to Emma who she wants to be with.

She can't choose you if she doesn't know you're a choice.

Mamma's echoed words are true.

I won't make Emma's choices for her.

But I'll be damned if I let him win her over without competition.

I have to toss my name in the hat. I have to step up and show her all the love I've been holding back. I have to quit hiding—let my guard down and show her my heart—even if it means she might break it in the end.

With a heavy sigh, I reach for my phone.

I'm not the kind of person to ask for help unless it's absolutely necessary. But I'm going to need all the help I can get. My original plan—asking Emma to dance at the Street Dance on Saturday—won't be enough. I'm going to need ideas of how to open up to Emma, and ways to show her that Garrett Waterstone isn't who he says he is.

I scroll to the group text between me, my siblings, and Lacey. I think to add my best friend Lars, but he's been pretty hard to reach since he started dating Amber back in December. He also can't keep a secret to save his life.

Lee: *I'm calling a meeting. Tomorrow. Noon. My house.*

Thankfully, the restaurant and Svea's shop are closed on Mondays, which means everyone should be available.

Svea: *A meeting? You're not voting to kick me off the group text chain again, are you? I promised I would stop using that Super Troopers meow meme, and I totally followed through.*

I roll my eyes.

Lacey: *Yes!!! Please tell me this meeting is because of Emma!*
Svea: *Wait, what?! What did I miss?*
Lee: *Just be there.*

I hesitate and then decide to be honest.

Lee: *I need help.*
Lacey: *Yes! We're going to get the girl!*
Will: *It's about time, man.*
Lee: *I know.*

Chapter Eight

Emma

"So, do you have any siblings?" I ask Garrett between bites.

I've never been good at small talk. I'm not a social butterfly. I'm more like an awkward stick bug trying to blend in with my surroundings so no one notices me.

Thankfully, Garrett doesn't seem to mind I'm not nearly as good a conversationalist as he is. And thankfully, I don't mind him doing most of the talking. We're a good match that way, I guess.

Garrett sips his iced tea. "Two brothers, one older and one younger," he answers with a less than authentic smile. "The older one is a lawyer, like our father."

"Oh, that's nice."

He nods, dipping a forkful of pot roast into his mashed potatoes.

The restaurant is packed now. It's a struggle to focus on Garrett with so many curious eyes on me. I'm used to flying under the radar, but that's impossible while I'm sitting across from someone as magnetic and charming as Garrett Waterstone. No doubt half of the people in here recognize him from the library event earlier, or they're wondering who this handsome stranger is.

It doesn't help that I'm rarely out with anyone besides my family. I don't think I've been on an official date since high school, and it was just to Cozy Roast with Brock Plafke. At the end, he asked me if he could copy from me in algebra now that we were dating. There was no second date.

I glance at Garrett's handsome face, my gaze snagging on his horn-rimmed glasses. He's probably been on a hundred dates—asking someone out every weekend without a thought.

"We're not that close," he adds, quieter. "My family doesn't have Sunday dinners or celebrate birthdays together. Everyone's too busy. Half of the year I'm holed up writing and the other half I'm promoting a book, you know?"

"Sure."

That makes me a little sad for him. Doesn't sound like he has a solid support system. I couldn't imagine not seeing Mom and Caitlin all the time.

I wonder who he spends all of his time with, if it isn't his family. Does he have hordes of friends he hangs out with in Minneapolis? Is he close to his assistant or his agent instead? Does he have famous author friends?

There's a part of me that knows he wouldn't mind if I asked him any of those questions. Garrett seems like an open book. But I can't find the words to explain my bewilderment at his family situation without it coming off incredulous or pitying.

Thankfully, he changes the subject.

"So, what made you want to become a librarian?"

I cut into a meatball. "Because I love reading," I answer easily, because it's literally the whole reason and really isn't more complicated than that.

"That's why I wanted to be a writer, of course." He flashes a grin, which fades into something more thoughtful.

Something about it makes me smile too. I like the way I can see him thinking. Thinking is my favorite, second to reading. Maybe that's why I've always been drawn to Lee, actually. I can tell he's always thinking about something, and yet his sentences are always so direct and to the point.

I mentally shake my head.

You're on a date, Emma. Stop thinking about another man—another man who would never ask you on a date or think about you twice.

"You know, for a while I wanted to be a screenwriter," Garrett tells me with a dreamy sort of expression. "I liked the idea of writing movies because that's the way I see it in my head when I'm writing. But my stage directions just became longer and longer until I realized I had half of a novel written around the dialogue." He chuckles to himself, and I join him. "Being an author isn't as glamorous as writing movie scripts, but it feels like home."

I smile at him. "Books feel like home to me."

Garrett returns my smile. "Precisely," he agrees. "I like having that in common with you, Emma. Not everyone thinks of books the way that we do."

He has a way of making me feel special and important that I'm not used to. This is nice. Validating, even.

This is going well.

"I'm really looking forward to spending more time with you this week. I have a feeling I'm going to love it here."

"So you're serious, then? About moving here?"

That too-blue gaze moves softly over the features of my face. "Yes, I'm serious."

Somehow the universe has aligned, it seems. I never thought a man like this would walk into my life with such openness and intention. It's a dream come true. It's everything I could hope for. I'm glad this turned into a date.

"*Trouvaille,*" he says then, smiling gently at me.

"Sorry?"

"It's French. It means 'something lovely found by chance.' That's what you are."

My cheeks flush. This man is perfection itself. He's a lover of words, just like me. What could be better?

"You speak French?" Somehow it wouldn't surprise me if he spoke a dozen languages.

He shrugs. "Just a little. When I travel abroad for book tours, I try to go to at least one new country so it gives me an excuse to dabble in other languages."

My eyebrows raise because there is not one relatable or normal thing about what he just said.

"Have you traveled much, Emma?"

I shake my head. "I've been to South Dakota a few times."

His eyes widen. "Isn't that like an hour from here?"

My attention drops to my plate, as if I don't make eye contact he won't notice my cheeks redden.

I'm not ashamed to be a homebody. Home is my favorite place, besides between the pages of a book. Looking after my mom is more important to me than traveling the world. Besides, travel costs money. I'd rather spend my money on things closer to home.

But I am embarrassed because my life probably seems...*small* compared to his.

Garrett clears his throat. "I suppose you'd prefer to stay close to your mom," he says belatedly. "That's admirable."

I nod, and for the first time there's a beat of silence. He clears his throat.

"You know, I don't tend to bring many souvenirs back with me when I'm abroad. My tourism is literary."

My brows scrunch in curiosity, awkward moment forgotten.

"Every language has a way of saying things, right? Some languages say it better than others. Like *trouvaille*." His blue eyes light up and my smile returns. "Or *dormiveglia*. That's Italian for the space between waking and sleeping." He winks. "I do my best writing between waking and sleeping, by the way."

My little word-loving heart picks up and I'm pretty sure it's showing all over my face because of the way he beams.

"One of my favorites is *cynefin*. It's Welsh. It means 'the place where you feel you belong.'"

The restaurant around us seems to hush just a little as he looks at me meaningfully.

"I think everyone is looking for that place," he says, just over the volume of the room. "I've been all over the world, and I'm still looking for it."

The idea that he's looked all over the world and somehow wound up specifically *here* with *me* seems nothing short of serendipity.

We talk long after our meals are finished and the bill has been paid. His friendliness and openness have me feeling like I've known him forever. It's easy to be smitten with Garrett, and I realize as we walk back down Main Street, the night air filled with the excitement of something new, smitten is exactly what I am.

I burst through the front door and quickly kick off my sandals. The kitchen is empty and the silence from the living room lets me know Mom already went to bed.

"Caitlin?!" I call out, probably the loudest I've ever used by voice before.

"Yeah?" comes my sister's response from the other end of the house.

I drop my purse, not even bothering to hang it up, and hustle through the living room. I head for the hallway and pass by my room, going directly for Caitlin's slightly ajar door. I can hear her talking as I push it open.

She's sitting on the edge of her bed with her phone pressed to her ear. Her blue eyes go a little wide when she sees my excited expression. I shut the door and lean against it.

"Uh...I gotta go," she says into the phone and hangs up. "What's going on?"

I bite my lip, hesitating because I can't even believe what I'm about to say.

Caitlin slowly stands up, studying me. "Emmy..."

My smile peeks out. "I—I just got back from a..." I swallow the lump in my throat and my voice fails me, coming out as a whisper. "A *date*."

My sister stares at me for a long moment. "A date with *who*?" Her tone is slightly confused, because I don't go on dates.

I clutch my hands to my chest. "With...*him*. With Mr. Right."

She blinks.

"It's like I manifested him, Cait," I say, still whispering. Pushing off the door, I come a little closer. "He's literally everything I described when we talked the other day. Like he materialized out of all the romance books I've read and walked right into the library."

Caitlin's mouth drops open.

"I know," I agree. "His name is Garrett. He's an author—the one Henry requested to come speak at the library. He's...charming and handsome and friendly..."

"And you went on a *date* with him?" she blurts out.

I nod. My heart beats a little faster as I remember him asking for my number and making plans to see each other tomorrow. When we said goodbye, he grabbed my hand and kissed it. I blushed the whole walk home. "He's going to be moving here from Minneapolis this summer."

"Oh my gosh," Caitlin whispers. "You *totally* manifested him."

"Right?"

"Wow..." She shakes her head slightly, like she can't quite get her mind around what I'm telling her. Frankly, I can't either. "This is...amazing!" Her face finally breaks into a big smile.

I smile a little bigger too, my heart fluttering, because it really *is* amazing.

"So, when are you seeing him again?"

"Tomorrow, at Open Mic Night."

She rubs her hand together excitedly. "Yay, then I'll get to meet him." Caitlin lets out a little squeal of excitement. "I'm so glad you listened to me, Emmy. You're really going for it!"

I snicker. "Thanks."

She hugs me. "Give this chance everything you've got, okay?" she says, and then pulls back. Her expression is shuttered. "Believe me, there aren't that many truly good men out there. Don't let one slip through your fingers."

"I won't."

I leave her room for mine.

Letting Caitlin's advice wash over me, I take in a deep breath and let it out slowly.

I'm proud of myself for taking action. For *doing something*. Something I wouldn't normally do.

I take in the comfort of my bookshelf stuffed with books. So much of my room is the same as it was in my childhood—books, comfy bedding, the small wooden desk by the window. Everything the way it's always been.

It's clear that I've been inactive in more ways than just dating. Reading was my solace after Dad died, and over time it's evolved into a place to hide. It's much easier to stay where nothing has to change—where I can pretend that Dad's just in the den reading and not really gone.

I wonder if Mom feels that way. If to her, he's just at work or fallen asleep in the recliner. If the dust on his books aren't proof of the passage of time, just a chore needing to be done.

Mom never intended for us to be her caregivers. She has nurses who help her and take her to her appointments. She's never been the one who's insisted we stay in the same house. But she doesn't push me or Caitlin to move out, probably because she knows this is the last place we were all a family. She can't ask us to leave the last place we lived with Dad.

But I've always known I can't live here forever. Caitlin too.

Despite the excitement of the evening, my shoulders tense as I sit down on the edge of my bed.

"Change is okay, Emma," I murmur. "Change is *good*."

I flop back onto the bed with a sigh. Garrett's handsome smile swims in my mind's eye. Butterflies fill up my stomach for a second, but then I remember how it feels like hummingbirds in my veins when Lee walks into the library.

Dating Garrett requires me to give up on the living daydream that Lee is for me. And something about that makes me incredibly sad.

Like reading your favorite book for the last time. Like losing the autographed hardcover copy of it and deciding not to look for it anymore.

But I know deep, deep down...there will always be a little place for him. No matter how unrequited, he's technically my first love. No one really gets over their first love...even when Mr. Right knocks on your door. Even if you'll always wonder what could've been.

Chapter Nine

Lee

I 'm pacing like a wild animal the next day as I wait for my siblings and Lacey to arrive. My stomach has been churning all day because...I *have to talk about my feelings for Emma.*

My shoulders drop as I sigh. I'm not good at being vulnerable, even with my family. Sometimes *especially* with my family.

Will figured out my feelings for Emma at some point, but he's only jabbed me about it every once in a while. I'm sure Lacey is well aware too, because she misses nothing. I have no idea what Svea knows.

But I know they'll do whatever they can to help. Svea can be a loose cannon sometimes, but she's crafty and thinks outside the box. Lacey is everyone's cheerleader and is always ready to help. And Will knows exactly how it feels to stick his neck out and go after what he wants. Not long ago he did just that, and now he's with the love of his life and owns a successful restaurant. He'll have lots of good advice.

And if they make fun of me a little or tease me about my feelings for Emma...well, I'll have to deal with it. Because this is my chance. If I don't take it, I might regret it for the rest of my life.

The door opens, halting my pacing. I look up to see Will coming through the door with two grocery bags. I thought nothing of his absence this morning because even on days the restaurant is closed, he's usually there doing something.

Lacey follows him, lugging a whiteboard under one arm and her purse in the other. Svea traipses in after them carrying a canvas-covered mannequin bust in both arms.

"What's all that for?" I grumble.

They put their things down on the kitchen island. I assumed I'd just be telling them my situation, and we'd talk it out. I wasn't expecting all this.

Will takes out containers of food from the grocery bags, smiling over at me. "We can't make a plan on empty stomachs, can we?"

Lacey pulls a foldable metal easel out of her purse and quickly gets it set up. She places the whiteboard on it and then digs back into her purse for a handful of dry erase markers.

"We can't make a plan without writing it down," she says brightly, tapping the whiteboard.

Svea slaps her hand down on the mannequin head. "I don't think this will be useful, but I like having a visual."

I blink, realizing how seriously they're taking this...and they don't even know all the information. For the first time since the Author Event yesterday, my shoulders relax. The panic and fear ease back. Just a little. Just enough for me to appreciate my family.

"Okay—I brought mashed potatoes and *västerbottenpaj*," Will says, popping the lid off the Swedish quiche-like pie. "And *kladdkaka* for dessert."

He must've made it all this morning, just for us. *Huh.*

Svea reaches for the container of *kladdkaka*, which is a kind of gooey chocolate cake, but Will swats her hand away. She scowls at him, and I can already see the wheels in her head turning, planning how to prank him.

Lacey grabs a stack of plates from the cabinet and brings them to the kitchen island. "Let's dish up and then we can get down to business."

"I don't think I can eat," I mutter.

Lacey grins. "Oh, he's so in love, and I'm so here for it!"

I give her a flat look and cross the living room. "You guys eat and I'll talk, alright?"

"I've never heard you volunteer to talk *ever*," Svea points out with glee. "Not gonna lie, bro, when you said last night that you needed our help, I thought for a second that maybe you were dying."

There's the ribbing I expected. I side-eye my sister but ignore her comment.

"Yes, I need help," I gulp out, my stomach souring a little more even as the delicious scent of buttery mashed potatoes fills the air.

Will shakes his head just slightly, doling out cheese pie onto four plates. "Never thought you'd ask, man."

"I know." I swallow around the knot in my throat. "That's how important this is."

Svea claps her hands, her green eyes alight. "Operation Get The Girl, yeah!" She hops over to the whiteboard and writes it across the top.

Lacey tries to hand me a plate, but I shake my head. She grins and sits down at the island. Will sits next to her with his own plate. Svea hands me the marker and gestures for me to take the floor. She snags her plate and sits on the living room rug in front of me.

I clear my throat, the tips of my ears burning hot.

"Well," I say, avoiding everyone's eyes. "I called this meeting because...I'm in love with Emma."

Lacey lets out a loud, genuine "awwwww" at the same time Svea snorts out a "duh." I narrow my eyes, but she just smiles up at me, chewing.

Taking a deep breath, I force myself to keep talking.

"Mamma says I hold back too much, and if I stopped doing that...then maybe..." I clear my throat again. "Maybe she would reciprocate."

Will nods thoughtfully, forking another bite of mashed potatoes into his mouth.

"I don't really know how to do that. But I know if I don't try...then I might lose her to one of the worst people I've ever met."

"Ferrett, you mean," Lacey supplies seriously.

My brother coughs out a laugh around his mouthful. "There's no way his name is Ferrett."

"It is! That's what he said!" Lacey insists, and then looks at me. "Right?"

My eyes roll up to the ceiling. "He's definitely a weasel of some kind, but no, Lacey. You're talking about Garrett Waterstone."

Svea perks up, eyes wide. "What? *That's* who you're up against for Emma's heart?"

"Wait, who's Garrett Waterstone?" Will asks her.

She whistles low and sets her plate down. "He's like the Brad Pitt of the book world."

Will's nose scrunches up, wrinkling his freckles. "I don't know what that means."

"It's bad news, that's what it means," Lacey exclaims, shaking her fork at him. He gently lowers her wrist.

"Easy there, big guns," he says, his eyes full of love and amusement.

"You didn't get a good look at him last night," she tells him. "He's a hunk. Like in a sort of nerdy, smart way that someone like Emma would totally eat up."

Bile hits the back of my throat.

"You're up against it, bro," Svea says grimly. "He's like the perfect man for her."

"This isn't helping," I growl, squeezing the dry eraser marker in my hand.

"You didn't let me finish," my sister asserts, getting to her feet. She leaves her plate on the floor and goes over to the counter where she left her purse.

I roll my eyes and pick up her plate, moving it to the island so it doesn't get stepped on.

Svea brings her phone over and reaches for the smart TV remote. A moment later, Svea's phone screen appears on the TV, where she's typing in Garrett Waterstone's name into Google.

I groan as his stupid face comes up with all of his writing accolades.

"*This* is Garrett Waterstone," Svea says, a small green laser circling his face on the screen.

Where did she get a laser pointer?

"He's published five books," she continues, "each one landing on the top of the *New York Times* bestseller list for weeks at a time. Is he handsome? Yes. Smart? Yes. Rich? Yes. Successful? Y—"

"*Svea*," I bark out, losing my patience.

"Hey," she barks back, her hands on her hips and the green laser pointing behind her at my bookshelf. "We need to know the facts. And not just about him—about you too."

She turns back to her phone, the laser blazing at the ceiling now. She scrolls and taps on a picture of me that she clearly took when I wasn't looking. Me at *fika*, shoving a cinnamon bun into my mouth.

Will and Lacey chuckle as I glare at Svea. She stifles her laughter as she circles my face with the laser pointer.

"*This* is Lee Christiansen," she says through a Cheshire grin. "Loyal brother, son, and friend. Good-looking in his own way, even with his signature scowl. Police officer. Book worm. Wet blanket."

My face twists into said signature scowl, letting her know just how unamused I am. She, as usual, is unaffected.

"Svee," Will says disapprovingly. "We went over this. No giving him a hard time."

My head snaps in his direction. *They went over this?*

"You said you would be on your best behavior if I brought *kladdkaka*," he reminds her.

Svea winces, and then whispers, "I lied."

Lacey snorts.

"You have ten seconds to redeem yourself or I'm kicking you out," I threaten.

Her mouth clamps shut for two seconds, eyeing me, and then she relents. "Garrett Waterstone sounds good on paper, but that's literally all he has going for him."

I blink, my spine straightening with a little bit of hope and a lot of interest.

"She's right," Lacey joins in. "He's shiny and new and exciting, but that's all he is to Emma right now. We can use that to your advantage."

"How?"

"You've already laid a foundation with her," Lacey answers right back, full of confidence. "Ferrett has nothing of any value."

"What foundation? There's nothing between me and Emma that extends past the library," I grumble.

"And do you know *why* it hasn't extended past the library?" Lacey asks, moving her hand in a circle to get me to keep talking, but I don't know where she's going with this.

"Because I'm an idiot?"

My siblings snort in unison.

"Yes," Svea says and points to the whiteboard. "Write that down."

Lacey sighs and moves closer, smacking her hand down on my shoulder. "It's because she thinks you barely know she exists."

My eyebrows disappear into my hairline. "What?"

She nods slowly, dropping her hand. "That's what she said at the Holly Ball, buddy. I told her she should dance with you, and that's what she said."

The room falls silent as I process.

She thinks I don't see her?

I rub at the ache building up in my chest...because I do see her. *She's all that exists.*

And I'm so bad at showing anything vulnerable that she has no idea.

Despair washes over me, smarting my insides like a thousand paper cuts.

"How do I...how do I change that?" I ask painfully, staring at the couch unseeingly.

Will gets up and takes the dry erase marker out of my hand. I look up, finding a gentle, sympathetic expression on his face.

"You have to..." He pauses, glancing at Lacey for a moment, and then looks back at me. "Lee, you have to just...*jump*. You can't just dip your toe in the water and expect her to feel such tiny ripples."

He steps closer to the whiteboard, writing as he speaks.

"You have to get vulnerable. Talk to her about things you've never felt comfortable talking about."

"Yes," Lacey chimes in. "Find ways to connect with her. A personal question or an inside joke can go a long way."

Will writes that down too.

"Smile at her. On purpose," Svea says. Her contribution feels just as serious as it does teasing.

"Talk about ideas, not just things or people," Lacey adds.

"Be around her as much as possible while Garrett is here," Svea suggests.

"Yes," agrees Will, pointing the marker at our sister. "There's all kinds of things going on this week for the Fourth. Let's do our best to get Emma to go with us so she doesn't have a chance to go with Garrett by herself."

I smile hopefully.

These are good ideas. Tangible, real ideas.

Maybe this could work.

"I have an idea you might not like, bro, but it would be effective," Svea says hesitantly.

All eyes turn to her. "We could get the gossip wheel involved."

"What do you mean?" I ask, one eyebrow raised skeptically.

"We start a rumor. We could make it a bad rumor about Garrett or...or a rumor that you have a crush on Emma. There's no way it wouldn't get back to her."

My neck heats up. "No," I say. "I don't want her to hear about how I feel from anyone but me." I glance back at the whiteboard thoughtfully, knowing what the right thing is. "And I don't think we'll have to start a bad rumor about him. I think his true character will shine through eventually...with a little pushing."

Lacey smiles in approval. "You're right. I can distract him with my own experience in moving here from the cities."

"I'll brag about all the awesome things you've done as a police officer," adds Will.

"I could prank him," Svea offers, all evil eyes.

I shake my head, smiling just slightly.

"Hey, isn't there Open Mic Night tonight?" Lacey asks. "We should go, just in case Emma's there."

Svea wiggles her eyebrows at me. "You should do something."

"Do something at Open Mic Night? Are you crazy?"

I don't sing, or play an instrument. I dabble in writing poetry, but I'd rather die than read my poor attempts out loud in front of anybody.

"Just read a poem or something," Svea suggests, like she can read my mind. "We could help you write it."

Lacey gasps, and I scowl at the dreamy expression on her face. "That would be so romantic, Lee."

"No."

"Yes," Will agrees with a sigh, like he knows how hard it's going to be to talk me into this.

"No."

"We'll help you write something," Lacey echoes what Svea said, clasping her hands together pleadingly.

"Absolutely not."

"You wouldn't have to dedicate it to her or anything," Svea says with a scoff. "Just stand up there and read a few lines of something—it would get her attention for sure."

My stomach hates this idea. But they're right. If Emma is there...it would be a good chance to have her full attention and let her know that there's more to me than my intimidating outer shell. Mamma said to show her...to let my walls down...

I let out a long sigh of resignation, which has everyone cheering.

"I'll get some paper," Will says cheerfully, already heading for the short hallway leading to our bedrooms.

"For what?"

He pauses and pins me with a "you're an idiot" expression that's almost as potent as Svea's.

"Uh, so we can work on a poem?"

Looks like I need to tell them.

My stomach clenches. I glance at each of them, hesitating as they all staring back.

"I...have something written already."

Lacey's mouth drops open. "*What*? You write *poetry*? Since when?"

I shrug. "I don't write regularly...just whenever the words strike me." I explain, mumbling through the last part of my sentence. They don't need to know about the flower book in my glove compartment. Yet...

My gaze shifts to Svea defensively, waiting for her to tease me.

But she's grinning. "I can't wait to hear it tonight."

I frown. "You guys don't need to be there."

Will comes back into the room, laughing. "That's funny, Lee. There's no way we're missing it."

"Yeah, we gotta be there to support!" Lacey chirps.

Will slings his arm around her shoulders and kisses the side of her head.

"You asked us to help," he reminds me, nodding toward the whiteboard.

"I know," I mutter, already regretting it.

Chapter Ten

Emma

About once a month, the Cozy Roast hosts an Open Mic Night. The event showcases the humble talent of the Larkspur community. And while I could never get up on stage for any reason, I enjoy being in the audience showing my support for those who do.

Tonight, the coffee shop is almost packed when Garrett and I show up. I usually can get a seat by showing up twenty minutes early, but tonight only a handful of chairs remain.

The three baristas are working hard fulfilling orders for decaf coffees, smoothies, and sandwiches. They look stressed, but I know this is good business.

"Have you eaten?" Garrett asks me over the deafening sound of the blender, nodding toward the counter.

I shake my head and follow him, getting in line.

He looks handsome as ever wearing a black V-neck T-shirt and the most pristine-looking pair of jeans I've ever seen. I've already noticed that his clothes are either very well taken care of or just mostly new. I wonder what he would buy if I took him across the street to Svea's Boutique, where every clothing item has been upcycled.

Garrett looks around cheerfully, glancing from the people sitting in the chairs to the small stage. He leans closer to me to speak, his spicy cologne briefly drowning out the coffee aroma.

"This is fantastic," he says, his blue eyes bright behind his glasses as his gaze flits here and there. "There's such a sense of community here.

An event like this in Minneapolis would be much bigger and therefore less intimate."

I nod, and we move up with the line. I like that he's seeing Larkspur with fresh eyes. It helps me to take notice too.

He digs into his back pocket and takes out a small notebook with a pen stuck in the spiral binding. I smile as he jots a few things down.

"For your book?" I ask when he closes it.

He flashes me a beautiful smile, all perfect white teeth. "Absolutely. I always have a notebook on me." He shoves it back in his pocket. "Do you write, Emma? Or just read?"

"Just read," I answer, clasping my hands behind my back.

"I love readers," he says warmly. "I'd be nothing without them."

I smile up at him, admiring his humility.

"Well, them and my agent." He chuckles and moves those unreal blue eyes to the menu boards over my head.

The blender goes off again, and I glance toward the door. Caitlin is coming directly from the salon, where she works as a hair stylist, so she can meet Garrett. Part of me wants her to meet him just to confirm I'm not imagining how great he is.

"What do you recommend?" Garrett asks.

"Um, it's all good," I answer vaguely. "I usually get the chicken Caesar wrap."

He nods, eyeing me for a moment. His usual smile dissipates into something softer. "You look beautiful, by the way."

My eyebrows lift in surprise, and my cheeks flush. "Thanks."

His charming smile returns, and we move up to the counter, our turn to order. He insists on paying, even though he paid for dinner last night, and he tells me to go grab us a place to sit while he waits for our food.

I snag three chairs together on the far side, keeping one eye on the door for Caitlin and one on Garrett. He's chatting with the other people waiting. It's clear he's one of those people who doesn't know a stranger. His confidence is something I admire but also envy. He probably hasn't felt shy a moment in his life. His intrinsic belief in himself is likely a big reason for his success.

Garrett makes his way over then with two water bottles tucked between his chest and one forearm, each hand clutching a plate. I stand up and wave him over. I take a plate and water from him.

"Thanks," I tell him as we sit, balancing our plates in our laps. "You don't have to keep paying for things."

"It's my pleasure, Emma." He winks, and then digs into his wrap.

We're about halfway through our meal when Carly Gustafson, the owner of Cozy Roast, comes to the stage. I glance around to see a dozen people standing in the back. Still no Caitlin.

"We have a lot of great things on the schedule tonight," Carly says into the microphone with a smile. "We have some of the usual performers, but we have some newbies tonight too."

Someone in the back shouts out a "whoop!" which makes everyone chuckle. I look back, recognizing the voice as Svea Christiansen. Before I can find her, Carly continues.

"So, first up we have John Lofton with a few original songs." She gestures to where John stands off to the side, with an acoustic guitar slung over his shoulder. He's the music teacher at the high school, but he also writes his own music and plays great cover songs too. He plays at least once a month at the Drunken Mallard.

Everyone claps as he heads over to the stage and points a weathered smile at the audience. "Thanks everybody. Here's a few you haven't heard before."

He jumps right in, strumming his guitar with practiced fingers and singing with a well-used voice.

Once we've finished our food, I take Garrett's plate and stack it on mine. I set them beneath my chair for now, not wanting to get up in the middle of John's performance.

Garrett bobs his head along with the beat of each song, a genuine smile stretched across his face, like there's nowhere else he'd rather be than listening to an amateur musician from Nowheresville. Halfway through the last song, he brings out his notebook again and writes something down.

"Let's give it up for John," Carly says, and applause rings out around the room. "Up next we have Alexis Martin on violin."

The applause picks back up as a high schooler comes to the front with her violin in one hand and bow in the other. She smiles, looking a little nervous, but once she brings her violin up into position, everything about her relaxes. She plays a rendition of "Nothing Else Matters" by Metallica that's beautiful and haunting.

When she finishes, everyone claps and cheers. Garrett leans over and says, "That was phenomenal."

I grin my agreement back at him.

The evening continues with Mona, one of the bartenders at the Drunken Mallard, singing a Mara Matthews song acapella. Then the high school English teacher, Ms. Overton, recites an excerpt of *Romeo and Juliet* while looking over at John Lofton the whole time. Garrett applauds vigorously for her.

Carly comes back onto the stage, her smile bigger than ever. "Alright, my friends. Up next, we have a newcomer to Open Mic Night. Let's make him feel welcome! Lee Christiansen will be reading an original poem. Where are you, Lee? Come on up here!"

Did she say Lee?

My neck swivels so quickly that it cracks. The applause is slow to start, mostly because everyone is caught off guard. It's rare for Lee to even attend Open Mic Night, much less take part in it.

My heart skips a beat as I replay what Carly said—that he wrote an original poem.

Excitement bubbles up inside of me.

I *knew* it. I *knew* there was more to him than meets the eye. I knew all the poetry he reads would be meaningful to him—enough that he *writes his own poetry*. I can't hold back my grin.

Lee walks by with a small sheet of paper in his hand, moving up to the stage with his usual no-nonsense, purposeful stride. Everything inside me sits up tall when he faces the crowd. His expression is the familiar pinched, grumpy one that I secretly have a lot of affection for. The only indication of nerves is the tight set of his wide shoulders.

He looks around, like he's looking for someone in particular—like he did at the library yesterday when he was looking for *me*.

Some instinct deep, deep down wants to raise my hand, so he finds me in this crowded room.

But then his eyes stop, pointing in my direction. I can't tell if he's looking directly at me or not, but either way, my heart goes crazy.

He clears his throat, lifts the paper, and nothing could have possibly prepared me for the words he reads slowly and deliberately.

There's dirt on my hands from all the flowers I've never given you
Violet irises, like the sweater you wear when it's cold
Crimson tulips, like your favorite color lipstick, bold
There's a whole world of colors I never noticed until I saw them on you

The breath leaves my lungs.

There's no way he's...

I have a purple sweater. It's my warmest...so I wear it often in the cold months of the year.

And...I wear deep red lipstick most days.

He keeps going, my ears pricked to the max so I don't miss a single word.

White daisies, like your sundress with the buttons black
Pink roses, like your cheeks under another blush attack

This time, a small gasp escapes me.

Because I have a white sundress with black buttons. It's my favorite...

And, sure, I'm not the only shy person in the town...but I blush every time I see him.

My poor heart beats so hard in my ears I can barely hear the rest of Lee's poem.

There's so many flowers I've picked and never given you
because I'm only the dirt on my hands to you

Lee lowers the paper and looks up, right over toward me again. Something in his eyes changes—a little of the typical hardness there dropping away—and for just one second, there's no one else in the room. Everything stops, like time itself is pausing just for us.

But then something comes down around my shoulders; Garrett has lifted his arm and settled it around me.

The volume of the applause rushes at me while Lee leaves the stage, tucking his poem into his pocket as he goes by me. His gaze stays on the floor, but I can't look away from him.

I turn my head to watch him disappear through the people standing in the back, including Svea, Lacey, and Will, who are all losing their minds with excitement. The door opens and I know he's gone.

And if this were a romance novel, I'd follow him.

I'd run after him down the sidewalk and dare to ask if those details in his poem were just a coincidence, or if...if he wrote those words about me. And in that quiet, stoic way of his, he'd touch my hair and tell me that of course he wrote it about me...because there's no one else for him.

Instead, Open Mic Night continues on. Carly comes back to the stage to introduce the next person, and Garrett leans closer.

"Not bad, but I could do better."

I look at him, some distant part of me grimacing. His expression is light, almost flirtatious. Confident. He's definitely talented enough to write poetry. He's a bestselling author. Garrett could write the most perfect poem in the world if he wanted to. But it wouldn't be Lee's.

Even if Lee's poem isn't about me—because the realistic side of my brain finally switches on and realizes that it's probably not—it's still a poem *he* wrote. He picked those words and deemed them worthy of being written and then spoken aloud. *He* is what makes them beautiful.

And I realize I'd choose Lee's writing—however amateur it might seem to someone like Garrett—over the most popular poet in the world.

I don't really hear the rest of the performances. I'm vaguely aware of them in the periphery of my brain, but all I can really focus on is memorizing the words Lee said. I don't know if he plans on being a regular at Open Mic Night, so in case he never reads another of his poems again, I replay his poem, over and over, again so I don't forget it.

When Carly tells us that's a wrap, most people get up to leave. The rest stay behind to talk to the performers, likely their family and friends. A few people who saw Garrett speak yesterday at the library come and say hello, so I take our plates over to the bin.

As I'm turning around to head back to Garrett, I spot my sister making her way toward me, milling through the people who are headed out the door.

"Hey."

"Hey," she says, glancing around. "Sorry I was late—I had to stand in the back."

"It's alright."

She raises her blond eyebrows. "So where's the guy?"

I nod behind her, where Garrett is chatting animatedly with a few people. I point him out to Caitlin, who whistles low when she spots him.

"Wow. You weren't wrong, Emmy, he's gorgeous."

I say nothing as we stand there, looking at Garrett's handsome profile. It's pretty rare to see someone that good-looking in the wild. He has a face for Hollywood movies—all perfect angles and flawless skin. There isn't anything I don't like about the way he looks, but...there's really nothing terribly interesting about being so handsome. Not once the shock wears off, that is.

Maybe I'm just more attracted to someone who doesn't look...perfect.

"Emma!" comes an excited voice from behind us. Svea approaches, Lacey and Will following behind her.

"Hi, guys," I greet them politely, turning around. Caitlin turns too but keeps her head pointed in Garrett's direction.

"Kind of an epic Open Mic Night," Lacey says with a big smile.

"Right?" Svea agrees. "I never thought I'd see the day that Grumpy Goose would read a poem in front of anyone."

"I didn't even know he wrote poetry," I tell her.

"Same," says Will, his arm draped around Lacey's shoulders from behind.

"So glad I got it on video," Svea adds with glee.

Will scoffs. "He's going to make you delete it, you know that."

"Only if someone tells him I have it." Svea raises her eyebrows at her brother in a challenging way.

I snicker at them.

"Caitlin, you came late. Do you want to see it?" she asks my sister, who whirls around at the sound of her name.

"Sure."

I don't even hide the fact that I'm watching it too as Svea holds out her phone. There he is, reading his poem in that deliberate, low voice of his. I'm aching deep down to have that video saved on my phone so I could watch it whenever I want.

"Wow, that's pretty awesome," Cait comments in surprise.

"Little did we know that the man of few words can actually string some beautiful ones together when he wants to," Svea says with a chuckle.

I smile at her and wonder how many other poems he's written. Does he keep a notebook with him all the time, like Garrett?

Glancing over my shoulder, I find Garrett still talking and not looking at all like he needs rescuing.

"What did you think, Emma? Did you like it?" Lacey asks me. "I'd love to get your opinion, being that you're so well-read."

I blush a little at the compliment. "I haven't read as much poetry as Lee has, but I liked it very much."

Caitlin frowns thoughtfully. "Do any of you know who he wrote it about? He's not dating anybody, right?"

My throat goes dry.

Lacey presses her lips together, like she's afraid she might say something she shouldn't.

"No, he's single. It's not for us to say who it's about," Will says carefully.

"You'll have to ask him yourself," Svea adds with a big smile pointed at me, like I was the one who asked and not my sister.

"Does your guy write poetry?" Caitlin asks me. Something swoops in my stomach a bit at her referring to Garrett as my guy.

"I don't know," I answer honestly.

"I didn't know you had a guy. Who's your guy?" Svea blurts out.

My cheeks burn as I look over at Garrett. He shakes hands with someone and then spots me. I wave, and he makes his way over.

"Uh, he's—he's not officially, you know, *my guy*..."

"But you did go on a date last night," Caitlin clarifies.

I nod as Garrett joins us, smiling at everyone in our little circle.

"Garrett, this is my sister, Caitlin," I tell him, and he reaches in front of me to shake my sister's hand. Caitlin's eyes go a little wide as she takes him in up close.

"So nice to meet you," he says with all his usual charm and warmth.

"And you remember Lacey. This is Will, her boyfriend."

Garrett grins and shakes his hand too. "Ah, yes. The chef from that delightful little café we ate at last night."

Will smiles politely.

"And this is his sister, Svea."

"Svea," he repeats, shaking her hand. "What a beautiful name."

I expect Svea to blush or at least look pleased at his compliment, but she eyes him suspiciously.

"Lee is our big brother," she says. "You know Lee, right? He was the one who read the poem about flowers."

Garrett stiffens just slightly beside me, and I notice how inflexible his smile becomes as he answers.

"Yes, I briefly met Lee yesterday at the library."

When he asked Lee if we were dating. The initial surge of humiliation dies off quicker this time...because of the way everything stopped after he read his poem.

Svea nods slowly, her eyes a bit narrowed. "He's a police officer," she adds for some reason—not quite a threat...more like a warning.

Garrett nods too. "A noble profession."

I smile. It really is a noble profession. Especially for Lee, who prioritizes helping others both on duty and off duty.

"Lee is very noble," Svea answers. "It's kind of annoying, actually."

Lacey snorts. "He's one of the good ones, even if he comes off a little grumpy."

"Sometimes women like that," Caitlin points out with a shrug.

"The strong, silent type," Svea agrees with a nod.

"I think a woman would rather have a good communicator," Garrett declares, shifting closer to my side.

"Who says a quiet guy can't be a good communicator? They just need less words to say what they mean, that's all," Svea defends, and suddenly this all feels awkward and too personal.

Somehow we're talking about Lee and also not talking about Lee at the same time.

Garrett studies her, his expression curious. "Are you seeing someone?"

Svea's expression falls a little, and she clears her throat. "Yes," she mutters, not sounding happy about it.

Hmm, maybe she and Clay are about to be off again.

Garrett nods. "Well, this has been lovely." He winks at me. "Thank you for inviting me, Emma."

"Sure," I say.

"I'm sure we'll see you around this week," Lacey tells him. "Did Emma tell you about all the things going on for the Fourth?"

"She mentioned a few things, yes. I'll go wherever she tells me to." He chuckles good-naturedly.

Everyone says goodbye, leaving me to walk out with Garrett and Caitlin.

I glance down the street, as if I might glimpse Lee somewhere, but he's long gone.

Chapter Eleven

Lee

Word travels fast in Larkspur. It's been about sixteen hours since I read my poor attempt at a poem, and the town was asleep for eight of those hours, yet...everyone at work has somehow heard about it. I've been on the clock for only a few hours, and Sherry, the dispatcher, has communicated with me over the radio two different times beginning with "roses are red, violets are blue..."

The gossip factor wasn't something I thought through completely. I didn't just read my poem to Emma, or even just to those in the Cozy Roast. I released it into the intricate network of chatty Cathy's who pounce on whatever snippet of excitement they can get their paws on.

Thankfully, I'm on patrol this morning and don't have to be stuck at the department where people can tease me to my face about it. Sanders already took his chance the second he saw me by telling me I need to do all my reports in poem format from here on out.

Ultimately, it doesn't matter what my stupid coworkers or the town gossips think. Their opinions are their own, and eventually something else will take precedence, and my poem will be forgotten.

But I did spend most of the night wondering about Emma's opinion of it. It's not like I can flat-out ask her. I purposely left right after I read it so no one would ask me about it. I didn't want to give anyone the opportunity to ridicule me or ask me who it was written about.

That's the worst part of it, though. There's no immediate reaction that I can bank on. I have to be okay with not knowing if she understood my poem was about her. The whole idea is to slow-play it...to show her how I feel with my actions.

The poem is just step one of the plan. I knew it'd be tough, but this is harder than expected. I kind of hate myself a little that it's this hard.

But I started this...I have to keep the ball rolling. This is my chance. I can't back out so easily.

Tonight there's trivia night at the Drunken Mallard. I couldn't care less about trivia night, but Lacey thought it would be a good thing to invite Emma to so she wouldn't have another date with Garrett. Svea is going to swing over to the library on her lunch break to invite her, encouraging her to bring Garrett.

Although I'd love to never lay eyes on that jerk again for the rest of my life, I need her to see the cracks in his façade. Sure, he dazzles women without even trying, but it'll be harder for him to do if I'm staring him down the whole time.

I take the squad car through town and go slower once I turn down the street leading to Larkspur Park. Storytime should be finishing up by now. As I get closer, I spot Emma doing crafts with about a dozen kids on the picnic tables near the statue of Charles Larkspur.

My heart stutters when I see she's wearing her white sundress with the black buttons.

A smile pulls at my mouth.

Did she do that on purpose?

I take a left and then another left, turning up the street which divides the park from the library.

Ahead, on the right side of the street, there's a kid driving one of those mini Hummers. His dad walks behind him, glancing up and down the street as they go, ensuring there aren't any cars coming. When he spots me in the squad car, he lifts a hand and I return it through the windshield.

I slow down, realizing as I get closer that the kid is driving a little police car. He must be three or four, if I had to guess, with the same brown hair as his dad.

Instead of pulling around him, I turn on the sirens and pull over behind the kid. He stops and so does his dad. They, along with all the kids playing at the park, turn to stare at me. I smile at the dad and turn off the sirens.

Grabbing my ticket pad, I get out and approach them. The little boy is staring at the squad car with round brown eyes. He swings them up to me when I stop next to him.

"Good morning," I say. He blinks up at me in awe. "Can I see a license and registration, sir?"

The dad chuckles and takes out his phone to record.

"I don't has a license!" the boy exclaims, hitting a button on his plastic dash, making a staticky siren sound.

"No license. Hmm." I come closer, making a show of examining his vehicle. "This car doesn't look road safe. And you know it's a federal offense to impersonate a police officer."

"Uh oh, Mikey, he might have to arrest you," his dad teases.

"No, I awwest *you!*" The boy shakes a plastic set of handcuffs at me.

I crouch down next to him and grab the pen from my chest pocket. "You're very tough," I tell him seriously as I write his name at the top. "You're going to make a good police officer one day. For now, you better leave it up to the professionals." I rip the citation off the pad and give it to him. "I'm gonna let you off with a warning this time."

Mikey takes the paper, looks up at his dad and then back to me, not sure what to think.

I smile at him. "You want to see the inside of the squad car, bud?"

His eyes go wide again and he nods vigorously. He gets out of his mini squad car and his dad takes his hand to bring him over. A handful of kids shout from the park and I look over at them.

"Can we see it too?"

"Please!"

"Yeah, can we?"

I glance behind them to where Emma is standing with the sweetest smile on her face, the skirt of her sundress blowing in the breeze.

"Is storytime over?"

Emma nods, gesturing for me to take them. It's not until then that I see Garrett must've tagged along, because he's sitting at one of the now empty picnic tables with a less than pleased expression pointed at me.

I wave the kids over and they rocket across the street. A few parents come over too, taking pictures with their kids in front of the squad car. Emma joins them, catching me off guard.

I let a few kids hit the sirens and pretend to drive. I let Mikey and his dad sit in the back seat. The kid is all eyes, taking everything in like this is the best day ever.

"Thanks, Officer," the dad says with a big smile, shaking my hand when I've shown them everything. "He'll be talking about this for months."

"No problem."

I shake hands and exchange nods with the other parents, who take their kids back across the street to the park again.

My eyes land on Emma, who's hanging back as the small crowd disperses.

"You want to hit the sirens, too?" I ask her, probably the first time I've ever said anything remotely teasing to her. It fills me with exhilaration.

Emma snickers, smiling, as I come closer. "You were great with them," she says quietly. "If you—if you ever want to do a storytime sometime, that would be really fun."

I blink in surprise.

"There would definitely be an audience for it," she adds, nodding toward all the kids. "We could read a book or two about police officers and then do some crafts..." She fidgets with her glasses in that shy way of hers. "Just an idea."

"It's a great idea. Tell me when and I'll be there."

She smiles up at me, her glossy black hair reflecting the sun.

"It's funny," Garrett says, coming across the street toward us with a stack of papers and a kid's library book tucked under one arm, "in the Twin Cities, no one is ever happy to see a police car. Not the case here, I guess."

I frown at him as he joins us.

"Oh, thank you," Emma says, taking the library materials from him.

"You know, I'd love to show you my typewriter," he says to her. "Maybe after you get off work, you could come over to the inn and I can give you a tour of it." He glances at me with a chuckle. "I mean, it's not a police cruiser, but I *do* have the same typewriter that Stephen King uses."

My breathing picks up. He wants to give her a tour of his typewriter? It takes everything in me not to scoff.

Before Emma can respond, I do. "Sure. I get off at six."

Garrett stares, obviously struggling with whether it would make him look bad if he tells me the offer was for just Emma. No doubt he was hoping to get her all to himself.

Over my dead body.

"Okay," Emma says, and I smile at her.

Looks like trivia night is off. I'm honestly not bummed about it.

"We could have a fire too," I suggest. "There's a fire pit in the back. I'll invite Lacey and Svea. Will's working, but maybe Lars could make it."

"That sounds great," Emma confirms.

Garrett forces a smile. "Yeah, great."

Pulling up to Larkspur Inn usually comes with positive emotions. This place is my parents' pride and joy, and even though Will isn't running it anymore, it still feels like a second home. Patty took it over in January, and she's been doing a great job. Even if someone like Garrett might call it "rinky-dinky," I've always thought it felt like an extension of my family.

The last time I was here was this winter when I delivered Lacey here in my squad car so she and Will could both quit being idiots.

Now they're together, happier than ever, and I'm here now, scowling at Garrett's stupid Mustang parked on the street and walking around the side of the house to the backyard, hoping to keep him and Emma apart.

The sound of chatting and laughter reaches my ears and I round the corner to find Lacey, Svea, Emma, and Garrett gathered around the fire pit in the middle of the small backyard. There's eight chairs pulled up around it. The fire has yet to be started, but Svea is arranging a small stack of kindling inside of the pit.

I make my way over, my footsteps muffled by the grass. The sun won't be setting for at least another hour, but it's low enough and tucked behind the towering pines, so the backyard feels hidden away from the rest of the world.

Emma's still wearing her white dress, and it still makes my heart pound. I'd be happier though if she wasn't sitting next to Garrett.

"There he is," Lacey calls, announcing my presence.

"Hey, bro," greets Svea.

"Hi," Emma says. I nod at her with a smile.

Just as I'm about to reach them, my phone buzzes, and I pull it out of my pocket to find Lars calling. I pick up with a frown, already knowing what he's calling to say.

"Hey, man," I answer, lingering behind one of the unoccupied chairs.

Lars sighs. "Hey, Lee. I know I said I would make it tonight, but I guess Amber has something going on, so I won't be there."

I turn away slightly from the group, frowning. I've barely seen him in the last couple of months. Amber has an iron fist on his free time. I don't know how to tell him her controlling tendencies worry me more and more as time goes on.

"That's a bummer. Feel like I never see you anymore."

He sighs again. "I know. Me too."

"You guys going to any of the stuff around town this week? Maybe we can meet up."

"I don't know, honestly. Amber changes her mind a lot."

I frown even deeper. "Well, not to sound like a jerk, but you *are* allowed to do things without her."

Lars says nothing for a long moment, hesitating. "Yeah, I know. It's just...easier to go with the flow sometimes. Hard to explain."

There's a deep exhaustion in his voice, worrying me even more. Some people start dating someone and, in the process, they become more themselves. Will is a good example. Lacey makes him better. She supports him in every way, and he's happier because of her. But Lars is slowly becoming less of the happy-go-lucky guy I've always known. Amber drains him and gets between him and the other people who love him.

"Lars, you know you can talk to me about her, right? If things aren't going that well, or whatever?"

"I know, man. Everything's fine, I promise."

I don't even think he believes that but before I can say anything else, he keeps going.

"I'll let you know about later this week—maybe we can meet up at the fireworks or something."

"Sounds good, Lars."

"Say hi to everyone for me. Later."

I hang up, pausing for a second before turning around to face everyone else, trying to figure out which of his family members I could talk to about him. His mom is one of the coldest people I've ever met, who spends all her time throwing pottery in their converted garage. Anders, his older brother, is almost as much of a jerk as Garrett, and not close to Lars. His dad is probably the best bet. Pappa has coffee with him and some other men at Alma's Diner once a week—maybe I'll start by putting a bug in his ear about it.

Pocketing my phone, I mentally shake off my worries and join everyone.

"Was that Lars?" Svea asks, kneeling with a match in one hand and a small scrap of paper in the other. The paper lights and she tucks it beneath the kindling.

"Yeah, he can't make it."

"Booo," Lacey whines, her fingers dipping into the bag of marshmallows. "I never get to see Lars."

"Yeah. He says hi."

"Oh, Lars—from Janssen Auto?" Garrett chimes in, seeming happy to be part of the conversation even if it has nothing to do with him.

"Yeah, that's him," I answer, eyeing him as I sit down next to Lacey. "Did he get you a new tire?"

I have only one goal in asking the question—finding out if he told Emma we met on the side of the road and not at the library.

"Yeah, he got me fixed up. Good guy," he tells Emma, not me. She doesn't give any indication Garrett told her about our unfortunate first meeting.

"He's Lee's best friend," Svea tells him, wafting at the growing flame with her hands. The scent of wood-smoke perfumes the air.

Garrett's eyebrows raise quickly. "Really?"

I raise mine too. "Yes."

"What do you mean, *really*?" Svea spits, glaring at him. I'm not sure if it's on Lars's behalf or mine.

"I—I just mean, Lars is very friendly and Lee is—"

Silence.

Not one of us—not even Emma—steps in to help Garrett from looking like he's about to insult me directly to my face.

Even without finishing his sentence, it's an insult. And I hate how much it stings.

Garrett clears his throat and laughs awkwardly, attempting to smooth things over. "Opposites attract, is all I meant."

"Yeah, and empty barrels are the noisiest," Svea growls. It's a Swedish expression to put him in his place.

My eyes move from scowling at Garrett to my little sister. My scowl softens. She gives me a hard time, but deep down she really does care.

Lacey takes the lead then. "You know, Lars and Lee came to my rescue once."

I lean forward a bit as Lacey launches into the story of how she wound up in Larkspur. "*Tack*, Svea," I mutter. It means "thank you."

She flashes me a murderous expression, like she would rip this guy limb from limb if I gave her the go-ahead.

"I swear on my life it was a baby Yeti," Lacey says with complete seriousness. Garrett is all ears, eating up her story.

My eyes stray to Emma across the growing fire, and my heart stops when I already find her eyes on me. For the first time, she doesn't look away, and neither do I. Her expression is...soft. Almost apologetic, like she's well aware I didn't deserve to be called out like that in front of everyone by Garrett.

"I thought I'd have to sleep in the jail for the night, but then Lee brought me here," Lacey says and lets out a wistful sigh as she looks up at the house. "And this is where I fell in love with Will. A month later I moved here and there's nowhere else I'd rather be." Lacey smiles to herself, then digs out her phone to no doubt text my brother.

"That's an incredible story," Garrett says with bright eyes.

"You forgot the part where we all conspired to get you back," Svea teases her.

"Conspired?" Emma pipes up.

Lacey giggles and puts her phone down. "Yes. Even Lee was involved." She smiles over at me. "He pulled me over on my way back into town and brought me here so I could talk to Will. Acted like I was under arrest and everything."

Svea snorts as the back door of the inn opens and Ben rushes out, a couple of grocery bags in his hands.

"There you are," Garrett says impatiently. "Took you long enough."

Ben says nothing, used to his boss's rudeness, and sets the bags down on an empty chair.

"Hey, Ben," I greet. He looks up, surprised at being acknowledged, and nods.

"Ben?" Svea asks, her head cocked to the side.

"Yeah, we haven't met Ben," Lacey adds, smiling.

"Oh, my apologies," Garrett says with a chuckle. "This is just my assistant, Ben."

Svea eyes Garrett. "Just?"

Ben waves a little nervously, like he isn't used to having this much attention.

"Hi, Ben," Emma says. "Nice to see you again."

He smiles at her. "You too." He starts taking things out of the bags. "Garrett sent me to get s'mores ingredients."

"Yes, just leave them there," Garrett instructs. "Then you can go."

"What?" Lacey asks, quirking an eyebrow. "No way, you should join us."

Ben tenses, shooting a glance at his boss.

Garrett's mouth squirms into a line, not quite a smile and not quite a frown. He's caught between trying to seem inviting and getting rid of Ben.

I do my best not to roll my eyes.

"Yeah, you should stay," Emma insists sweetly.

Garrett clears his throat, switching the charm back on so quickly and completely that my shoulders tense. "Of course. You're welcome to join us."

Ben hesitates, watching his boss carefully. He, like me, can probably tell Garrett doesn't actually want him to stay. Instead of sitting down, he makes himself busy with unwrapping the s'mores things and then takes over stoking the fire as conversation picks up again.

I watch him until Emma snickers at something Svea says, drawing my attention to her sweet face. The flames of the fire reflect on the lenses of her glasses. I desperately want to know what she thought of my poem. I wish I could read her mind so I don't have to find some way to ask her.

But ultimately I know what I have to do tonight. Somehow I need to talk to her alone, so I can address something that's been bothering me since Lacey said it the other night. Emma thinks I don't know she exists, and I need to make sure she knows that's the furthest thing from the truth and it always has been.

Chapter Twelve

Emma

I inhale the wood smoke-scented air and sigh, my body relaxing. Garrett and Lacey chat across the fire, talking about her move from Minneapolis and how she likes Larkspur much better. Svea tosses in funny anecdotes here and there. Ben makes himself useful whenever he can. And Lee sits quietly, listening and saying nothing, just like me.

Lee often wears a serious mask, but tonight the fire sharpens the way his expressions shift—a flicker of thought or a hint of amusement—and I can't help but wonder what's behind it. When his eyes drift to the flames, is he thinking about beautiful poetry, or is he just considering moving the logs with a poker?

I've thought about him all day, first because of his poem, and then because of the way he was so kind to the kids at Larkspur Park. It's not often I see him interact with kids, and my heart melted because he took a few minutes out of his day to give them all a positive experience.

As soon as I got back to the library, after Regina confronted me about the gossip going around about me and Garrett, I talked to Henry about Lee doing a storytime sometime soon. He loved the idea and I can't wait for it to happen. His dad and Will have done storytime the week of Christmas, many times over the years, and I always love it. But this will be even more special, because kids bring out Lee's softer side. I'm desperate to see more of it.

I had no idea he's a poet and is so good with kids. I'm learning so much about him this week.

"This is silly," Lacey says, standing up. "Let's switch seats, Emma, then I don't have to talk over you and Svea."

"Oh, sure." I stand up too, and we scooch past each other so I can have her seat between Svea and Lee.

Garrett's pleasant expression falls away when I sit down, but Lacey continues their conversation and he turns his attention back to her.

Lee radiates almost as much heat as the fire. Garrett's magnetism is strong, but not like this. Next to Lee...my whole self turns toward him like a flower following the sun.

And I think about him standing up on stage last night, letting down that iron guard of his enough to say his beautiful poem out loud. It took courage to do that. Would he have the courage to answer me if I asked him why he loves poetry? Would he answer if I asked him who he wrote it about?

Do I have the courage to ask him?

Garrett seems to be enjoying his conversation with Lacey. Svea has her phone out, texting. So I take in the way the fire casts shadows on some of Lee's features while highlighting others. There's something rugged and wild about his thick eyebrows and high cheekbones. His mouth is a dark red slash, but when his eyes catch mine, it curves upwards as if to let me know that he doesn't mind me looking at him.

"I liked your poem," I whisper, my voice betraying me like it usually does when I speak to him. It's only four words, but they feel chaotic leaving my mouth.

Lee watches me carefully, but I don't know what he's looking for. Sincerity? Honesty? I watch him right back, wishing I could look closely enough to see his thoughts scrolling on his forehead or in his eyes.

After a long moment where I forget about the four other people sitting around this fire with us, he finally says, "I hoped you would."

He hoped I would?

I'm not sure how to translate. Does he mean me personally? Or librarian me? Are they one and the same to him? How do I exist in his mind?

A firefly swoops between us, landing on the back of his left hand where it lays on the arm rest. His skin glows beneath it and I smile.

I bet he could quiet the most ferocious beast. He could soothe a crying baby or a scared cat. He might look like thunder, but there's some other intense, nameless force inside of him, just as strong but all quiet and calm.

"How long have you been writing poetry?" The question slips out before I've really even thought about it, which is a rarity. But Lee is drawing me out of myself by leaving me a lot of breathing room to think and speak.

"I don't write that much," he says, his deep voice low and growly even though his tone is gentle. "Just a line or two when it comes to me."

Garrett laughs at something Lacey says, but the warm sound of it feels a long way off. Like hearing it from the next room or on the other side of a closed door.

The firefly lifts from his arm, its bioluminescent light winking on and off in the falling light, and then lands on my knee.

Here's my chance.

"Why poetry?" I keep my eyes on the firefly as I ask it, because it feels personal and I don't want to cross some invisible vulnerability line.

Lee leans forward to rest his elbows on his knees. His eyes stay on the firefly as he answers, but I can't look at the little glowing insect anymore. I want to see his face when he explains.

"Poetry uses the fewest words possible to say the most important things."

I smile. Of course. A man who uses his words so sparingly wouldn't enjoy reading more words than are necessary to explain something.

"My favorite thing is reading a line of poetry that puts words to something I've never been able to." He smiles. Just a little thing, but it brightens his face more than the fire does. "Makes me feel connected to everything else when that happens."

"I love that," I say.

His brown eyes meet mine. My heart pounds.

As if the firefly can tell it's no longer being paid attention to, it flits off my knee. The glow of it gets bigger in my periphery a second before the firefly lands on the tip of my nose.

I stiffen, startled.

The most incredible sound rumbles up out of Lee's chest. He laughs. It's this rusty, gruff, huffing laugh that I've never heard before, and I forget all about the tickly, incandescent insect on my nose.

His laugh draws the attention of everyone else, and their laughter breaks the intimacy of our conversation. Suddenly their presence rushes back in and my cheeks heat up, even as I laugh too.

The firefly takes off and zips behind us toward the tree line where a few of its friends are blinking around the branches.

And when I look back to the group, I wish it was just me and Lee. I wish the spell hadn't been broken.

"There's a word for this," Garrett says, looking around at everyone and then at the fire with a gentle smile on his classically handsome face. "*Blazemoche.*"

"What?" Svea asks in a flat, disinterested voice.

Ben makes a surprised choking sound in response to her.

"It's the tranquility one feels when listening to a crackling fire." He grins at me and I smile back.

"There's a word for everything, huh?" Lacey says thoughtfully and then screws up her face. "That sounded really dumb, but you get what I mean."

Garrett chuckles softly. "Absolutely. That's what I love about my profession. It takes a certain kind of research to find just the right words. It's a skill, really, because I find, most of the time, those words aren't in English."

"Oh, *håll tyst,*" Svea mutters.

Lee snorts.

I don't know what she said but from her tone I can tell she doesn't care for Garrett's flowery language. I could see some people thinking that Garrett's way of speaking is boastful or self-important. I think he just loves what he does.

"What was that Svea?" Garrett asks politely, his blue eyes alight because she said something in Swedish.

Lee coughs. "Nothing."

"How about some s'mores?" Lacey jumps in. "The coals are hot enough now, I think. Let's go find some sticks." She gets up.

"Oh, that's alright. Ben can get us sticks," Garrett decides.

Ben stands, ready to do as his boss says.

"It's more fun to pick them out ourselves," Svea insists, getting to her feet.

"Yeah, poor Ben doesn't need to fetch us sticks," Lacey chimes in. "Pretty sure that's above and beyond the call of duty."

She's right. I smile at her.

Garrett frowns at Svea and Lacey in a way I don't understand. After an awkward moment, he relents. I eye him and his assistant, wondering if Ben is expected to go above and beyond like this all the time. I can see Garrett being a demanding boss, but in this case, I hope it's just because he doesn't want to get his hands dirty finding a stick.

The rest of us get up and make our way toward the tree line. I stay close to Svea as the others split off down the other direction.

"What did you say?" I ask her, keeping my voice down.

Svea rolls her eyes in the dim light and bends to grab a stick off the ground. "I just said *shut up.*"

My eyes widen a bit. Wow, she doesn't like Garrett?

She examines her stick, bending it slightly to test for strength and then tosses it away. "I don't mean to be rude, but he talks a lot." She pauses, her eyes flicking upward. "Actually, I kind of mean to be rude. I just don't have the appetite to be around another man who thinks he's the best of all the men who have ever lived. Like, calm down. Not everyone needs to be as in love with you as you are with yourself, you know?"

I reach down for a stick and stand up again to look at her. "I think he's just...confident."

Svea scoffs, and I move with her as she continues her search for a worthy stick. The others are down the other way, Lacey's voice and Garrett's laughter carrying across the yard.

"Trust me, Emma. Men who want people to fawn all over them don't know the first thing about how to love someone else." She waves her stick like a sword, giving it two clean swipes through the air. "And how dare he talk about Lee like he's some troll? Lee's a good man. I mean, he's a little rough around the edges but he's good to his core, you know? There aren't many people like him out there."

She's completely right about Lee. He didn't deserve to have his character called into question just because he isn't as friendly as Lars. But I don't think Garret intended to insult him...I think it probably just came out wrong. Svea is most likely worked up because she's protective of her family, and I can't fault her for that. I know if someone said something against Caitlin, I'd feel the same way Svea does right now.

"Yeah, Lee is one of the good ones," I agree. We walk a little further and I spot a better stick than the one I have, so I snatch it up. "Who's the other man who thinks he's the best of all men?"

She sighs in exasperation and snaps her stick in half. "Clay. He's an idiot. Why do I only attract *idiots*?"

I suddenly get the impression she was texting with Clay before and he must've upset her. Maybe she's just taking out her frustrations with Clay on poor Garrett.

Deciding not to read too much into Svea's assumptions about Garrett, I try to comfort her the way I would want to be comforted.

"There's someone great out there for you, Svea," I tell her softly. She stops her stick pursuit, and even in the darkness away from the fire I can see the pain in her eyes. "The real thing will find you. And I hope when it does, it's everything you hoped it would be."

Svea stares at me for a long beat. Just long enough to make me think I've said something wrong. But then she drops her stick and moves toward me, flinging her arms around me in a tight hug.

Surprised, I hug her back.

"Thank you," she murmurs, then pulls away. She swipes at her eyes with the back of her hand and my heart breaks for her.

"I—I'm sorry—I didn't mean to—"

"No, it's okay. You're so sweet," she says, waving me off and going to pick up her stick again. Then she turns back to me, links her arm through one of mine, and leads me toward the fire.

I glance over my shoulder to where the others are heading our way, my eyes connecting with Garrett's. He smiles and lifts one hand in a quick wave. I smile and wave back.

Svea releases my arm and we sit down.

"Your dress is adorable by the way," Svea says, grabbing my attention as she skewers a marshmallow on the end of her stick. "The black buttons are such a nice touch."

"Thanks." I appreciate her interest in my dress. Her compliment goes a long way since she makes clothes. I've frequented her boutique many times since it's opened and always find something beautiful there.

Svea glances at the other four, halfway to us and still out of hearing distance. She turns back to the fire and makes a thoughtful sound in the back of her throat. "Lee had a line in his poem about a white dress with black buttons. Hmm."

My heart races a little as I look down at the skirt of my dress. "Yeah," I acknowledge weakly. "Probably a coincidence. White dresses aren't uncommon."

She eyes me for a long moment. "If you say so."

Garrett takes the chair next to me, sitting where Lee had previously. "I haven't had a s'more in decades," he says with a big childlike smile. "I think I was maybe five years old? My grandparents had a house on Lake Minnetonka and we had s'mores right there on the shore. It was magical."

Ben, who in the darkness actually shares a passing resemblance to Garrett, smiles. I realize it's the first time I've ever seen him do it.

Svea torches her marshmallow and brings it out of the fire, watching the blaze devour the sugary confection. When it's good and black, she blows it out and assembles her s'more. Lacey's stick is slightly too bendy, so her marshmallow is dangling off the end of it. She holds it a bit too far from the coals for it to brown quickly, but her expression is happy. Lee holds his stick at just the right spot, expertly, patiently, rotating the marshmallow.

I focus on roasting my mine with difficulty. Mostly because all I can think about is what Svea was insinuating. Nothing good can come from me leaning into her narrative. Lee wouldn't...he wouldn't have written a poem about me. A lot of women wear white dresses, especially in the summer. It would be a dangerous thread for me to follow...because my poor heart couldn't handle it if I were wrong.

Chapter Thirteen

Lee

"It's the only thing I write on," Garrett says to me, Svea, Lacey, and Emma. Ben excused himself to his own room. We're all crammed into his guest room upstairs in the inn, standing around a folding table Patty must've hunted down for him. It's placed at the end of the bed with a typewriter sitting on it.

After we finished our s'mores, he not-so-smoothly tried to get just Emma to come up here to look at it. Obviously, the rest of us came too.

"Don't your fingers get tired?" Svea asks, stepping closer to look at the keys.

"Yeah, you have to lift your fingers so high and push them so far down," Lacey agrees, pushing the A-key down with her pointer finger. A satisfying *thwack* rings out as the mechanism stamps a lowercase A on the blank paper.

Lacey looks up at Garrett with wide eyes. "That was so fun!"

Svea snorts. "You need to get out more."

"What if you make a mistake?" Emma asks, looking up at Garrett. I can't help the way I scowl when he leans toward her, too close to her for my liking.

"Mistakes are just happy accidents," Garrett answers warmly. "Some of my best works have come out of a mistake."

"Your whole life is a mistake," Svea mutters next to me, low enough so only I can hear her. I think she's trying to make a joke, but the edge in her voice says otherwise.

She's ripe tonight. At first I thought she was just really dialing up the ridicule of Garrett, because that was part of the plan, but it's more than that. She's in a sour mood.

"Honestly, just writing on the same typewriter that Stephen King uses is enough of a muse to keep me on task. I don't make mistakes much."

I give him a flat look that he doesn't notice. I think it's at least the third time I've heard him say he uses the same typewriter as Stephen King since he's been in town. He included it in his speech at the library. His need to repeat it takes away all the possible clout he thinks it gives him.

Typewriters are interesting, sure. But I can't imagine he actually writes his entire manuscript on one. Having *one* copy of a manuscript is a terrible idea—what does he do, mail the whole thing to his editor? How does he edit things? None of it makes sense.

I wouldn't be surprised if this was just a prop, similar to his Mustang that he apparently only takes to events.

Downstairs, the front door opens and closes.

"*Hej alla!*" comes Will's voice. He must've closed the restaurant and come straight over.

"Upstairs, buttface!" Svea shouts back.

Garrett flinches at the volume of her voice and probably her nickname for Will.

I try not to smile.

Emma's face goes pink, and then she lets out a quiet giggle I can barely hear over Will thundering up the old staircase. He appears in the doorway with a big smile, nodding at everyone in greeting. His attention stops on Lacey, and they smile at each other like two love-struck idiots. I'd never admit how happy it makes me to see them like this.

"You all have to teach me some Swedish," Garrett says, grinning at Will.

"I'll teach you something," Svea pipes up, sounding sincere this time and not like she wants to slap him.

"*Släng dig i väggen,*" she says, and Will smacks his forehead.

Garrett does his best to repeat it, interested.

"What does it mean?" Emma asks.

"The literal translation is 'throw yourself into the wall,'" Svea tells her smugly. "But Swedes use it to say 'get lost.'"

Garrett's expression falls slightly. He was probably hoping for something conversational like, "how are you?" or "my name is Garrett." Not an insult.

"Damn, Svee," Will chuckles with widened eyes.

Svea's pocket rings, and she takes out her phone with a loud sigh. I watch her carefully as she reads the text. She gasps and looks up.

"I have to go," she blurts out, and sprints from the room. Her steps are loud as she races down the stairs.

Will and I look at each other, puzzled and suspicious.

The front door opens and closes, and then I hear a car door slam out front. Without hesitating, I rush over to one of the two windows and look out. Svea is down on the lawn, arguing with Clay, who appears to have just arrived.

Will and Lacey look down from the other window, concerned. Garrett is trying to peek over them. Emma hasn't moved, but her gaze is on the window behind me.

"They need to break up for good," Will says with a heavy sigh.

I look back out the window and have half a mind to go down there. None of us like Clay, and honestly, Svea doesn't really seem to like him either. I don't pretend to understand anything she does, but her dating life is especially mysterious. In a way, it reminds me of Lars, because his dating life is also a mess.

"Something is wrong," I say. "She wasn't herself the whole night."

"She's not normally like that?" Garrett asks, sounding a little relieved.

I raise an eyebrow at him, but he's still trying to see what Clay and Svea are doing. Instead, I catch Lacey's gaze, and I don't like her worried expression. She and Svea are roommates and business partners. There's no doubt she probably knows more about what's going on with Svea than anyone else.

"She did seem upset earlier when we were picking sticks," Emma tells me. "What can we do?"

My chest warms at her desire to help.

"I'll talk to her," Lacey volunteers.

A car door slams again and we all look out to see Clay's car pulling away. Svea is getting into her own car. When she's gone, we all move away from the windows.

Will clears his throat awkwardly. "Well, I guess you're going to need a ride home, huh, big guns?" he says to Lacey, who carpooled over here with Svea from the boutique.

"Thanks for showing us your typewriter," she says to Garrett, who smiles.

"Thanks for the good conversation. It was nice to hear about how you ended up in Larkspur."

My brother throws his arm around Lacey's shoulders and they head for the door.

I quickly realize Garrett and Emma will be alone together in this room if I leave, and that's definitely not happening if I have anything to say about it.

"I'll walk you out, Emma," I say, nodding toward the door.

"She can stay if she wants," Garrett challenges, even tilting his chin as if accusing me of being domineering. It reminds me of our lovely run-in on the side of the road, making my hackles rise.

"Some of us have to work in the morning," I remind him in a low voice.

He glances at Emma as she nods somewhat apologetically.

"He's right," she says gently. "It was a fun night, Garrett. Thanks for getting everyone together over here."

He slides me a flat look, because we both know it wasn't his intention whatsoever for tonight to be a gathering of more than just him and Emma. And I bet tomorrow night he'll have the same intention.

"You guys coming to the 5k tomorrow?" I ask.

"Oh, that's right," Emma says. "Are you running?"

I nod.

She smiles up at me. "Where's the best place to watch?"

Her interest feels like winning the lottery, making me forget Garrett's awfulness. I smile back, hoping it's enough for her to tell how pleased I am she'll be there to watch me run.

"Anywhere on Main Street," I tell her.

"We'll be there," Garrett declares with a tight smile.

"See you tomorrow," Emma says to him, and turns to leave.

I follow her downstairs and outside, glad to be rid of Garrett finally.

The porch light illuminates most of the sidewalk leading to the street where my truck is parked. My heart beats hard as we walk side by side, and I realize this is my chance to say something important to her with no one else around. I got to tell her about poetry earlier, and it was something, but...I need to set things right in her mind about where we stand. Where she's always stood for me.

I glance down the street a bit and find her car parked on the intersecting street.

"You don't have to walk me all the way over there," she says quietly, peeking up at me.

"I don't mind."

We turn onto the city sidewalk, and somewhere in the back of my mind I'm relieved we'll be out of sight from the window of Garrett's guest room.

My footsteps seem loud beneath me as we walk, the distance between us and Emma's car closing in sooner than I want.

Don't choke, man.

I've spent years having moments like this with her—where I wanted to say something personal or even ask her on a date, and I've always chickened out at the last second.

I can't do that this time.

So, I take a deep breath in, hold it for five seconds, and let it out.

"Emma?"

"Mhm?" she answers back sweetly.

My chest is tight as I touch her elbow, quickly tapping three times, indicating she should stop. She looks up at me when my skin meets hers, and she turns toward me. Then it's just us, standing on the sidewalk, looking at each other while the rest of the world goes away.

Breathing becomes difficult as I prepare myself to speak.

"Lacey said something to me the other night that's been bothering me." My voice comes out breathy and low.

She lifts her eyebrows curiously.

Can she tell how hard my heart is pounding? Even hear it outside of my body? Can she see all the things I'm feeling on my face?

"She...she said that at the Holly Ball, you told her I didn't know you existed."

Her beautiful eyes go wide behind her glasses. Even in the low lighting, I can see her blush. For some reason, it comforts me. Makes me wish I could kiss her.

"So, I just want to say..." I clear my throat, aware of my pulse in every fingertip. "You couldn't be more wrong about that. And I—I'm sorry if I've made you feel like you don't exist."

Something relaxes in her expression—maybe some of the surprise or nerves.

"If I've seemed aloof, it's just that I...know how I am, and how I come across. Not everyone enjoys being around me." My gaze drops, realizing I've never said that out loud before. "I haven't engaged much because I've never assumed you would like being around me either."

When I look back up at her, I find the most beautiful, open expression on her face. Not a hint of shyness or self-consciousness. Just...Emma. And I love her.

I love her.

"Lee," she whispers, smiling just slightly. "You couldn't be more wrong."

Everything goes a little haywire then. My heart ricochets around in my chest. My brain goes a little fuzzy.

Why are my knees tingling?

"Really?" I rasp out.

"Yeah." Her lips purse into a sweet smile. Her fingers twine together behind her back. "I know how I can be too," she murmurs.

Perfect?

"Sometimes people think I'm stuck up but I'm just...quiet."

"I don't know anyone who thinks you're stuck up."

She giggles at my instantaneous response, her shoulders lifting as she laughs. I wish I could push her shiny black hair over her shoulder. Run my fingers through it.

"You are hands down my favorite librarian."

She laughs again, and though I don't consider myself a funny man, I'd do anything to keep her laughing.

"You're my favorite policeman," she throws back, but the blush creeps back onto her face again. Because somehow we're flirting. Somewhere in our words there's something more than friendship.

"You're my favorite poet, too," she murmurs, blushing full force now.

I smile softly, wishing I could say what I'm thinking next.

You're just my favorite.

For the first time, I hope she sees it on my face. For the first time, I try to *show* it. But I don't know exactly how...so there's a good chance the meaningful expression I'm going for is coming off a little manic. I lower my eyebrows, just in case, and try not to hate myself for how bad I am at this.

Thankfully, Emma smiles back at me and doesn't give any indication she thinks I'm a weirdo. "So, just to make sure we're clear—I like being around you, and...you know I exist."

You have no idea, Em.

"I like being around you, too," I amend. "I'm glad we're setting the record straight."

"Me too."

We resume walking and I can't feel my feet as I escort her to her car. She shoots me a sweet smile and a thank you before getting in. I watch her pull away and rub my hand over my chest, feeling like my heart is with her in the passenger seat and not under my ribcage.

I can see now, I can't let her in if I don't let my walls down. I see now she'll be gracious with me—and maybe she isn't so put off by my intimidating personality like I thought.

Maybe Garrett doesn't stand a chance. I don't know what they talk about, but it can't be better than this. It can't feel like home, like this does. Sure, he probably has better stories to tell, but...does the quiet between their words feel like this? Charged and electric, like lightning without the fear of the answering thunder? Like...fireflies?

Does *she* feel the fireflies? Or is it all just me?

Chapter Fourteen

Emma

I dig around in my purse as I sit beside Garrett on the curb in front of Svea's Boutique. It's swelteringly hot. A terrible night for a 5k if there ever was one. Tonight would've been much better for the fire department's water fight, but that's tomorrow instead.

But we're here to support Lee and watch him run, and I'm not sure how I won't burst into a huge smile when I see him. I don't even remember driving home last night. I was so in my feelings about what he said...about how he looked at me with so much intensity. It was like he was...*trying*. Despite his quietness and tendency to use as few words as possible, he went out of his way to set me straight about how I've always assumed he saw me. I couldn't be more thrilled to be wrong about something.

My fingers close around the pencil I'm looking for, and I bring it out, immediately gathering my black hair and using the pencil to twist it up into a bun.

"That's possibly the most librarian thing I've ever seen," Garrett teases me, nodding toward the pencil, and I blush a little because he was watching me. "If I ever write a book with a librarian in it, I'm going to use that."

I snicker and turn my gaze down the street. Little groups of people are scattered on both sides of Main Street to cheer people on as they run. The 5k doesn't start for another ten minutes, but Garrett wanted to come early so he could familiarize himself a little more with downtown Larkspur. We walked past all the shops, and I told him as much as I could remember about them and their owners. Maybe I *could* be a tour guide.

Even as we sit here, I can see his blue eyes taking in everything, like something he's never seen before. I guess I would do the same thing if the roles were reversed, and I strolled through Minneapolis with him. His interest in Larkspur makes me pay more attention to everything I'm so used to.

To be fair, I spend most of my time with my eyes pointed at a book. It isn't often I purposely look around the way Garrett inspires me to.

"Are you enjoying your time in Larkspur so far?" I ask him.

He smiles that Hollywood smile. "It's been lovely," he answers softly. "I appreciate you letting me tag along everywhere. I hope I'm not being a bother."

"Oh, of course not," I assure him quickly. "It's been...nice having you here. I'm usually a homebody, but playing tour guide has been fun."

He turns toward me a little more, adjusting his glasses on his nose. He's wearing a cream linen shirt that looks much cooler than the forest green sundress I'm wearing.

"I can see you being a homebody," Garrett says warmly. "Would you believe me if I said I'm a homebody too?"

I raise my eyebrows just slightly, and he chuckles.

"I know. I seem like Mr. Congeniality. I certainly do like being around people, but there's nothing better than being home." He pauses, those too-blue eyes taking in my unfortunately perspiring features. "Speaking of homes, I toured a couple of houses today with a realtor."

For some reason, my stomach drops. Maybe it's a reality check, because he's really going to stay here. He isn't just a tourist...he wants to be a resident. A permanent fixture here.

"And h—how did that go?" I stammer, because he's looking at me like I'm a piece of furniture he's trying to find a place for in his house.

"Well, the two I saw were pretty humble. There isn't much to choose from here, especially when I was hoping for something secluded and peaceful."

"Like a cozy cabin in the woods?"

"Exactly." He smiles. "Know of any by chance?" His tone is light and a little sarcastic.

"Sorry," I answer, smiling too.

After a moment, he shrugs and looks back down the street. "No matter. I could always just build what I have in mind. I'd rather not, though, because new builds always feel sterile and lifeless." He pauses thoughtfully, and I realize his opinion about new builds means he's familiar with them. "There's just something about an old house, you know? There's always some kind of history left behind by the previous owners. A dent in the wall or pencil marking the heights of their children...those are the kinds of things I like to be surrounded by, especially when I'm writing."

"You must love Larkspur Inn, then," I say.

"Well, there's a difference between 'lived in' and 'run down,'" he claims loftily, even snorting dismissively at the end of his sentence.

My eyebrows scrunch. He thinks the inn is run down? Why does that hurt my soul a little? Why does his critical opinion of a Larkspur institution spoil some of my good opinions of him? He's allowed to not like things. I can't expect him to blow in from the cities, where everything is sparkly and exciting, and love everything about Larkspur.

But he's made it seem so far like he thinks Larkspur is great. He wants to *move* here. He has to like it enough to be looking at houses.

Maybe it's just that I'm partial to anything the Christiansens are involved in. Will's restaurant, the inn, Svea's shop...I'm protective of those things, I realize. They're good people and they don't deserve to be disparaged, even in a flippant way like this.

"What's with all the gnomes, by the way? It's kind of a creepy décor choice for an inn, if you ask me," he adds, not catching on to my distaste for the direction of this conversation.

"I...think it's a cultural thing," I answer quietly. "Lee's parents own the inn."

Garrett's eyes snap to mine. "You've got to be kidding me," he mutters.

I frown. "What?"

He shakes his head and looks away with a bitter smile. "Nothing."

We sit quietly for a moment. It isn't a comfortable silence, at least not for me. It's the first time I've ever really seen anything ugly in Garrett. No one is all good or all bad, but I don't like whatever problem he has with people I care about. Sure, Svea wasn't very kind to him last night, but she's definitely going through something and was taking it out on him. I try to see the best in others, and sometimes I forget not everyone else does.

Maybe Garrett is more sensitive than he lets on. Maybe Svea had him pegged when she said he wanted everyone to love him.

My stomach sinks, weighed down by something unsettling and heavy.

Down at the other end of Main Street, a whistle screams and there's lots of shouting as the runners take off. We watch as a group of twenty people scatter, running down the middle of the closed street. The route is a loop. The runners will lap twice, and finish where they started. It only takes me a second to recognize Lee's strong body at the front of the pack, running with long strides.

I smile, happy to have an excuse to study him. Sometimes I see him running around town on his days off, so I know a 5k for him is probably easy. He certainly makes it look easy, though time will tell, especially in this heat.

My heart beats a little faster the closer he gets, his rough face taking me back to last night. Our conversation has been on my mind all day...because he apologized. Hearing him talk about himself the way he did—negatively, like there's something wrong with him—broke my heart. There's nothing wrong with Lee's personality. I actually like his gruffness. He can be funny, and I've always known him to be virtuous.

Lee and the others approach, and it's then that I realize his eyes are sweeping the sidewalks on either side. I suddenly wish I had made a sign so I could wave it at him. Instead, blushing to the max, I draw in a deep breath and use it to shout.

"Go, Lee!"

His head turns, and he finds me almost instantly. One corner of his mouth pulls back in a little smile that, for him, is actually pretty big. He nods at me and jogs past us a block down before turning and disappearing.

Garrett is silent, though I didn't expect him to cheer.

The rest of the runners trail off down the street, following the route, and still Garrett says nothing. I peek over at him, finding a thoughtful, almost shuttered expression on his face.

"There's a word I like in Welsh. *Hiraeth*," he says, the previous edge of his tone gone and replaced with something vulnerable. He doesn't look at me as he continues, his eyes pointed ahead of us unseeingly. "It's a kind of homesickness—sometimes for a home you can never go back to. Sometimes, for a home that maybe never existed at all." He takes another moment, choosing his words, and goosebumps rise all over my body when he finally looks over at me. His eyes are glassy behind his horn-rimmed frames. "I don't want to feel like that anymore. I want to belong somewhere. I want to belong...to *someone*."

I stare at him, stunned, with no idea what to say.

"And I know I'm being forward, Emma, but...when I look at you, I can see it," he says. His usual bravado and charm is gone. The absence of it makes his words just that more powerful. "The more time I spend with you, the more it comes into focus."

He reaches over and takes my hand in his. My chest squeezes tight.

"I can see you being the person I talk through my outlines with. I can see your profession complementing mine. We could be a team in every way, without competitiveness or resentment. I can see us supporting each other well because we both appreciate the same things."

Oh dear, he's not messing around.

Not about Larkspur and not about me. He knows exactly what he wants and isn't afraid to go after it. I feel flattered or honored, because I really *do* see it.

My life wouldn't have to change much. I'd still be in Larkspur, working at the library, devouring books, and visiting my family. But Garrett's presence would elevate everything I'm used to. I can picture a little cozy house in the woods, like he said, with me sitting in our home library going through his manuscripts and offering suggestions. I can imagine how amazing it would feel to have my ideas taken seriously...how it would feel when he comes home from a book tour or meetings with his publisher.

It's a perfect picture.

I couldn't realistically ask for anything better.

It's a romance novel kind of happily ever after.

It's everything Caitlin and I talked about...everything I didn't think could be possible.

But my mind flits back to standing on the sidewalk with Lee. I think about how much work it took him to say what he wanted to say, and how it made what he said so much sweeter. His brown eyes were so warm as he looked at me. I remember the sweetness of his voice when he told me he hoped I liked his poem. I can still hear his laughter when the firefly landed on my nose. I couldn't forget it, even if I tried. I couldn't forget *him*.

And I would have to, for things to work with Garrett.

Cheering from down the street lets us know the runners are completing their first lap.

Garrett's thumb smooths over the back of my hand, as if asking me not to look away. "I know what I'm saying seems a little...crazy. But I can't deny how I feel, Emma." He smiles. "What do they call this trope? Insta-love?"

Despite the seriousness of this conversation, I chuckle softly.

He lifts my hand and kisses it, those deep blue eyes still on mine. "Think about it, okay? Think about us and how we could be together."

Nerves swamp me, but I still agree to think about what he said.

Even in my periphery, I recognize Lee running past. Even with my eyes focused on Garrett, absorbing all of his amazingness, I'm still fully aware of Lee heading away from me.

And I recognize that a fork in the road is coming my way soon.

The door to Svea's shop opens behind us, breaking the moment. Svea plops down next to me on the curb.

"Did I miss much? I was in the zone working on a dress," she says, looking up and down the street.

"I think Lee went by twice already," I answer.

"Oh, let's go down to the finish line then." She jumps back up, pulling me with her.

Garrett follows suit, falling in beside me with Svea ahead of us on the sidewalk.

As we walk, I wonder if Lacey talked to her about Clay. Svea seems more cheerful today, but it could be because she was hard at work doing something she loves. Maybe she's fine if Clay isn't around. I hope everything is okay, and she doesn't keep settling for someone she isn't actually happy with.

I fan myself with one hand, the heat baking me from the inside out. I don't know how the people running are handling it.

We pass the antique shop, the butcher, a law office, and The Swedish Chef before coming to where most spectators are gathered at the starting line, which is now the finish line. Across the street are Mr. and Mrs. Christiansen, taking advantage of the shade from the awning over the hardware store.

It's almost ten minutes before the first few runners cross the line to cheers and shouts. I keep looking down the street, expecting to see the familiar shape of Lee emerge any second, but ten more minutes pass and almost half of the runners have finished. How could he have fallen so far behind when he was leading the pack during the first two laps?

Worry prickles in my stomach. What if something went wrong? Did he trip and fall? Or is the heat too much, and he's sitting in the shade somewhere, trying to fight heat exhaustion?

"Where is he?" Svea asks, concern and confusion lacing her words. "Did we miss him?" She looks at all the runners who have finished, but there's no Lee.

But then I see him. He's walking slowly beside a teenager, using his arm to support the boy. The teenager's face is flushed and red, washed in sweat. He clutches Lee's arm tightly, his steps unsteady.

"There he is!" I gasp, and Svea swivels to look.

Lee's mouth is moving, his attention solely on the kid as they go. As they get closer, I can make out his words, and my heart melts. He's saying, "You've got this. Just a little further. Come on, don't give up." And then he lifts his head toward the finish line and shouts out, "we need some water over here!"

One of the 5k volunteers runs over with a bottle of water and opens it for the exhausted runner. They help him cross the finish line, all the bystanders screaming their heads off in support. As soon as the kid gets across, Lee helps him over to the shade and begins barking orders. His parents crowd in close too, Mr. Christiansen retrieving more water as Lee tells the kid to sit down and take off his shoes and his shirt. He tells someone to run into The Swedish Chef to get ice and a wet towel. Mrs. Christiansen stays close to the runner's mom, whispering comforting things to the anxious woman.

Svea, Garrett, and I stand back out of the way as Lee takes charge. After a few minutes with a wet towel over his head and more water, the teenager revives enough for Lee to move him into the air conditioning of the restaurant.

I share a look of relief with Svea, but when I glance at Garrett, he has his little notebook out. He's writing something down, seeming pleased with whatever idea he's had.

"Well, city boy, have you yet to experience a smalltown bar?" Svea asks him.

Garrett looks up in surprise, because Svea's tone is pleasant and friendly, a complete turnaround from how she spoke to him last night. He glances at me, as if trying to clock whether I've noticed the shift in her too. Or maybe he's trying to gauge whether I'm interested in going.

"The Drunken Mallard sure is an experience," I tell him with a wry smile. I don't frequent the only bar in Larkspur that often, but I've been known to watch karaoke or attend a meat raffle there from time to time.

He shrugs. "All right then. I'm in."

We head that way, my mind on the contents of that little notebook.

Chapter Fifteen

Lee

Swinging the door open to the Drunken Mallard, loud TVs, laughter, the jukebox music, and so much talking greet me like a wall of sound. A lot of the people who were out for the 5k ended up here. Happy Hour is over, but the place is so full I have a hard time finding Svea and everyone.

The last time I was here was probably a month ago with Lars. I wonder if Svea invited him tonight.

My shoulders tighten as I look around, already overwhelmed by the packed bar and wishing I was at home. It's been a long day between work and the 5k. The only reason I agreed to come out was because Svea texted and mentioned Garrett and Emma were here too.

Finally, my gaze snags on familiar straight black hair and glasses. I edge my way between the bar stools and the row of occupied tables to their spot by the window. Lacey cheers when she sees me, and I roll my eyes because I know she's about to make a big deal about what happened at the 5k.

It's been more than an hour since I helped Robbie Fitger cross the finish line, and I'm still pissed off. The 5k shouldn't have happened tonight. It was way too hot, and even though I expressed my concern to the Chamber before the event started, they ignored me, and because of their negligence, someone was put in harm's way.

"Job well done, Officer!" she shouts out over the racket of the bar.

Will raises his glass of beer. "Way to save the day!"

"Three cheers for Lee!" Svea adds, a glint in her eye, because she knows I hate being the center of attention.

But it's the familiar voice shouting, "hip hip hooray!" from behind me that catches my attention. I forget about my embarrassing family and the woman I'm in love with sitting next to Garrett. I whirl around to see Lars grinning at me with a beer in his hand.

"Hey man," I greet, truly happy to see him. I stretch out one arm to hug him, noticing Amber isn't with him. "Good to see you."

He claps me on the back. "You too, Lee. Sorry it's been so long."

I smack him on the back too as we break apart. "I'm gonna grab something to drink."

As I wait for my Sprite, everyone near me quiets down, like usual. Where before there was boisterous laughter and loud talking, now people are sitting a little straighter, watching me out of the corner of their eyes.

One of the tough things about being a police officer is that I'm never really off duty. Not to other people, anyway. People don't relax around me in these situations. I can't blame them. I just wish my profession wasn't another reason for people to keep their distance from me. My personality does that well enough.

The bartender hands me my Sprite, and I wind my way back down to my friends. Emma's eyes are on me, her lips tilted up in a soft smile, even as Garrett's arm moves around the back of her chair in a way that's supposed to look casual and easy, but is really him trying to mark his territory like he did at Open Mic Night.

I take the last chair next to Lars, squeezing around the table meant for six people, currently hosting eight. I glance around at all the faces, all but two of them making me glad I'm here.

Lars is to my left, with Will and Lacey beside him, making out like teenagers. Across the table are Emma, who is studiously not looking at the lovebirds, and Garrett. He and Clay are busy chatting like they've known each other their whole lives. Two peas in a pod, talking about which hair products they use. Svea sits between me and Clay with a smile, which I take to mean she and Clay must've talked through whatever they were fighting about last night in front of the inn. *Shame.*

"It's good to see you, man," Lars says again, drawing my attention from the rest of the group.

"Yeah, you too. What's been going on? How are you?"

He adjusts the backwards Twins baseball cap on his head, his smile turning tight. "Ah, you know. Amber keeps me busy."

"That's not vague at all," I point out.

Lars snorts and sips his beer, avoiding my eyes. "She's..." He flicks his blue eyes at me, hesitating. "She's a lot, but...it's better than being alone, you know?"

I raise one eyebrow at him. "No."

He chuckles that time. "I guess I'm just at the point where I can't be picky if I want to settle down. Small towns make for small dating pools."

I rest my elbow on the table, turning toward him a little more. "You really don't think there's a better fit for you out there?"

His eyes move behind me for just a fraction of a second as Svea laughs at something stupid Clay is saying. "Believe me," he says, lowering his voice so I almost can't hear it over all the other noise around us, "if there was a perfect girl for me, I would be with her already. Everyone else is off limits or taken. I'm just doing the best with what I have."

My chest hurts hearing this. He deserves to be with a woman who makes him happy, not one who will force him into a tense and resentful marriage like his parents'. I know he wants what Mamma and Pappa have, but it seems like he's given up on finding it. Maybe Amber has convinced him she's the best he'll ever get.

And here I am, aching for the woman across the table. My literal perfect girl...and all this time I've stayed back because I thought she would never want someone like me. Because I've been too *chicken* to take the chance.

I've been a fool, that much is obvious. It's terrifying to keep putting myself out there like I have been lately, but the risk of losing her to *Todd Weiner* is worse.

I have to show Lars the kind of love he wants is out there. Somehow I have to convince him not to give up and rush into settling down with someone who only causes him stress.

I've never been the matchmaking type, but for the first time my brain flips through the single women in Larkspur. I realize immediately that my tendency to tune out the Larkspur gossip has worked against me. Maybe it would be better to ask Lacey or Svea.

That would only be part of the solution though. Lars would have to break up with Amber first before he could date anyone else. Obviously, that's the hardest part, because Amber knows full well Lars is a good guy and I'm sure she has no intention of letting him go.

I sit back in my chair a bit, my mood returning to something angry and bitter. But I don't get up. I don't go home. I stay for the next hour, wishing it wasn't so loud in here, so I could say something to Emma without shouting.

Eventually, Garrett goes to the bar to get a refill, and Clay follows him. When they haven't returned after ten minutes, I turn around in my seat to find Garrett in his element. He's telling a story at the other end of the bar, the handful of people around him riveted.

"He really is an entertainer, isn't he?" Svea says, looking down the bar too.

I grunt in response. "He and Clay sure hit it off."

Svea rolls her eyes. "Doesn't surprise me a bit."

I watch her for a moment, her green eyes still on her boyfriend.

"Why are you with him, Svee?" I ask, lowering my voice a little even though Lars is in conversation with Will, Lacey, and Emma.

She raises her eyebrows at my directness. She bites the inside of her cheek and faces forward. "I don't know," she says.

With a sigh, I look over at Lacey, wondering how much she knows about Svea and Clay's relationship.

Emma's hand comes up to cover the yawn escaping her mouth. She blushes a little when she realizes I've caught her, but I smile. With Garrett so distracted by his little audience over there, I figure it's safe to try to get her out of here.

My heartbeat ramps up as I lean forward. "You want to go, Emma? I can walk you out to your car," I offer.

She glances behind me, probably at Garrett, but then smiles at me. "I walked."

"A ride, then?" It's dark out now, and I don't like the idea of her walking home alone, even in Larkspur.

Emma nods to my glass. "You're okay to drive?"

"It's just Sprite."

"Okay then. Thanks."

I nod, getting to my feet. Slapping Lars on the back, we say our goodbyes to everyone else.

Emma and I slip out the back door. As soon as it closes behind us, the quiet of the night soothes my eardrums, and I let out a sigh of relief. It would feel even better if the night air wasn't still warm and humid.

"You okay?" she asks softly as we follow the sidewalk around the back of the bar to the street.

"Just loud in there."

She nods.

When we get to the street, she follows me to the right. She walks beside me, and everything in me wishes I could reach over and slip my fingers between hers.

"The 5k was exciting, huh?" she says, with a hint of sarcasm, making me feel lighter inside.

"Don't remind me," I mutter.

She snickers softly. "Good thing you were there."

I just nod, still too angry the Chamber ignored me. Instead, I change the subject.

"How's your mom?"

"She's good," Emma says with a smile. "The ramp in front of our house needs to be fixed, but she's been using the one in the garage instead."

"What's wrong with it?"

"The bolts just need to be tightened, I think. They've come loose over the years."

I nod, already deciding I'll be heading over there tomorrow to look at it. I have the next three days off with nothing but the community picnic on Friday.

"Do you go to the Drunken Mallard often?" she asks as we pass beneath a streetlight. The dark green of her dress just brings out her beautiful eyes, and she doesn't know how much it kills me.

"I used to go once a week with Lars before he started dating Amber," I explain. "I try not to be there too much. Mostly because I don't really drink, but also because people can't relax when I'm there."

Emma blinks up at me. "Oh. I guess I didn't think about that."

"Most people think of me as a police officer first, you know? Even when I'm not on duty."

She hums thoughtfully from the back of her throat, as if it's never occurred to her. *Hmm.* Maybe she doesn't think like that about me. Maybe to her I'm a person first and not my profession. Just the possibility of that fills my chest with something warm and fuzzy.

At the truck, I open the passenger door, and am rewarded with her shy sweet smile. She climbs in, and I shut her door. My heart pounds in my ears as I walk around to the driver's side and get in.

How often have I spotted whatever library book on the passenger seat, and wished it was Emma instead?

And now here she is.

Dreams really do come true.

I swallow down the excitement humming through me, and put my keys in the ignition.

"When you go with Lars, do you drink then?" There's something hesitant about her voice that has me glancing at her as the engine fires to life.

"One beer with my burger," I say. "I don't usually finish it."

She nods, her eyes fixed on the glove compartment, her dark eyebrows scrunched a little behind her glasses. I watch her for a long moment, the truck idling. It's not hard for me to understand why she asked that question.

Her family was blown apart because of a drunk driver. It's a sore subject for her.

"I take drunk driving very seriously," I tell her, kicking myself for how growly my voice comes out. I've never figured out how to make my voice sound soft or warm. Probably never will.

Emma looks at me. "I know." She gives me a tight smile. "Thank you." She looks away again, and I put the truck in Drive.

I pull out onto Main Street and then take the next right. As I drive, she sinks into her thoughts and pulls away from me.

My stomach pangs with nerves.

I need to tell her.

But saying it would require me to lower my walls all the way down. It would require me to be more vulnerable than I've ever been before, even with my family.

Isn't that what I'm trying to do? Be vulnerable? Let down my guard?

But once I do, there's no going back.

Even if she ends up with Garrett, I can never take this back if I put it in her hands right now. It's personal for me, but it's personal for her too.

I clear my throat as we approach the intersection. She tells me to take a left.

Nerves assault me from within, and I squeeze the steering wheel tightly, trying to keep my breathing even.

"Drunk driving is the whole reason I became a police officer," I tell her quietly. I'm so aware of my pulse I can feel it beating throughout my body.

Emma's head turns to look at me, and I find it best I don't make eye contact in case I chicken out.

I turn left, taking us down Emma's street.

"Really?"

I nod once.

"I didn't always want to be in law enforcement," I explain. "It just found me in a moment when I was lost, I guess."

"What did you want to do then?"

I glance at her self-consciously. "I wanted to be a Kindergarten teacher."

Emma's eyebrows go up a bit, but then she smiles warmly, almost like she can picture me herding a bunch of five-year-olds on a field trip.

"The guidance counselor said I was too intimidating to be working with kids though and told me to pick a different career." A prickle of bitterness nips at the back of my neck. "I was..." I hesitate, focusing on the road. "I was gutted, really, and I didn't know what I should do instead."

I swallow hard, because the next part is something I've never told anyone. Words I've literally never said aloud.

Emma's house comes into view down the block, and the glowing streetlights pass like a countdown—a reminder that time is passing and I need to explain even if it won't be comfortable for me to do it.

I pull into the driveway where Emma indicates, glancing at the wheelchair ramp she mentioned, and throw the truck into Park. I focus on the steady idle of the truck to keep my breathing steady.

"I know we weren't friends in high school," I say, my eyes following the curve of the steering wheel. "But...I noticed how you changed after he died. Before you loved reading, but then after it became your escape."

Emma's entire body locks up in my periphery.

My chest squeezes, making it harder for me to draw in a full breath. With difficulty, I keep going.

"I saw how your family was never the same," I add, quieter, "and how it all could've been prevented." I shake my head. "How I wished I could've prevented it."

Taking the deepest breath I can, I finally look across the bench seat at her. She stares back, wide-eyed and stunned.

I slowly reach across the bench seat, setting my hand next to hers. I let my pinky touch the side of her hand, needing some small, comforting touch. Courage to say what I need to say next.

The only way for her to ever really love me is to crack myself open wide in front of her.

"I became a police officer because of your dad," I murmur, driving the point home—so there's no misunderstanding. I've never felt more like a wrecking ball than I do right now, and that's why I stayed silent.

Her breathing goes shallow, her gasoline and honey eyes shining with unshed tears in the darkened cab. In a split second, she unclips her seatbelt, flings open the door, and races out.

My heart jackhammers in my chest. Panic lances through me, making my hands shake.

It was too much.

I unleashed something too personal—too close to home. But I couldn't soften it—make it less than what it is. Because underneath it is love, the fiercest thing I know—the hardest thing to tame.

And in this moment, with the most vulnerable part of me flayed open, I can't think of a single word that could adequately describe the pain I feel as Emma rounds the hood of my truck to get away from me.

Chapter Sixteen

Emma

I can't breathe.

All of the oxygen inside this truck has disappeared as I stare at Lee, his words echoing in my head.

I became a police officer because of your dad.

Everything quiets around us, like the entire world is holding its breath because of what he said.

Last night, he said I was wrong when I assumed he didn't know I existed, but now I really understand how deep his awareness of me and my family goes. I can't believe it.

Lee sees me. Really sees me. And he always has.

It's like he's taken off the chainmail armor, exposing his heart. This is him giving me the same raw, nameless force I felt when we were around the fire talking about poetry, but this time it's blazing out of him like a flamethrower.

And as he looks at me with so much vulnerability, that force whispers its name from somewhere inside of me. It reminds me that it looks an awful lot like what held my parents together. So strong it remains even after death.

Words fail me.

All I know is he's too far away from me to hug him the way I want to.

I unbuckle my seatbelt and throw open the door. The outside world rushes back—the warm, humid summer air and the fireflies lazily floating around the front yard. The darkness of the night is illuminated by his headlights and the porch light.

My heart pounds in my ears, louder than my footsteps as I cross in front of Lee's truck. I wince as the headlights bathe me in light and then the driver's side door opens.

"Emma—wait!" Lee chokes out, exiting his truck too.

I jog over to him and catch just one second of confusion on his amazing face before I launch myself at him, jumping so I can throw my arms all the way around his broad shoulders. Our fronts crash together, and I grip him as tightly as I can, standing on my tiptoes to reach.

For one split second, Lee freezes. Then he breathes in a hoarse gasp, and those strong arms surround me in the best hug of my entire life.

Tears spill over as I squeeze my eyes closed.

Why doesn't he feel unfamiliar in my arms? Why does it feel like we've hugged a thousand times like this? Why does it feel like my first genuine experience of peace?

He says something—and at first I think I missed what he said because of how quietly he murmured it, but then I realize it wasn't English.

One of Lee's hands moves to cup the back of my neck, some of his fingertips dipping into my hair. I grip his T-shirt in my hands in response.

His rapid heart beats against me, which means he must feel mine beating just as fast. He smells a little earthy, like Earl Grey, and dryer sheets. But there's something else too—something that's just *him*.

I'll never forget it—even if I never hug him like this ever again, I'll always remember exactly how he smells and how hard and warm his muscles feel all around me. I'll never forget how the legacy of his life hinges on the legacy of my father's death.

"He would be so honored," I whisper, because it's the only thing I can think of to say. I sniff, releasing his shirt with one hand so I can remove my glasses and wipe at my cheek with the back of my hand. Once my glasses are back on again, I wrap my arm around him where it was.

Lee's hand strokes the middle of my back, his thumb smoothing back and forth three times. He lets out a long breath, a cousin to a sigh of relief. "Never told anyone that," his rough voice rumbles. "I was scared to say it."

My *heart...*

I clutch him even closer.

Lee being scared of anything is almost too unbelievable. I've always viewed him as a fearless, brave man who takes danger in stride. His fear of telling me this changes my long-held view of him. He isn't immovable, like I thought. He isn't all one thing, but rather something more complicated. And I would die to know all of his intricacies.

I squeeze him tighter. "You never have to be scared with me," I say without a thought.

But in saying the words out loud, a deep, crushing fear rushes in like a tidal wave.

The soft, fleshy part of my heart is instantly walled up like an ancient city.

Releasing my grip on his shirt, I pull back. I drop from my tiptoes down to my heels again. His strong arms loosen enough to let me, his hands moving to my hips as mine move down his chest and then away. I stare up at him for a long moment, my heart hammering in my chest, before his hands drop away from me.

I gulp, not sure how to transition away from this. Ultimately, I revert to good manners.

"Thank you for sharing that with me."

Lee watches me so closely he doesn't see the firefly land on his shoulder. "Can I see you tomorrow?" He clears his throat. "At the water fight?"

I nod, my stomach clenching when I remember I'll be going with Garrett.

He nods too and finally catches sight of the firefly as it takes off and flits between us, then away.

I take a step back. "Good night, Lee."

He does too. "Night."

I can feel his eyes on me as I turn around and head to the front door. I open it, and when I glance back, he's still standing there with one hand on the open driver's side door, looking at me. I probably shocked him with that hug, and in a way I'm shocked at myself too.

I give him a little wave and then go inside. A moment later, his truck door slams and then his truck reverses down the driveway. I watch from the kitchen window as his headlights disappear down the street.

I'm still staring out the window when Mom rolls into the room.

"Emma?"

I flinch just slightly and shut my eyes, turning around to face her. She's there, parked in the little hallway leading to the dining room. When I don't smile at her or say anything, her expression changes from pleasantly neutral to concerned.

"What's wrong?"

My nose tingles and I sniffle. My eyes start to sting. My heart aches.

I don't know how to answer—to explain I just looked love straight in the eye and I'll never be the same. How do I tell her what Lee's done with his life because of her husband?

Do I even have permission to?

"Do you regret falling in love with Dad?" I squeak out like a rusty faucet. "If you had known what would happen—would you have still..." My vision blurs as a soft sob escapes me.

Mom blinks in surprise and immediately wheels herself closer to me. She takes my hand and squeezes. There's pain in her expression but softness too. "No, sweetie. Why would I regret loving him, hmm? Just because he's gone?" She gives me a small smile full of grief and memories of the love she lost. "He doesn't need to be alive for me to still love him."

I sink down to my knees in front of her. "But he can't love you back anymore."

She wipes my cheek, and I feel like I'm five years old again. Something about that is comforting.

"I know. But that doesn't mean he loved me any less when he was alive. If anything, his death just highlights all the ways he loved me well."

How can she see it that way—be at peace with loving someone who was taken from her too soon? How can she look back over her life with him and not be filled with anything but anger and indignation?

I sniff. "Aren't you mad? You found your soulmate and then the universe ripped him away from you."

Mom chuckles, surprising me. "It's very easy to be angry, Emma, but what good does it do? I promised I would love him for the rest of *my* life, not for the rest of *his*."

I shake my head. Every answer she's giving me is so simplified. Her wisdom has sharpened everything into well-worded phrases. The kind that Lee would appreciate.

"But you're *alone*, Mom," I whisper. "It hurts *me* to watch you being alone. It has to hurt for you too."

"Sometimes," she acquiesces with a sigh. "Sometimes I miss him so much I can't breathe. But most times I think of him and smile."

"It isn't fair that love has to hurt so much."

Mom frowns thoughtfully. "It does hurt...but it's still worth it. Love is the only thing that makes life worth living."

I swallow around the lump in my throat.

"What's all this about, hmm? What's really going on?"

I don't want to say how I feel about Lee out loud. Then it'll be real and I can't take it back. I would have to deal with it if I spoke about it.

"I wish I was as strong as you, Mom," I say, resting my chin on her knee. "If I was in your shoes, I don't think I could do it."

"There were a lot of times I didn't think I could do it either," she admits quietly. "But I had two daughters to look after and, well...like it or not, time marches on. I didn't exactly have a choice." She tucks my hair back behind one ear, wobbling my glasses just slightly as she does. "I don't know what brought all of this on, Emmy, but my advice is that if you love someone—really love someone—don't hold back."

Mom's blue eyes cloud over with tears, but she smiles down at me.

"If you fall in love, Emma, then love that man with everything you have and hold nothing back."

I don't know if I can.

I let out a deep breath, conflicted but comforted by Mom's words. Lee's choices have excavated some painful wounds, and Mom has given me a lot to think about.

But I don't want to think about it. It *hurts* to think about it. I want to go read until all these feelings go away.

I force a smile and stand.

"Thanks, Mom." I kiss her on the cheek and head for my room.

"Night, honey," she calls after me.

The tension creeps back into my body as I open my door and go inside. I rip off my clothes and get into my pajamas as fast as I can, then I'm reaching for the book on my desk like it's a lifeline.

My eyes drink up every word, but none of them stay in my brain. I reread a paragraph half a dozen times before finally moving onto the next. The silence of my room is loud. I can't focus.

Why isn't this working?

Reading always whisks me away when I need it to.

But I can't stop thinking about Mom's words.

I abandon my book, angry at it for failing me, and turn off the light.

I try to sleep, but I'm awake for a long time thinking how Mom doesn't regret the thing that ended up hurting her the most...because it was worth it. I can't reconcile that no matter how hard I try.

I sigh up at the blurry white ceiling above me.

Part of me just wants to run away. I'll go live in a cabin all by myself. Just me and my books and a mug of London Fog. I've spent most of my life alone in my head, anyway. What's the difference, right? I can bury myself in books and abandon everything else.

Everything was easier when I just lived vicariously through the characters I read about. Why did I listen to Caitlin? Why didn't I think about the *consequences* of taking action? I was just proud to have made a choice by going on that date with Garrett, and now...

Now I'm *feeling things*. And it isn't nearly as fun when it isn't fictional.

I roll over, staring at my bookshelf.

I'm getting ahead of myself. Sure, Lee became a police officer because of my dad. But that doesn't mean...

Lee has never said anything concrete about how he feels about me, except to tell me that he knows I exist. Garrett has been incredibly upfront with me about his intentions. There's nothing left unsaid with Garrett.

Garrett is the one I went on a date with. Because he asked. Lee has never even hinted that he wants to be more than friends. I exist to him, and he cares. That's all.

Eventually, I sink into a restless sleep that leaves me groggy in the morning when I get up for work. I slog through a shower, drag my feet through getting dressed and putting on my make-up. Though I'm typically a tea drinker, when I get to the kitchen, I seriously consider stealing a bit of Mom and Caitlin's coffee.

I'm standing there at the counter, frowning at the coffeepot, when I hear something outside. I turn around, looking out the kitchen window curiously. With a yawn, I move closer, leaning over the sink to get a better look around the front yard.

A metallic *clunk* sounds out, and I glance down to see a pair of muscly legs sprawled out on the grass in front of the ramp.

My eyes widen, and the breath catches in the back of my throat.

More metallic clunking and then some squeaking too. I skitter around the kitchen peninsula to the front door to look through the peephole. I see Lee's truck parked on the side of the street.

What?

I go back to the kitchen window, leaning over the sink as far as I can without falling in. Lee's lying on his back, half of his body under the ramp.

He's...fixing it. Because last night I mentioned the bolts needed to be tightened.

I step back from the window, my heart beating off kilter.

His kindness makes my eyes sting.

The danger with Lee is in what he doesn't say. Because he isn't much for talking, he shows what he wants to say with his actions. And by being here this early, I'm assuming on his day off, to fix the ramp for my mom, he's saying an awful lot without saying even a single word.

The metallic clunking changes then, and I see his head go past the window once. I belatedly think of ducking or hiding, but he's probably leaving. But then I see him go by again in the other direction, and I realize he's checking his work—making sure the ramp is sturdy and nothing else needs to be fixed.

Then, I dart out of view, hiding beside the fridge. I wait, expecting him to knock on the door or something, but his truck starts up and when I peek around the fridge, I watch it go down the street.

Gathering myself, I go out and give the railing a shake. Where before the whole thing moved, now it holds strong. I put my foot on it, and it doesn't sag beneath my weight like it used to.

I smile, something warm and light filling me up.

Mom is going to be so excited. I turn around, intending to go tell her, but I stop. In my haste to check out Lee's work on the ramp, I missed what he left on the porch.

A single red chrysanthemum he must've picked from the flower bed and laid right in front of the welcome mat.

The breath catches in my throat.

What am I supposed to do about a man who says nothing but does things like *this*?

Chapter Seventeen

Lee

M y face feels weird today.

I keep catching myself smiling, even when I'm not replaying the hug Emma gave me last night. She permeated every layer of skin and muscle, and I swear I can still smell her sweet, sugary vanilla scent on me even though I showered this morning. If I close my eyes, I can still feel exactly how tightly she hugged me—using it to say so much more than the words she said about her dad being honored by my career choice.

Will left for work about an hour ago, and I'm glad. I didn't want him to tease me for being so blatantly happy. After I got back from fixing Mrs. Mackenzie's ramp, I sat on the back porch pretending to read. Once he was gone, I tossed the book aside and have been sitting here ever since.

No poem could capture my feelings when I was hugging Emma last night.

Now I have hope. She hugged the hell out of me, overwhelmed by my confession. I never thought I would get the chance to hug her, much less hug her like the world was ending around us and it didn't matter even a little.

It was a glimpse. A peek into what I always hoped could be between us. It was perfect.

No way Garrett has any skin in the game. Not now.

There I go, smiling again.

My phone buzzes from inside my pocket. When I see that it's a notification from the group chat I'm in with my siblings and Lacey, I let out a disgruntled sigh.

Will: *Status report? How are we doing? Do we need to revise the plan?*

I stare at the message for a long moment, not sure how much to say.

Lacey: *I talked Ferrett's ear off the other night about my move to Larkspur. What else can I do?*
Svea: *That was real smooth giving her a ride home last night, by the way.*

The tips of my ears burn.

Will: *Garrett was really mad when he came back to the table and you guys were gone. He tried not to show it, but I could tell.*
Svea: *Surprised you even noticed with your tongue down Lacey's throat. [Goat lolling its tongue around meme]*
Lacey: *That's an exaggeration.*
Will: *Meh. Pretty spot on, actually.*
Lacey: *Will!*

I shake my head at their antics, and finally reply.

Lee: *Things are going fine.*
Will: *That doesn't sound encouraging at all, dude.*
Lacey: *Yeah, what does "fine" actually mean?*
Lee: *It means I think our plan is working.*
Svea: *Yeah? She's into you being more vulnerable and stuff?*

I swallow hard, hesitating with how much I'm comfortable sharing with them.

Lee: *She hugged me last night.*

As soon as I send it, I regret it. I set my phone down as it vibrates on and off for a full minute with their responses. I hold my breath when I finally pick it up again, and instead of reading each of their messages, I gloss over all the exclamation points and caps lock words. I dive back into something concrete.

Lee: *She said she'll be at the water fight tonight, so let's continue trying to keep her and Garrett apart.*
Svea: *Did you see him put his arm around her last night? As soon as you walked in, Lee, he did that. He knows you're a threat.*
Lacey: *He's totally jealous of any attention Emma gives you. He's on to you and how you feel about her.*
Will: *Hopefully, Emma is picking up on how you feel too.*

I look out over the lawn with a sigh. I hope so too.

My phone buzzes in my hand with another message. It's from Svea, outside of the group chat.

Svea: *I just wanted to tell you that after you left, Amber started calling Lars nonstop. He left, and he seemed upset.*

My stomach sinks.

Lee: *I'll text him.*
Svea: *I'm worried about him, bro.*
Lee: *Me too.*

Though to be fair, I'm worried about her too.

Lee: *You sure everything is good with Clay?*
Svea: *Yeah, fine.*

I scoff. That's really convincing. But she can be a lot like me when she wants to be—clammed up, quiet, stubborn. Even if I asked her about the incident in front of the inn the other night, she would give me some lame answer. At best, it would be truth-adjacent and watered down. I could ask Lacey, but I don't want to go behind Svea's back.

Svea: *I'm proud of you, you know. It's really awesome to see you putting yourself out there.*
Lee: *Definitely not easy.*
Svea: *It's gonna pay off, I'm sure of it.*

Time will tell, I guess.

Every year the fire department puts on a water fight where there are teams who use their fire hoses to move a ball strung up high on a wire. Sort of like tug of war, but with water. It's always a lot of fun, and the kids in the community especially love it.

The weather is perfect for a water fight—not windy and plenty warm. They usually do it on the north side of Larkspur Park, so the street has been barricaded off already.

Because I know the guys from the fire department, I came early to help them set up. Besides the water fight, they're also serving free root beer floats, so I end up tasked with helping set up the table in the gazebo. I'm grateful for the shade and the vantage point it gives me to monitor the library, where Emma will likely be coming straight over once the library closes.

My skin tingles just thinking about how it will feel to see her. I think she understood how personal it was for me to tell her what I did last night, and her hug is enough to get me to hope that things between us will keep going in that direction. I'm dying to know if she'll look at me differently. Will she hug me again when she gets here?

I shake my head slightly.

I need to lower my expectations. Just because hugging her was life-altering for me doesn't mean it was for her. I'm confident enough to know that it meant something to her, but I can't assume it steamrolled her like it did me.

Just play it cool. That's all I can do.

Around 6, people start to show up. I help make the floats and hand them out with Ginny, one of the firefighter's wives.

"Are they just for the kids?" comes a familiar voice, and I look up to see Pappa standing there with a big grin.

I chuckle and hand him a red Solo cup.

"My money is on Derek's team," he says, nodding towards the fire-fighters.

"We'll see."

He pats me on the shoulder and joins Mamma, who's chatting with the Gustafsons. Pappa hands her the cup and kisses her head.

I smile softly at them until I see Garrett approaching. He's wearing pressed white shorts and a stupid white short-sleeved dress shirt with pink flamingos all over them. He beams at everybody he passes, including my poor sucker of a father. His biggest fan. If only he knew.

Leaving Ginny to man the table, I go over to join them. The Gustafsons take off, headed toward where people are gathering to watch the water fight.

"Well, I've never seen a water fight like this, but I'm intrigued," Garrett says conversationally, glancing over his shoulder at the fire trucks.

"It's a lot of fun," Pappa comments with a smile.

Garrett looks over at me then. "Lee, nice to see you again."

I give him a flat look and say nothing. Pappa pats me on the back proudly, and I slide him a small smile.

"I suppose you met at the Author Event, did you?" he asks. "And have you met our other two? Will and Svea?"

Garrett smiles warmly. "Yes, I've had the pleasure of seeing them a few times already this week." He glances at me, narrowing his eyes slightly behind his glasses, like it suddenly occurs to him, it was no accident. "You have a beautiful family."

"Yes, we do," Mamma confirms almost in defense, watching him closely.

His gaze catches on something behind me. His stupid face lights up, and I just know he's spotted Emma.

"Here she is," he says, holding one arm out expectantly as Emma reaches us. She goes to Garrett's side and hugs him, probably to be polite, but it still stings a little. Even if it was nothing like our hug.

She faces everyone else, her black hair fanning over her shoulders. "Hello, Christiansens," she greets us with a sweet smile, her beautiful eyes moving shyly from my parents to me.

My heart squeezes in my chest. She's wearing a pale pink, gauzy skirt and a white t-shirt with little black polka dots on it. I instantly memorize that pale pink color. Maybe, I can find a flower at the community garden to match it.

A lazy smile lifts the corners of my mouth.

Did she find her flower on the porch?

The first one I've ever had the guts to give her.

She gives me no indication that she did, or that she hugged me after I opened myself wide. If anything, she seems more reserved than ever.

Mamma smiles wide at her. "*Hej*, Emma. Where's your mom? I haven't seen her in forever."

"Caitlin is bringing her. They'll be here soon," she explains with her small, shy voice.

"Oh, I can't wait to meet your mother," Garrett chimes in with a big smile, snaking his fingers through hers like it's nothing.

My shoulders tense. Mostly because she doesn't seem very surprised he's holding her hand, and she doesn't take any action to separate them. I do notice she avoids my eyes after.

I try not to let the hope deflate out of me, but that's a pretty strong message. Holding someone else's hand after we had such a big moment...was last night too little too late? Did it mean more to me than it did to her?

Suddenly I wish I could go back in time to this morning and say something different in the group chat. Clearly, we *do* need a new plan.

Because more than ever I can picture Garrett being the one at the end of the aisle. The one she smiles at and exchanges vows with and spends her life with.

My parents notice Garrett's display of affection, and Mamma frowns at me. Pappa's eyebrows go up behind his glasses in delight, much more delight than I'd like. But he doesn't know how I feel about Emma. Apparently, Mamma said nothing to him about the little talk we had at the library.

"Look at this," Pappa says with a grin, making me want to throw up. "You and Emma? What a perfect match."

Emma blushes, her shoulders hunching inward just a little like she wants to disappear.

Garrett beams. "That's what I've been telling her," he says happily, looking at Emma and squeezing her hand.

She puts on a polite smile, but it's tight and not meaningful.

Heat floods through my veins as my entire body stiffens.

What else has he been telling her? What have they talked about? What has he been putting into her head?

"Emma was telling me you own that charming little inn," Garrett says loudly, with all the friendliness and personality I don't have.

"We do indeed!" Pappa exclaims. "How are you liking your stay?"

"Oh, it's been just amazing. Patty is so helpful and welcoming."

I can't keep myself from snarling. His intentional flattery is more than apparent and less than genuine.

"And the gnomes," Garrett adds with an easy-going laugh. "So adorable."

Emma studies his smiling face, blinking at his comment.

Mamma side-eyes him, and I couldn't love her more because, boy, does she see right through him.

"*Tomten*," she corrects him.

"Sorry?" Garrett asks, leaning a little closer to her in a good-natured way.

"They're *tomten*," she repeats sternly. "They protect my family from disaster and bad luck."

Garrett's blue eyes go a little wide before he catches himself. "Oh. Well, that's wonderful."

"*Hej Mamma!*" calls Svea from behind us.

"*Hej Dotter!*" she calls back, waving with her free hand.

Svea, with Lacey in tow, make their way over, weaving between the other people. When they get close enough to see that Garrett and Emma are holding hands, Lacey squawks and slaps her hand over her mouth. Svea's mouth drops open and then snaps shut as she lets out something resembling a growl. Then they look at me, and all I can do is look back, helpless.

My phone rings inside my pocket as everyone exchanges greetings. I'm surprised to find Lars's name on the caller ID. Maybe he's here somewhere and wants to meet up. With a surge of guilt, I realize I forgot to text him earlier when Svea told me about how he left the Drunken Mallard upset last night.

Stepping away, I accept the call and sweep my gaze around the park, looking for him.

"Hey man," I say into the phone, my back to the group.

A few seconds pass without him saying anything and I pull my phone away from my ear to make sure the call didn't drop. It didn't, making me wonder if he butt dialed me. I put the phone back to my ear.

"Lars? You there?"

I hear something. Not his voice. Something else.

A...sniffle?

Confusion and concern ripple through me.

"Lars?" I try again, my voice dropping low.

There it is again—a sniffle, this time louder. Lars clears his throat. "Lee, I don't...know what to do..." he rasps out slowly, his voice milky and stuffy sounding. Like he's been crying. The only time I've ever seen him cry was at his grandpa's funeral.

My heart lurches. "What happened?" I snap, already moving away from my family and toward my truck. "Where are you?"

"At home," he answers, sounding so unlike himself that I almost don't recognize his voice. "I need your help." His voice cracks on the last word and he lets out the saddest, tiniest cry.

"I'm coming—I'll be right there," I assure him quickly, breaking into a run toward my truck, parked at the end of the block. "Are you alone?" I wrench the door of my truck open and throw myself inside.

"Yeah, she left..." he says as I switch to speakerphone and put my phone in the cupholder.

I turn the ignition and pull out onto the street, heading toward his house. I have to keep reminding myself that I'm not in my squad car. I can't speed. But goddamn do I want to.

"What happened, Lars? Talk to me," I say, mostly to make sure he stays on the line.

He sniffles again. "I don't know how to talk about it," he says brokenly. "You'll see when you get here."

I make the final turn down his street, flying down it once I see there are no other cars. His house comes into view on the right—a little two-bedroom rambler with light green siding. I skid to a stop in front of it, throwing the truck into Park and killing the engine as quickly as I can.

In the middle of hurrying around the front of my truck, I stumble to a stop when I find Lars sitting on the top cement step with his head in his hands. The front door has been left wide open.

The hair on the back of my neck stands up. All of my police training rushes forward as I quickly take in the front of the house, and my best friend. He looks unharmed, and so does the house, but the open front door makes me nervous as hell.

I move closer, going slowly, and he doesn't look up. His shoulders are shaking just slightly. His phone is sitting next to him, the call still going even though I left my phone in the truck.

"Lars," I say, trying to keep the adrenaline coursing through my body from shaking my vocal cords as I speak. "What's going on?"

Keeping his face down—*why won't he let me see his face?*—he lifts one hand and thumbs behind him at the house.

Trying to take a deep breath, I climb the steps next to him and approach the open door. Just one quick glance inside tells me everything.

Shoes and motorcycle boots are strewn around the living room—one pair of sneakers hanging from a ceiling fan blade by its tied laces. Books and car manuals have been knocked off the bookshelf by the window, their pages creased on the floor. The TV screen is cracked. Shards of broken dinner plates cover the dining room floor. There's a couch cushion on the kitchen counter and various potted plants knocked over, dirt spilling out onto the linoleum next to the sliding glass door. Thankfully, the pots aren't broken—I know his mother made them herself.

My blood boils. It's obvious who did this.

I pivot back to Lars. He's still slumped on the front step, and there's a weird ringing in my ears as I move toward him, my breathing ramping up as if I've run a marathon.

"Are you injured?" My voice is low, quiet, almost strangled.

He shakes his head just once, and it doesn't convince me.

I go past him down the steps again and turn so I can face him. "Look at me, Lars." It's a command. No-nonsense. Ninety percent police officer and ten percent best friend.

Lars sniffs and slowly drops his hands away from his head. Just as slowly, he lifts his head so I can see his face. The left side of it is red, like he was struck—by an object or a hand, I'm not sure. My hands shake, but then I see his eyes. How long has he been sitting here crying for his eyes to be that swollen? *How long did he sit here before he called me?*

His eyes are bloodshot too and he won't look me in the eye. Placing my hand on his shoulder, I breathe in through my nose to rule out alcohol. He's not under the influence. He's just broken.

"What happened?"

A tear slides down the irritated side of his face. He stares unseeingly toward my Larkspur Inn t-shirt.

"We were fighting," he whispers. "She throws things when she's mad sometimes, but this time—this time she..." He shakes his head, his eyes closing and dark eyebrows scrunching.

I squeeze his shoulder.

"I didn't know what to do...so I called you."

"Do you want to press charges?"

He slowly shakes his head. "She'd just retaliate, I think."

I don't doubt he's right about her retaliating. But I hate the idea that he's okay with letting her get away with this.

Lars lets out a long breath. "I can't do this anymore, Lee. I've tried so hard to make it work, but...I can't handle this." He ducks his head and lets out the same tiny cry he did on the phone.

"How long has she been like this with you?"

Lars shrugs. "She's always been a little fiery, but for the last couple of months she's been pretty unpredictable." He wipes his nose, still keeping his head down. "Throwing things, testing me, looking through my phone."

Frowning, I release his shoulder and stand up straight. "You should've told me it was this bad."

"I know." His fingers thread through his longish brown hair, gripping it. "She broke my grandma's plates," he grits out miserably. "The ones she got when she married Grandpa. I can never replace them..."

I wince. I know Grandma Janssen, and when she hears about this, it'll absolutely break her heart.

"Let's not worry about that right now, okay?" I glance back at the open door. "I'm going to take some pictures of everything, just in case you change your mind about pressing charges."

Lars says nothing in response, so I go back inside and take at least a hundred pictures. It's going to take a lot of work to clean all this up, and I don't want him to do it alone. I also don't want him to be alone here tonight. I wouldn't put it past Amber to come back in the middle of the night to cause more mayhem.

When I go back outside, he hasn't moved.

"Go pack some stuff," I tell him. "You can stay with me tonight, and then tomorrow we'll come back over and clean everything up."

After a long moment, and what seems like a lot more effort than it should, Lars gets to his feet. I go in with him. He doesn't look around as we go through the living room to the small hallway where the bedrooms are. I stand in the doorway of his room as Lars grabs a few things and puts them in a backpack.

He locks up the house, and as we're pulling away to head over to my house, I have one fleeting thought of Emma...*she's with Garrett*. but then I focus back on my best friend.

Tonight, the plan will have to wait.

Chapter Eighteen

Emma

M y stomach is in knots as Lee makes a beeline for his truck.

I hope everything's okay.

Maybe it was work related, but I could've sworn I heard him say Lars's name.

I'm not the only one who noticed the abrupt way he left. His family and Lacey all exchanged anxious glances. Garrett kept the conversation going without skipping a beat.

He's still holding my hand when I see Caitlin and Mom. Her blue eyes immediately zone in on our hands, and then she's smiling at me in understanding as she wheels herself forward.

Something squirms inside of me as I realize she's putting puzzle pieces together from two entirely different puzzles. She thinks I was asking her about Dad last night because of Garrett, when it couldn't be further from the truth.

Caitlin smiles in approval too, though hers is less meaningful and more excited.

I wave at them, drawing the attention of Lee's parents. His mom has been side-eyeing Garrett and me, making me feel like I've done something wrong. It's a relief that someone else has her attention.

"Silvie," Mrs. Christiansen says warmly, going over to bend down and hug Mom, who returns it with a smile. "So good to see you."

"You too, Elsie," Mom says as they pull apart. She looks at me expectantly, and I hear Garrett clear his throat, like he's preparing himself to be introduced.

Instead of focusing on that, all I can think about is how excited Mom was when I told her Lee had fixed her ramp this morning. She said something broad, like I usually do, about the Christiansens being so helpful and selfless. I couldn't get myself to say anything in reply, because deep down I know what Lee did was as much for her as it was for me.

"Mom, this is Garrett," I say, the words coming out weaker than I want them to. "Garrett, this is my mom, Silvie. And you remember my sister, Caitlin."

Garrett drops my hand so he can shake Mom's. He gives her his best smile as he leans over a bit to meet her eyes.

"It's an absolute pleasure to meet you," he says in that friendly way of his. "Emma speaks so highly of you."

Mom glances at me with a wink. "As she should."

Garrett chuckles and straightens up, stepping back next to me again. His warm hand rests gently on my lower back.

I'm a little surprised he's being so touchy with me in front of everyone. When he held my hand yesterday at the 5k, it felt intimate and sweet—purposeful, even, because of what we were talking about. I didn't expect him to hold my hand or be so comfortable with his hand on my back now. He told me to think about a future with him, and I assumed he meant the ball was in my court.

By touching me so publicly, it's almost as if he's assumed I've already decided in his favor. Or maybe he's trying to sway me by turning up the affection. Either way, I shouldn't be surprised by his confidence. Though I am a little put off about it.

Garrett stiffens suddenly, and I follow his narrowed eyes to find Ben walking toward us. Though he's dressed much more casually than his boss, there's something just as classically handsome about him. Maybe men from Minneapolis are just a cut above other men when it comes to good looks.

"What are you doing here?" Garrett calls out to his assistant, his voice polite but just barely. I frown at him.

Ben shrugs, hands sinking in the pockets of his jeans. "I'll keep to myself," he promises as he reaches us and doesn't slow down, like he plans on going over to the crowd by himself. But then his eyes snag on my hand in Garrett's and he instantly stops. Ben blinks at his boss and then looks at me with widened eyes.

"Hi, Ben," I say.

A slow frown moves across his mouth, his eyebrows drawing together in concern.

That's weird.

Garrett clears his throat, catching Ben's attention. They stare at each other for an awkward beat, the rest of the group staring at them.

"You can hang out with us if you want," I tell Ben.

He keeps his eyes on Garrett's. "You know, I forgot I have a call I need to make." Without another word, Ben turns around and walks away.

Tension settles into my stomach. I've only seen Ben a few times, but this was the first time he wasn't tripping over himself trying to do what Garrett wanted. I didn't like the way they looked at each other, and I don't know what to think of it.

Garrett frowns after him for a moment and then rolls his shoulders back. The frown switches back to a smile as he looks around at my family and the Christiansen's like nothing happened.

"What was I saying?" He chuckles.

"I'll be right back," Svea blurts out suddenly, darting away from the group.

Lacey frowns, but shrugs it off. "This is my first water fight," she tells everyone excitedly. "Will said to wear something I don't mind getting wet." She's wearing a navy T-shirt with The Swedish Chef logo on the front and jean shorts. It's very casual compared to the trendy and stylish way she usually dresses. She and Svea both wear clothing they've made themselves. I admire their talent for reworking fabrics.

Garrett's flamingo shirt looks expensive, but I know nothing about clothing. Not like Lacey or Svea would, anyway.

"That's part of the fun," Mr. Christiansen assures Lacey with a shrug and a fatherly smile.

Something about it hits me square in the chest. It's been twelve years since I saw the same look on Dad's face pointed at me. I suck in a breath, attempting to keep myself from getting emotional. I'd literally rather die than cry in public.

Garrett's hand makes small circles on my back. Rather than comforting me, all it does is remind me of the way Lee's thumb felt smoothing back and forth there instead.

"Come on, let's go find a spot," Caitlin says, and I follow everyone brainlessly.

I struggle to keep my mind in the present and not on the two men who aren't here. The two men who, to me, are inextricably linked now.

Desperate for a distraction, I reach for Garrett's hand. He curls his fingers around mine and smiles, not in surprise, but in delight.

I wish it helped. I wish touching him had enough of an effect to distract me from my grief. But all I can think is that holding Garrett's hand is...nice. Pleasant. Easy.

My shoulders slump. *Why is nice such a letdown?*

There's a crowd on the lawn of Larkspur Park, facing where the water fight is set up. Mom, Caitlin, Garrett, and I congregate on the edges of the crowd. Mr. and Mrs. Christiansen and Lacey opt for a closer look and move toward the middle. Svea joins us right before the fire chief lets everyone know they're about to get started.

I smile at the group of kids who are front and center, many wearing their bathing suits and some holding squirt guns.

I forget every year how powerful the water hoses are, and from Garrett's wide eyes, I can tell he wasn't prepared for it either.

Both teams aim their hoses at the ball in the center, trying to move it down the wire with their spouts. People cheer and shout, especially the kids. The breeze carries droplets of water and spray, landing on my glasses and Garrett's.

He chuckles, taking them off to wipe the lenses on his shirt.

It only takes a few minutes for one team to win, but they'll do it multiple times. I think the winner is the best out of seven. This way, the community gets a good show.

On the last try, everyone gets riled up and shouts their lungs out. Most of them know that after it's over, the firefighters trade the fire hoses for super-soakers and try to get the crowd. Usually they go for the kids, so I'm not super concerned about getting more than a little splashed.

"This is amazing," Garrett comments with his dazzling smile pointed at my community. I'm sure he's about to pull out that little notebook to write something down but then a firefighter points his super-soaker our way.

"Watch out!" Svea cries out with a laugh, just before a firefighter unloads his super-soaker directly all over Garrett.

He tries to dodge and cover his face, but there's really no use. I get some of it and so does Caitlin, but by the time the firefighter darts away, Garrett's brown hair is soaked, and so is his pink flamingo shirt.

"That was so harsh!" Svea says through a fit of giggles.

Garrett grimaces, water dripping down his angry face as he rips his glasses off. I've never seen him in any condition other than pristine and perfectly collected. But now his face is red, and he looks...*embarrassed*.

For some reason, he glares at Svea. Without a single word, he turns and stomps away.

Poor Garrett... If it had happened to me, I would be humiliated.

I call after him to wait, rushing to catch up as he flings one arm out and then the other, trying to get the excess water off of him.

"Not now, Emma," he barks, his tone unrecognizable from the usually friendly, warm, charming way he speaks. My feet slow for just a second, shocked, but I quickly remind myself he's acting this way because he's so embarrassed.

"It's okay," I say, reaching for his back to comfort him. His shirt is plastered to his fit body, the white background translucent against his skin while the pink of the flamingos just pops even brighter.

"No, it's *not*," he snarls, wiping the water from his face with his free hand. "I've never been so humiliated in my entire life."

"I'm sorry," I say, like it's somehow my fault. "I—I should've told you not to wear something so nice."

He's still stalking ahead at full speed, with me just barely keeping up. I don't know where he's going—maybe back to the inn to change?

"Not that many people saw it happen," I assure him, but it does nothing to calm him down. I look back toward the park, two blocks away from us now, and pick up my pace to match his. "It's just us now. It's okay."

Garrett turns at the intersection, and we cross the street, Larkspur Inn down about four blocks from here. My concern fades when he says nothing else and doesn't even glance at me.

I remember what Svea said about him needing everyone to love him, the same way Clay does. Maybe that's why this is hitting him so hard. He's probably used to being adored wherever he goes—like he was last night at the Drunken Mallard—so being singled out in a humiliating way must be harder for him to take in stride.

When we get to the inn, he charges up the stairs, still ignoring me and still fuming. I stay downstairs, glancing around at the homey living room, not sure if I should give Garrett space or stay to try and make him feel better.

Friendly chatting drifts through the open windows, probably other inn guests in the backyard.

I let out a long, uncomfortable sigh. I'll wait for a few minutes to see if he comes back down. I'm not one to judge, but his reaction seems a little dramatic.

Just when I'm thinking he won't reappear, a door opens upstairs and Garrett stands at the top of the staircase in dry clothes.

He looks down at me calmly, most of the anger gone from his handsome face. Instead, he seems...tired. He lifts one hand, gesturing for me to come up.

Taking a deep breath, I climb the stairs and meet him at the top.

"Are you okay?" I ask quietly, noticing his blue eyes pointed downward and that his signature smile is missing.

Garrett takes my hand and sighs. "I'm sorry for that," he says, not meeting my eyes. "I shouldn't have spoken to you like that. I just...don't like being the butt of the joke."

My eyebrows go up. "There was no joke, Garrett. That guy just got carried away," I assure him, referring to the firefighter who drained the super-soaker all over him.

He looks up at me with flat eyebrows. "Don't be naïve, Emma." His voice is quiet but harsh. "Svea was talking to him before the water fight started. She obviously told him to do that."

I blink. My first inclination is to deny that Svea would do something like that, but then I remember her reputation for being a prankster. I wince at him apologetically.

"She likes pranks," I explain, almost whispering.

Garrett glares. "She doesn't like me," he argues.

"It's not that she doesn't like *you*. You just remind her of someone she doesn't like." I don't mention the person she doesn't like is her boyfriend. Because it makes no sense at all.

He lifts one eyebrow suspiciously, not convinced.

"In a way, it's sort of a compliment. She doesn't prank people she doesn't feel comfortable around."

Garrett rolls his eyes, and I frown up at him, discouraged. Apparently nothing I say helps. Sometimes Caitlin is like this—she doesn't *want* to feel better. She just needs time to get over it. I try to extend the same grace to him as I would my sister, but I find it much harder.

He sighs and tugs my hand, bringing me into his room. He leaves the door open and leads me to sit next to him on the bed. Those bright blue eyes are focused on where our fingers are twined together and resting on his thigh. His expression is serious and almost resigned.

"I'm realizing that our childhoods were probably very different," Garrett says softly. "I spent mine at museums and art camps, traveling to bigger cities with more culture." He swallows. "From a young age, I was expected to be perfect. Thinking about it now, I realize my parents expected me to act like an adult. I never got to be messy or disorganized or silly."

His thumb moves over the back of my hand absently, and everything inside of me quiets, listening hard as he goes on with a vulnerability even deeper than what he showed me last night when he talked about wanting to belong somewhere.

"Even now, my parents expect a lot. You'd think being a bestselling author would make them proud, but no matter how many weeks my books spend at the top of those lists, it's never enough." He bites the inside of his cheek for a second and then continues in a small voice. "I didn't like that you saw me being imperfect. I don't like feeling out of my element. I'm sorry for how I acted."

I squeeze his hand. "No one is perfect. Thank you for your apology."

He looks at me then, unblinkingly. "You forgive me?"

"Forgive you for being embarrassed and mad? For not being perfect?" I clarify, raising my eyebrows with a little smile. "Yes, Garrett."

He swallows, his Adam's apple bobbing, and the most tender smile takes over his mouth. He makes a soft sound in the back of his throat and leans forward, pressing a quick kiss to the center of my forehead.

It doesn't rock me, that little kiss. It feels just as pleasant and nice as holding his hand.

Garrett releases my hand and moves his arm around my shoulders, pulling me in against him so my head rests on his shoulder. The strong scent of his expensive cologne overtakes my senses. He lays his cheek on the top of my head. It would be a perfect moment if my glasses weren't smashed against the side of my face.

"You're amazing, you know that, Emma?" he murmurs. "Every time I see you, I'm realizing more and more how beautiful you are inside and out."

My cheeks get a little warm. I admire how good he is with words. He writes well, of course, but he speaks well too. In the back of my mind, though, I note—he made an assumption of what my childhood was like and didn't ask me. He doesn't even know how Mom ended up in a wheelchair or why there's no father in my life. Not that I couldn't have brought it up... Maybe it's both of our faults.

"When I met you at the library that day, I..." He chuckles quietly, the sound smooth and nice. "I almost said the wrong name when I introduced myself. I took one look at you, and my brain stopped working for a second."

I close my eyes, half of my heart whispering...*this is good enough*. This is enough to make me happy. His pretty words are enough.

But the other half wonders if that's all they are—just pretty words. If compliments are his attempt at getting back into my good graces after he reacted so harshly before.

"It feels like you've been here all this time, waiting for me," he continues, his voice warm and sweet like honey.

I bite my tongue, because I was, in a way. I told Caitlin I was waiting for Mr. Right to show up on my doorstep. It's even more fitting his path crossed with mine at the library. I manifested this, whether I meant to or not. I said *yes* to this.

But I realize in this very sweet moment, tucked beneath the arm of one of the most handsome men I've ever seen, the deepest part of me is completely untouched.

For the first time, I wonder if I'm doing it on purpose.

Chapter Nineteen

Lee

My best friend sits on the back deck, a half-full mug of coffee beside him. He's been out there for an hour, watching the sun rise and staring at the grass. The only thing he's said to me so far this morning is he called in sick to work today. He seems...shell shocked. Hollow. It worries the hell out of me, and more than anything, I feel guilty.

He's been through breakups, but nothing has ever shaken him like this...extinguished his spark. Part of me worries he'll never be the same.

I join him on the steps. "I'm sorry, Lars," I tell him.

"For what?" he mumbles.

"For not helping you get out before this...before it got this bad."

He shakes his head, glancing at me. "I wouldn't have listened before this." He clears his throat, but it does nothing to make his voice any less cracked and broken. "I texted her and told her it was over. I blocked her number, but...I don't know what she's going to do."

My shoulders slump in relief. It's *finally over.*

His face is stricken with fear, and my protective instincts kick in. "You can stay here as long as you want, Lars. Will won't mind." Will didn't come home last night, so I assumed he stayed over at Svea and Lacey's apartment. If I had known, I would've offered Will's bed to Lars, but oh well.

Lars just swallows hard and says nothing, because he's not comfort-ed. I'm scared to death that she's gotten so into his head he won't feel safe no matter where he goes. There's so much I don't know. *What else has she done to him?*

"I can clean everything up, if you want. If...you're not ready," I try again. "Or we can just leave it for now, too. It's up to you, man."

He just nods.

I have to be at the community picnic tonight, but I have nothing else going on today. I would've gone to the library to return my book and see Emma this morning, but I don't want Lars to be alone, unless he specifically asks me to give him space.

Amber's vandalism couldn't have come at a worse time.

I grimace at how selfish that is, but half of me is dying. I haven't spoken to Emma since I told her why I became a police officer. And...I got a text from Svea last night. It said, "May Day! May Day! My prank backfired!"

I don't know what she did to Garrett, but it's the first time my sister has pulled a prank on my behalf. In my absence at the water fight, she apparently took the baton and tried to sabotage Garrett and Emma. Even though she said it backfired, I still appreciate the effort.

I take a relieved breath. *I'm not in this alone.*

But time is ticking. The Street Dance and fireworks are tomorrow, and if Garrett and Emma dance together, I won't survive it. I have to go with the momentum I've been making, even if Garrett has been gaining momentum too.

I don't know whether she'll be at the community picnic tonight, but I'll be serving food there. Once the sun sets, there's a movie projected onto the side of the community center, and people bring lawn chairs to watch. It seems more likely that she and Garrett would attend that event than the community picnic.

"Should—" Lars starts, to say and then stops. He swallows hard, hesitating. "Should I file a restraining order?" The way he whispers the question breaks me a little.

"If you want." I watch him carefully. "It wouldn't stop her from trespassing, but having a restraining order would allow us to prosecute her if she violates it."

He scrubs his hand through his brown hair with a sigh. "I'll think about it."

I nod. "I'm here for you, Lars. You know that."

He throws me a tight smile.

My expectations sink. I don't want to leave him alone for too long. I have to help at the community picnic because the police department runs it, but the movie is definitely optional. And I don't think Lars would want to go. It seems like he won't leave my house at all today.

My chest squeezes tight with stress and more than a little panic.

The stakes are high for me with Emma, and time is running out. But I can't in good conscience abandon my best friend when he's at his lowest.

Maybe I can see if Svea or Lacey will invite Emma to the picnic. At least I'll get to see her, though I won't be able to talk to her much.

It's something. She would be a sight for sore eyes after witnessing the nightmare Lars is going through right now.

With a pat on his shoulder, I leave my best friend to his thoughts.

After lunch, Lars stays behind, and I go over to his house to clean up. Thankfully, Amber didn't come back, but the mess she left was more than enough damage.

I'm low-key depressed by the time I finish bagging up the things she ruined and putting his belongings back where they were. I try to do it with care, hating that cleaning up the mess won't reverse the pain she caused Lars. But this is all I can do for him right now and it feels good to help, even if I'm stressed about Garrett and Emma getting closer while I'm currently unable to do anything about it.

I leave directly from Lars's house to go to the police station.

I'm getting out of my truck when my phone rings. It's Mamma.

"Hello?"

"Lee," she says sternly, and I brace myself, loitering by the tailgate.

"Yes, Mamma?"

She's silent. I wonder if she somehow knows what happened to Lars. But no. She's all knowing, but she's not *that* all knowing.

"Tell me what happened between you and Emma."

I pinch the bridge of my nose and squeeze my eyes shut.

"She was holding Ferrett's hand last night."

One eye peeks open.

Ferrett? Lacey must be keeping her in the loop.

"I'm trying, Mamma. Just like you said, I'm showing her."

Mamma sighs, and I drop my hand away from my face. "You're showing her. Good. Now you tell her too."

My shoulders sink. My stomach rolls. But she's right. I need to put words to my actions, so she understands...understands it's all on purpose. And not just because I'm trying to be nice. I have to tell her I want to be a choice.

"Tell her, Lee," she insists when I say nothing. "Before it's too late."

Every year, most of the town comes out for free food and giant lawn games at the community picnic. There's a huge hopscotch court drawn out on the parking lot behind where the buffet line is, as well as giant Jenga and multiple cornhole sets in the grass.

Svea said she swung by the library on her lunch break and invited Emma to come with her and Lacey. She reported back saying Emma said she might. But after an hour, I'm doubtful Emma will come.

And then there's Lars, who's been alone at my house for most of the afternoon. The worry I feel about that is constant in the back of my mind.

My mood lifts briefly when Mikey comes through the line for food and he blinks up at me with wide eyes. This time he's with an older woman, probably his grandma.

"Hello there, Mini Officer," I say to him. He grins, obviously thrilled I remember him.

"Say hi, Mikey," his grandma says with a big smile. I recognize her from Silver Estates, where Lars's grandma lives. Before Amber, I would sometimes go over with him and play cards with Grandma Janssen and her friends.

"Hiiii," he calls out loudly.

She chuckles and shakes her head at me good-naturedly.

"Wanna hogs-scotch?" Mikey asks, pointing behind me.

"You...want me to play hopscotch?"

He nods quickly.

"Maybe later, Mikey," his grandma says, setting her hand on the top of her grandson's head so it stops moving. "Officer Christiansen is serving food right now."

Beside me, Sherry pipes up. "It's slowing down a bit. I can handle it. Go ahead."

I narrow my eyes, but she gives me a surprisingly strong shove for being near retirement age.

"Yeah!" Mikey cheers, thrusting a fist upwards.

"Alright," I mutter, shooting the kid a smile.

Mikey and his grandma follow me over to where about a dozen kids are on various parts of the hopscotch court. Chief drew it himself, purposely making it crazy so it loops and crosses itself in several places.

I grab a small rock from the pile next to the starting line and squat down next to Mikey. I offer him the rock. "Throw this very carefully, okay?" I warn him, and he takes it confidently.

Some of the stress and worry melts away as I follow Mikey; our rocks quickly vetoed in favor of hopscotching itself. With each jump, some of the tension leaves my shoulders. By the time we get to the end, I'm smiling more than I have all day.

That's what I love about kids. Being around them helps me remember the important things in life. The simple things.

This is why I wanted to be a Kindergarten teacher.

Mikey's grandma comes over and high-fives him.

"Again!" he says, and races back to the starting line.

She laughs next to me, folding her arms. "You're very good with kids," she says, watching her grandson.

A dull ache moves through my chest. She said it so genuinely. Without any surprise that someone as intimidating as me could be good with children.

I look around at all the kids, grieving a bit for the dream I once had. Simultaneously, I'm buoyed by Mikey's grandma's positive assessment. I'm not warm and fuzzy, but I'm not intimidating either. I'm *lagom*. Maybe that's enough. Maybe one person's opinion of me doesn't need to dictate the rest of my life. Maybe Mamma was right; the guidance counselor was wrong about me.

"Come on!" Mikey calls, waving at me wildly to hopscotch some more.

Not being able to deny the little man, I oblige, even though I'm the only adult playing. Halfway through, someone cheers for me.

"Go, Lee!"

I look up, recognizing Lacey's voice. I find her standing to the side with Svea. And there—there's Emma too.

My heart lifts, especially when I realize she's smiling softly. Admiringly.

Smiling even more, I follow Mikey through the rest of the course. His grandma convinces him to go get some water, and I glance back at the food tables. Sherry is doing fine, so I go over and say hello.

All three women are grinning as I weave between people, heading their way. My eyes stay on Emma, not even caring how obvious I'm being about how glad I am to see her. Her smile fades a little as I join them, like she suddenly realized how big she was smiling.

"Evening," I say to them, still focused on Emma. She's wearing a plum-colored sundress tonight, her black hair twisted up into a neat knot on the top of her head. My whole being sighs in relief when I realize Garrett isn't with her.

"That was adorable!" Lacey blurts out. "You need to have a hundred kids."

I side-eye her as Svea lets out a loud guffaw.

Emma's eyes are wide behind her black frames.

"I think four is my limit," I deadpan.

Lacey chuckles. "You're almost as cute with kids as your brother." Her brown eyes get all dreamy then, and I shake my head slightly.

"Did you guys eat?" I ask them.

Emma nods while the other two answer yes.

"Svea, let's play cornhole," Lacey says suddenly, and drags my sister away by the strap of her purse before she can respond.

Wow, she's not subtle at all.

Emma shares a shy smile, and glances away. Her admiring smile from before is gone. I try not to read too much into it...even though it doesn't bode well.

Maybe she isn't as happy to see me as I am to see her.

I clear my throat. "How are you?"

She nods, looking back at me, but not sustaining meaningful eye contact. "Good. You?"

Watching her carefully, I decide to be honest. "I'm glad to see you."

Her dark eyebrows raise and her cheeks blush. She says nothing though. It's not like I was expecting her to admit she's glad to see me too, but a man can dream.

"I was looking forward to hanging out at the water fight, but something came up," I add, pushing my hands into the pockets of my jeans.

She nods. "Everything okay? Was it work?"

I give her a tight smile. "No, it was..." I hesitate and check to ensure no one is paying us any attention. Lars might not be able to keep a secret, but I take his privacy seriously. Amber trashing his house isn't something he needs to hear is going around town. "Lars and Amber broke up," is what I settle on saying.

"Oh." Emma watches me, maybe trying to gauge whether she should offer some kind of condolence.

"It's for the best. They weren't a good match."

"A good match is hard to find," she says, mostly conversationally. But my mind flits back to last night—to when she and Garrett were holding hands.

Has he convinced her they're a good match? Has all of his smooth talk and warmth won her over?

I don't want to deal with the possibility she and Garrett are really a thing, but I might have to.

My throat constricts.

"No Garrett?" I grit out.

She shakes her head. "He's at a showing with his realtor. He said he'd try to make it but his appointment ran over." She pauses. "Must mean he's interested in making an offer."

I swear the sun overhead flickers dark as she gives me this information. The noise of laughing kids and people playing lawn games goes quiet. The tangibility of Emma's future without me in it becomes more pronounced in my mind, and I'm reeling.

"Oh," is all that comes out of my mouth.

She finally holds my gaze, something pained in the way her eyebrows are just slightly scrunched. "Yeah."

Silence stretches between us as the world continues, like my whole life isn't about to fall apart.

I don't know what to say.

Did I come on too strong the other night?

I want to know if it's over. If...if I've run out of chances. I want to know what Garrett is to her and what plans they're making.

Instead, I steer away from saying anything more about him. I lean back into the way she hugged me the other night. I focus on the concrete things between us.

"Listen, I want to ask...after the other night. I—I just want to make sure we're good," I stammer, kicking myself for how hard it is to just say things.

She blinks.

"We talked about some pretty personal things," I hint, pulling on the back of my neck nervously. "I hope I didn't make you uncomfortable."

Emma is quiet, watching me for too long, and I cling desperately to the fact that if she says nothing, there's still a chance I'm reading this wrong.

At last, something shifts in her expression. The pained, sort of scrunchy look relaxes into something gracious and sweet.

My heart pounds.

"Of course not," she says, her voice so quiet I almost can't hear it. "What you said was—" She stops, fidgeting with her glasses. "What you said was okay. I promise."

It was...okay? As in allowable? Or okay as in...just fine?

She clears her throat and tries again. "It means a lot to me—what you—why you've made the choices you have. Thank you...and thank you for telling me."

I take a slow breath, trying to calm my heartbeat. With so much nervous energy I'm sure she can feel it radiating off of me, I take one step closer.

Her dark eyes widen just slightly.

Tell her.

But the words dry up.

Every single one I could use to tell her—*poof*—gone. Just like that.

No. Don't chicken out.

I suddenly wish the book in my glove compartment was magically in my back pocket. I wish I could put it in her little hands and tell her to read it...because if she did, she would understand. It wouldn't be as romantic and forward as a bouquet of fresh flowers. The pages are warped and dirt smeared, but there are words in there... There are thoughts and intentions. There's love in it. All the love I've wanted to show her, but didn't think she would want.

Emma's phone rings from inside her purse. She looks down and digs it out, answering with the last two words I want to hear.

"Hi, Garrett." She aims a tight, slightly apologetic smile at me, then turns away, giving him directions as she heads toward the parking lot.

Chapter Twenty

Emma

"Oh, you're too kind," Garrett says modestly to Mrs. Flannigan, yet another fan of his books. We've been at the community picnic for an hour now and he's had no less than six different people compliment him on his books.

No wonder he likes it here.

I've mostly followed Garrett around while he charms and jokes and laughs with everyone, the way he always does. I should be enjoying myself, but all I can think about is Lee.

Garrett welcomes a hug from Mrs. Flannigan and then looks around, as if expecting to find a line of people awaiting him. Instead, most people have left. I sneak one glance across the parking lot where Lee is cleaning up the food tables.

"Well, what now, my dear?" Garrett says, linking his fingers through mine with an affectionate smile that does nothing at all to my insides.

"Um, they're showing a movie at the community center. That's why everyone is leaving," I explain.

"Perfect. Let's go."

"Alright. I can drive," I offer. "I'll drop you off after the movie."

"Sounds like a plan." He swings my hand back and forth as we head over to where I parked my car.

As soon as we're inside and on our way, he launches into the house he toured today, like he's been holding in his excitement the whole time we were at the picnic.

"It's a little further out of the way, but that's kind of what I wanted, right?" he says, glancing out the windows as we drive. "Privacy is necessary when you're a celebrity, so the house needs to be more secluded, but I do wish it was closer to town." He chuckles as I side-eye him for referring to himself as a celebrity. "Not that I can't afford the gas."

He's on cloud nine. He has been all evening. I'm happy for him—he found a house he likes and can move forward with his plan to move here.

But for me, reality is hitting hard. The Garrett road is coming more and more into focus, materializing in front of my eyes, even though I keep sneaking looks down the Lee road.

I can't shake Lee's expression when he asked if we were good, and said he hoped he hadn't made me uncomfortable. He's probably confused by my behavior—how I went from hugging him to distancing myself. Guilt churns in my stomach.

"Did I mention all the beautiful landscaping in the backyard? It's a dream—I can see myself sitting out there writing," Garrett gushes, not noticing this conversation is completely one-sided.

I turn into the community center parking lot. Most of the spots are full already. At least fifty lawn chairs are set up in the grass, all pointed at the blank exterior wall. Even with my car windows closed, the salty, buttery scent of popcorn wafts through the open front doors of the building.

The sun won't set for another hour, but the beginning of the sunset casts a faint orange, golden glow onto everything. It's a warm, slightly breezy evening. Perfect for being outside.

I find a parking space, and Garrett gets out before I even turn the engine off, still talking.

"And the windows! Huge, wide windows," he exclaims, holding his arms apart. "The natural light is incredible!"

His voice momentarily ceases as he closes the passenger side door, and I reach into the back seat for the blanket I brought along. I take an extra few seconds to grab it, taking in a deep breath and letting it out as I appreciate the quiet.

My door opens, and Garrett is standing there expectantly, those blue eyes lit up as he offers me his hand. I give him the blanket instead so I can grab my purse, lock up, and get out. He tucks it under one arm as I push the door shut. Then he's lacing his fingers through mine and tugging me forward.

Nice, is all I can think.

Holding hands with him is *nice*. He smells *nice*. Listening to him speak is *nice*. Reading his books is *nice*.

There's nothing wrong with *nice*. Nothing at all. Most people would be thrilled with *nice*.

Be thrilled, Emma.

But that's the thing, isn't it? Nice isn't thrilling. It's...*safe.*

Maybe what I really find appealing about Garrett is how safe I feel from him. Not in the murder mystery kind of way, but...in the way his affection for me isn't incredibly deep or personal. He could never reach the depths of me, and some part of me doesn't believe he would try to.

He's a safe choice.

Garrett finds a spot to spread out the blanket, a perma-smile on his handsome face. We sit down and settle in, waiting for the movie to start. They project *Independence Day* every year on the Fourth of July weekend. I could quote the speech Bill Pullman's character gives at the end of the movie word for word.

"This is quintessential small town," Garrett says, beaming as he takes in everyone gathered and waiting for the movie to start. "Better than a drive-in movie theater."

I smile at him, but I can feel how weak it is.

"Do I smell popcorn?"

"Yeah, they're selling it inside."

He chucks my shoulder lightly with his fist. "Well, I better get some. Be right back."

Garrett gets to his feet, and makes his way to the front doors. Once he's gone inside, I let out a heavy sigh and look down.

I smooth the skirt of my dress over my legs. I fidget with my glasses. Smooth my bun. Straighten the blanket.

A painful electric flutter fills my lungs, like an allergic reaction without the allergy. I realize it's nerves, but not the usual shyness or the good kind, like excitement. This is...harsher. Deeper.

Everything is fine, Emma. You would have a nice life with him.

But the problem is...I saw Lee hopscotching tonight, smiling and playing with those kids, like he should've been doing all this time. He's a police officer because of my dad. And in some way, because of *me*. And now I know what it feels like to hug him. *Really* hug him.

No amount of Garrett hugs could come close to just one Lee hug.

Just one Lee hug tore through every layer of me, and there's no amount of walls I could erect around myself to keep him out. I can't protect myself from him. He's all deep, raw, intense energy. By far, the most dangerous choice.

So why can't I stop thinking about him?

Why does the Garrett road look less enticing when it's the safer choice?

With a heavy sigh, my shoulders slump.

Garrett makes his way back a minute later, carrying a greasy paper bag of popcorn with him. He sits down next to me again, still smiling, and holds the bag out for me to take some.

"This is great," he says, so over the top happy, he selfishly doesn't seem to notice my lack of it. "Everything is falling into place now. I found a great house, a great small town to study for my novel, and—" He looks me in the eyes fondly. "A phenomenal woman by my side. What more could I ask for?"

"I'm happy for you," I say and take a few pieces of popcorn.

The bag lowers slightly as he rests his hand on his knee, turning toward me a little. "I hope you've given what I said the other night some more thought."

My nerves ramp up, feeling like buzzing bees all over my body, as he looks at me in the falling light.

"I just keep thinking, if I hadn't come here, I never would've met you." The fingers of his free hand lift and graze affectionately across my jaw. "And what a terrible shame that would've been, Emma."

His eyes move around my face—appreciating my glasses, my hair, even my nose, and then my mouth. I keep mine on his impossibly blue eyes, a hurricane of nerves stirring up inside of me. When he meets my eyes again, there's a question there. A romance novel question.

Garrett's warm fingertips follow the curve of my jaw down to my chin.

My lungs shudder, the breath leaving them. Not because Mr. Right is about to kiss me and I'm excited, but because I already know what kissing him will feel like.

Nice.

I'm pretty sure any other man's kiss but Lee's would feel *nice.* Because Lee's would obliterate me.

Garrett leans closer, smiling softly. He's gently pulling me forward by my chin, and I realize he's not going to give me the choice to say no.

A red flag goes up in my mind, because...*he didn't technically give me the choice to say no to a date, did he?* He decided it was a date once we were already at The Swedish Chef.

Popcorn rains down on both of our heads. Garrett pulls back in surprise, releasing me before our lips meet.

"Oh, I'm so sorry!" comes Lacey's frantic voice.

I look back and see her helping Ben up from the grass behind us.

"I must've tripped you—I'm so sorry," she says again, sounding truly apologetic.

"It's fine," he says, dusting himself off.

"What the hell, Ben?" Garrett exclaims, brushing popcorn off his shorts.

I frown at his harshness. "It was an accident."

"It was all my fault—" Lacey says, bending down to press napkins to Garrett's shoulders and hair, trying to blot any butter the popcorn may have left.

He takes the napkins from her and mutters something under his breath that sounds like...*unbelievable.*

"Accidents happen, *boss*," Ben grumbles, glaring down at him. "No one is perfect."

"Exactly," I agree, pinning Garrett with a meaningful look. But my hopes for him to be as understanding with Ben as I was with him last night are quickly dashed.

Garrett's mouth pulls back into a scowl, his brows pulling together behind his glasses. "What are you even doing here?"

Lacey's mouth drops open.

"No," Ben says firmly, folding his arms. "Try again."

Lacey folds her arms too. "Yeah, try again. Say something nicer."

Garrett's face flushes with an anger I don't understand.

I thought he treated his assistant well, but after their weird moment at the water fight last night and now this...? I'm not so sure.

I frown as his mouth presses into a thin line. *Why is he being like this?*

Clearing my throat, I look up at Ben and Lacey, hoping to smooth things over. "Why don't you guys join us?"

Garrett makes a shocked sound in the back of his throat.

"Thank you, I'd love to," Lacey says instantly, ignoring him. She sits next to me.

Ben stays where he is, glancing between Garrett and me.

"I mean it," I encourage him. "You're welcome to stay." I give Garrett a pointed look. "I'm sure it's boring being at the inn by yourself all the time."

Garrett flicks one unimpressed glance my way.

Okay...

Ben smiles slightly, shaking his head in almost disbelief. "You're way too nice for him," he mutters.

"Hey," Garrett exclaims, getting to his feet with a scowl. "No one asked for your opinion."

"No one ever does," Ben answers, giving his boss an identical scowl. "That's the problem."

"Oh, you have a problem with the way we do things, huh? Is that it?"

Lacey snags the forgotten bag of popcorn and stuffs a handful in her mouth, eyes staying on the men arguing above us like *this* is the movie we came to see.

I'd be more entertained if I wasn't so worried Ben might about to be getting fired right in front of me.

"I have a problem with a lot of things," Ben says, stepping closer to his boss.

"Well, *now* isn't exactly the time to deal with it, wouldn't you agree?"

Ben looks down at me, hesitating. "Fine," he huffs. "We'll deal with it later." He shoots one more glare at Garrett and then turns around, walking toward the parking lot.

Garrett's fists clench and unclench at his sides and then he smooths his hair, adjusts his glasses, and sits down again.

"Sorry about that," he says, clearing his throat. "He's been wanting a raise for a while now."

Lacey mutters, "interesting theory."

"We won't let Ben ruin our night," Garrett continues, not hearing what Lacey said. He takes in a deep breath and lets it out, then his usual Hollywood smile returns like he wasn't yelling at his assistant just a moment ago.

"Right. Because *Ben* is the problem," Lacey agrees with thinly veiled sarcasm.

When I look at her, she lifts her eyebrows once to indicate who the real problem is.

"Exactly. Thank you," Garrett says, and looks up at the blank wall where the movie should be starting soon.

You're way too nice for him.

My stomach squirms at what Ben is insinuating—that Garrett isn't nice at all and has just been pretending with me.

No doubt Ben would think that, given how charged his interactions have become with Garrett the last couple of days. Is Garrett usually so combative with his assistant? I sift back through all of their interactions but am distracted when Lacey clears her throat.

"I don't think I've seen this movie," Lacey says, trying to move on but her usual brightness is still dim from Ben and Garrett's argument. "Will told me it's good. He'll be here soon." She looks over toward the parking lot, like she's hoping he'll appear just because she's said his name.

I look too, part of me hoping I'll see Lee's figure emerging from the darkening parking lot. He's probably staying behind at the community picnic to clean up. Ben is gone, likely pulling out of the parking lot on his way back to Larkspur Inn.

"Are you guys going to the parade tomorrow?" Lacey asks, turning back to us. "Supposed to be a hot one, but they're going ahead with it."

"Oh, I'd love to see a smalltown parade," Garrett answers cheerfully, Ben seemingly forgotten. "I'm sure it's nothing like the Macy's Thanksgiving Day Parade." He chuckles to himself, and I can't tell if his comment was meant to be a dig or not.

"It'll be my first one, too!" Lacey grins and then she nudges me. "I told Will to do a float, but he's still crazy busy with getting the restaurant up on its feet. Maybe next year."

I smile, grateful Lacey is here. "What about Svea?"

She snorts. "I told her we should but she said no. I thought it would be so fun to do a moving runway with people modeling our clothes." She bounces her eyebrows at us. "Shame."

"Do you have men's clothing there too?" Garrett asks, leaning around me slightly.

"Some, yes. We do alterations too."

"I'll have to stop by," he says warmly and then rolls his eyes. "If Svea doesn't mind, that is."

Lacey cocks her head. "Why would Svea mind?"

He levels an expression at Lacey I don't like. It's pure condescension.

"Because she doesn't like me." His tone is condescending too, like Lacey's an idiot for not understanding.

She frowns at him, and I do too. We talked about this, but apparently he's still sure Svea was the one behind him getting soaked yesterday.

"You don't seem to like her much either," Lacey fires back.

Garrett's eyebrows shoot up, like he can't believe Lacey called him out.

"And for some reason, you *really* don't seem to like Lee."

My heart beats a little harder as Lacey brings Lee into this conversation.

Garrett scoffs, all of his charm gone up in smoke, just like when Ben arrived. "And for some reason *you* keep showing up wherever we are." He gestures between us. "All of you do, actually, and I'm thinking it's on purpose."

"What are you talking about?" I ask, my voice tinged with shock.

"Listen, buster," Lacey growls. "This isn't the city. This is a small town. Everyone goes to everything. Emma is my friend. So if you're planning on moving here, then you're going to have to get used to seeing me and Svea and Will and Lee. If you don't want to be friends with us, fine, but that doesn't mean we're going to stop being friends with Emma."

A small smile lifts the corners of my mouth. Svea is usually the feisty one, but I like Lacey's feistiness too. To know she thinks of me as part of her friend group means a lot. Being shy really has its disadvantages when it comes to making friends. I'm grateful Lacey isn't one of those people who mistake my shyness for disinterest. Knowing I have a genuine friend in her is like being wrapped up in a warm blanket, especially right now when I'm seeing so much more of Garrett's rude side.

I also like her drawing a line in the sand. Just because Garrett's trying to stake his claim on me, doesn't mean she's going to let him dominate my already small social life.

To my right, Garrett sniffs in derision. It's clear from his sharp scowl, he didn't like a single thing Lacey said. His eyes are narrowed on Lacey, but then he pins me with the same look. He widens his eyes and raises his eyebrows, as if he's hinting I should say something to defend him.

But what Lacey said is true. He's going to be seeing a lot of them, not just me, when he moves here. If he's serious about us, having the future he wants, then he'll need to get along with people.

And the idea of him *not* getting along with someone seems so anti-Garrett that I wonder if I know the real Garrett at all. If his friendliness and warmth are genuine or just a way for him to get people to like him. If, like Ben insinuated, he's really as great as he seems.

He looks good on paper, but what's really written between the lines?

"She's right," I whisper with an apologetic grimace.

His mouth drops open. "*What?*" Garrett looks back and forth between my eyes like he's never seen me clearly before.

"You don't have to be friends with everyone—you'll make your own friends, I'm sure," I add, trying to salvage...something from this conversation. "And besides, you'll be away at your house writing most of the time, anyway."

My words do nothing to help. He snaps his mouth shut, and keeps right on scowling. "I would *never* be friends with the people who are actively trying to come between us, Emma." He turns his glare to Lacey. "That's what's really happening here."

Lacey shakes her head in my periphery.

"That's a big accusation," I say. "Why would my friends want to come between us?"

His condescending face moves back to me. "*Because they don't like me*," he seethes, each word coming out slow and deliberate. Because apparently I'm the idiot now, not Lacey.

A hot strike of anger churns in my stomach. I break into a sweat—for the first time my face flushes with anger and not shyness.

"Hey!" Lacey barks. "Don't talk to her like that. And for the record, I like you just fine when you aren't being a condescending *jerk.*"

My head is spinning as I stare at him.

"I'm not a condescending jerk!" he claims defensively. "I'm not the one who's meddling in someone else's relationship—you are! And Svea, Will, and Lee, too. You've all done everything you can this week to make me look bad, and here we are again. I'm sick of it!"

Despite how much I dislike the way he's talking to me and Lacey right now, there's a small part of me that realizes he might be right. Svea hasn't hidden her ill feelings about Garrett at all. Lacey has been friendly and nice, but she's certainly taken over a lot of conversations with Garrett. Will hasn't said or done anything suspicious I can think of, but Lee hasn't been overly friendly with Garrett either.

And of course Garrett wouldn't take well to any of it because he feels like he has to be perfect. He doesn't like people seeing his imperfections, especially me.

Maybe it isn't that he isn't as nice as he seems—maybe it's just his frustration with my friends that's bringing out his unkind side.

Garrett's theory might hold true, because I've seen more of everyone this week than usual. Obviously, Lee comes to the library every week. I run into Will at the grocery store or Lars at the post office, sometimes. I see Lacey and Svea around town quite a bit, and they invite me to do things with them, but this week I've seen them every night.

Is it because they don't want me to be alone with Garrett?

Some of my anger extinguishes. Poor Garrett has been trying to spend time with me and has been repeatedly interrupted. And until now, he's been a pretty good sport even though he's been frustrated about it.

"I'm sorry," I say to him, setting my hand on his wrist.

His head snaps to me, his face finally losing its ugliness.

"*What?*" gasps Lacey.

I shake my head slightly at him. "I didn't realize...I didn't know you were feeling like this. I'm sorry."

Relief soaks into his features, those too-blue eyes softening. He covers my hand with his.

With a smooth, soft voice, he asks, "can we go somewhere else, just us?"

"Sure."

Chapter Twenty-One

Lee

I weave my way out of the police station, running into Chief who asks if I can help with traffic control tomorrow at the parade, and finally make it outside. The sun is nearly down, and I grimace at it.

I check my phone as I walk across the parking lot to the street where I parked my truck. Lars hasn't texted me, and I hope it's because he's just lying low.

I unlock my truck, noticing a familiar red Mustang parked a little ways down. He must've carpooled with Emma to the movie.

Pocketing my phone, I walk over to it. With a small smile, I reach into my wallet and pull out the stupid twenty-dollar bill he gave me. I tuck it under his wiper blade. Feeling a small sense of satisfaction and only a small amount of disappointment that I won't see his face when he finds it, I go back to my truck.

My phone rings as I open the driver's door, and I quickly dig it out of my pocket. But it's not Lars. It's Lacey.

Something twists in my stomach. The last time she called was to tell me Emma and Garrett were on a date. What are the chances she's calling for a good reason?

I slide the green button, bracing myself.

"Hello?"

"Lee!" she yells, out of breath like she's walking fast.

My stomach drops.

"What's wrong?"

"It's a disaster," she gasps. "He's onto us, buddy, and Emma left with him—I don't know where."

"What do you mean he's onto us?" I assume she means Garrett.

"I mean, he called us out! Right to my face—in front of Emma! How we're coming between them on purpose and everything." She pauses and lets out a long wail. "And he almost *kissed* her, Lee! I just barely stopped it in time."

My chest shudders like I've been shot. I turn and sit on the seat, the door still open as I try not to hyperventilate.

It's worse than I thought. *Worst nightmare, even.*

"I'm getting in my car right now, okay? I'll meet you at your house and we can try to figure out what to do," she says hurriedly, the beep of her car unlocking in the background.

"No, not my house," I say belatedly. "Lars is there right now."

"Oh, that's great! He can help," Lacey blazes on.

I clutch my chest, focusing on my breath. "No, Lacey. He's not—he's not okay. He and Amber broke up last night."

There's a split-second of silence as she processes. "Oh, thank everything thread and sewn," she mutters in a rush.

I don't know what to do. I don't want everyone over—I don't think it's what Lars needs right now. He doesn't even know what's been going on this week or that Emma is my dream girl. But if ever we needed to figure out a new plan, it's now.

"I'm going to go home and see how he's doing, alright? Maybe he's asleep for the night and I can come meet you guys at your apartment." I reach for the door and pull it shut.

"Okay—I'll text Will and Svea." In the background, Lacey's car starts up. "Talk to you soon."

We hang up, I quickly buckle my seatbelt, and get on the road. My mind races as I drive home.

Something in my gut is saying it's too late. I opened up too late. Tried too late.

A frustrated growl rumbles from my throat.

But there has to be something else I can do.

She can't end up with Todd...she can't.

Turning into my driveway, I quickly take in the house. The lights are off, and I go inside to find the open living space dark. I try to be quiet as I go down the short hallway into the kitchen. I look to the right, expecting to find my best friend on the couch, but it's empty. The TV is off. Frowning, I glance toward the bedrooms. Maybe he's in the shower?

But the bathroom is empty, and so are the bedrooms.

He's not here.

I go back to the kitchen and flip on the light. I see a note on the island and snatch it up.

Going to stay with my folks for a bit. Thanks for letting me crash here. —Lars

A huge breath of relief rushes out of me. I immediately shoot him a text saying I'm around if he wants to talk. Then I text my siblings and Lacey.

Ten minutes later, they all show up, bursting through the door like there's an ice storm outside.

Svea's green eyes are wide as she looks at me. She throws her hands down on the kitchen island. "He almost *kissed her*?" she screeches, like I was the one who saw it happen.

Nausea hits me hard. Thank Mamma's *tomten*, I wasn't there to see it.

Will is pacing behind her, one hand on the back of his neck.

Lacey throws herself down on the living room carpet, starfishing her limbs out dramatically. "What are we going to *do*?" she pleads with the ceiling fan.

Looking at all of them panicking makes me feel like it's all over.

This won't be the story of how I won Emma over. This will be the story of how I lost her to one of the worst human beings I've ever met.

I'll never get to dance with her. I'll never know what it's like for her to love me back. I'll never be more than a library patron who she hugged one time. I'll never hold her hand, kiss her, fall asleep with her, or spend the rest of my life with her.

My hands shake as I clear my throat. "We tried," I croak out. "At least we tried."

Lacey lifts her head off the floor to look at me, and once my defeated words process, she covers her face and lets out a sob. Will quickly goes to her side, kneeling beside her and pulling her upper body off the floor so he can hug her tightly.

Svea stares at me. "Lee," she whispers, her tone almost murderous.

I look at her wearily. "I can't make her love me, Svea."

Her face turns bright red, eyebrows slamming down over her eyes. "You're just going to *give up*?"

"Svee—" Will pipes up, trying to defend me, but she talks right over him.

"No. No. You can't do that! Will can't be the only one of us who gets to be with the person they love." She sniffs, her face still red and glaring.

Lacey looks up from where she had her face buried in Will's shoulder. "Svea..." she murmurs.

"So maybe what we tried hasn't worked as well as we thought," Svea continues, looking from me to Lacey and Will, then back to me. "But that just means we need a Hail Mary."

I slowly shake my head.

All I'll ever have of Emma is one life-changing hug. My bookshelves will fill up with books full of dried flowers and unspoken words. I'll have to live my worst fears and watch her fall in love with *him*—waste all of her sweetness and love on someone who can never give it back to her in full. I'll fill my days hoping maybe someday she'll leave him.

"Like what?" Will asks over his shoulder.

Svea levels me with her gaze. "You have to tell her."

My shoulders tense.

"You have to tell her you love her. That the poem was about her. That she's everything you've ever wanted. That no one will ever come close to her in your mind."

My throat constricts, as if my vocal cords themselves protest the idea.

"I think she's right," Will admits quietly. He kisses Lacey on the forehead and stands up, helping her to her feet as well. "You have to put it all on the table."

"I'm not good with my words," I remind them. "I'll never be able to say it perfectly...I'll mess it up." I palm the back of my head, my heart jackhammering as I imagine trying to articulate the tangle of things in my mind.

"Maybe she doesn't need perfect words, Lee," Lacey encourages softly. "Maybe it'll be enough to just tell her that you love her."

I hold her teary eyes for a moment, considering.

"You've already been showing her," Will adds, his arm sliding around Lacey. "Maybe putting those words to it will make it all click."

"Hearing a lot of 'maybes' in this Hail Mary plan," I mutter, mostly to myself.

"Well, *maybe* you should use the smart part of your brain," Svea says, "because if you did, you'd realize there's no one else on this earth who can love Emma better than *you*, Lee."

My sister's words scramble my brain for a second.

I've never heard a truer sentence.

I may not be well-spoken, or overly good-looking. I may not be smiley, charming, or rich and famous. But I'm honest. Hard-working. Humble. Loyal. I try to be a good person wherever I go, whatever I'm doing. And I might not tell her with pretty, perfect words how I feel, but I know how to show it. I know how to try.

I know how to put flowers down in a notebook, dirt and all.

It's still there—out in the glove compartment. A book she's never read. One full of intentions and colors and love. The best of my attempts at poetry and all the flowers I picked for her. All the bits and pieces of how deeply I love her.

"I know what to do."

The room stills.

Without another word, I leave the house. I go out to my truck and fling open the passenger door.

"What are you doing?" Svea shouts from where she, Lacey, and Will are all crowded at the front door.

I open the glove compartment and take out the book with my whole heart in it.

Taking a deep breath filled with both hope and terror, I close the door and bring it back to the house.

My favorite people scurry from the doorway into the house as I approach. Once we're all back in the living room, staring at the wrinkled, warped-paged book in my hands, I tell them what it is.

And then we make one more plan.

Chapter Twenty-Two

Emma

Where the drive to the movie was filled with Garrett's endless, excited chatter, the drive away is completely silent.

My brain works overtime, sifting through everything, trying to determine if Garrett's version is true, or if he's twisted it with his own insecurities.

Ultimately, I don't want to believe my friends—most of all Lee—would try to make him look bad, or to get between us. But if they did...is it because they don't see the romance hero I see in Garrett? Am I being blinded by his charm and humor? Was Ben trying to warn me?

I don't know what's true.

"Do you really think they've been trying to get between us?" I ask quietly as I pull over in front of Garrett's shiny red car.

He doesn't look at me as he answers. "Of course. They haven't exactly been subtle about it."

"I don't like thinking they would do something like that." I put my car in Park. "In some way, I'm sure they were just trying to help."

Garrett scoffs softly and adjusts his glasses. "It's impossible for you to think ill of anyone, isn't it? Even people who have hurt me?"

Guilt tightens around my shoulders, but then his words sink in.

I can't think ill of anyone.

My heart pounds at that realization.

"If I can't think ill of anyone—including you—then maybe they're just trying to look out for me."

His head snaps up, his nostrils flaring in outrage.

"I'm not saying they were right to interfere," I add quickly.

Garrett sighs and shakes his head. "It's not my place to tell you who you can be friends with, but I can't be second to them. I'm going to set that expectation right now."

My eyebrows shoot up. "I don't know about you, Garrett, but I don't like to *rank* the people I care about."

His brows slam down behind his glasses into an ugly scowl. He unbuckles his seatbelt and opens the door. "Get out," he orders. "I can't talk to you like this." He slams the door shut and waits for me in front of my car, his arms crossed.

I do as he says and join him face to face. Nothing about his harsh expression has changed.

"What I'm saying is that I'm going to be a priority to you or nothing at all."

The finality of his sentence leaves no room for argument.

Heat rises from my chest. I look away from him, toward his classic car illuminated by the streetlight.

It's fair for him to expect to be a priority, but for him to *demand it*? It just reminds me of what Svea said about him and Clay—how they need to be loved above everyone else.

Garrett touches my hand to get me to look at him again.

"I'm not one to waste my own time. If I can't have it all, then it isn't worth having," he says firmly. But then his face softens. "Because I look at you and I know exactly what I want, Emma. I've made a connection with you that I haven't made with anyone else, especially not this soon. It would be a mistake not to fight for it. That's what I'm trying to do here, okay? I'm trying to fight for what I want—for what I know we can be."

His words are romantic and possessive in a way most women—especially my sister—would die to hear.

But instead of calming me, I see how he's trying to trap me with pretty words.

It would be a nice cage.

I shake my head and take a deep breath.

"My first priority will always be my family," I tell him evenly. "Maybe it isn't something you understand because you aren't close to your family. But I've lost a core member of mine, and almost lost another. That kind of loss changes a person, and I don't want to be away from my mom and my sister, ever."

It hits me then.

Dad wouldn't have liked him.

He would've seen right through Garrett's friendliness and warned me away from someone who *demands* to be my only priority. He would've paid attention to how Garrett treats his assistant and the people he can't charm.

Garrett listens closely as I continue, not interrupting me even though I can tell he wants to say something.

"So I need you to understand, nothing will take me away from them. You might travel all over the world for your job, but I won't be going with you. My family is *here*. My place is *here*. I'm happy *here*."

Garrett stares at me for a long moment. "You wouldn't travel with me? You don't want to see the world, Emma? Even just every once in a while?"

I shrug. "I love my life here, Garrett. This is where I want to be. I'm setting that expectation right now."

He blinks at me. His eyes lower.

Even while we're entrenched in a conversation I'm barely comfortable having, I can't help admitting how handsome he is when his brain is working.

After a long moment, he bobs his head. "I see." He looks back up at me, his mouth flattened in a bitter line. "I'm glad to know where I stand."

Then he turns and walks toward his car, stuffing his hands into the pockets of his chinos. After a few steps, he pauses in the middle of the street and waits, his back still to me.

What is he doing?

He throws his head back with an annoyed sigh. "This is the part where you say 'wait, Garrett! Don't go! We can figure this out!'"

My eyes widen.

Wow. He's more dramatic than my sister.

When I say nothing, because frankly I'm too stunned by his immaturity to speak, he scoffs and starts walking again.

I shake my head, watching him cross the street.

But then he stops again.

My hands squeeze into fists. *Is he seriously waiting for me to stop him...again?*

Garrett grumbles and stalks over to his car, messing with his windshield wiper. He whirls around, shaking something in his hand.

"*This* is what I'm talking about! This right here!" He screams.

Despite myself, I go over and see what he's so mad about.

"Is that money?"

"Yes. It's a twenty-dollar bill!" Garrett lets out a strangled growl.

I'm a little worried about his sanity. "Garrett...what?"

"I don't know why I'm surprised, honestly. Of course he would give it back to me." He shakes his head at the sky.

"What are you talking about?"

"*Lee*, Emma. I'm talking about Lee." He growls again.

My brows knit together in confusion.

"I got a flat tire on the way into town, and he helped Ben change it for me. But when I offered to pay him, he refused. When he wasn't looking, I put this twenty under his windshield wiper and took off. And *here it is!*"

I shake my head, overwhelmed by this new information. "You tried to *pay* him? When he was on duty?"

"Does it matter?"

"Wait, I thought you met at the library."

Garrett produces his wallet and wrestles the bill into it. "No."

"But...you acted like you hadn't met him before."

"Well, he didn't exactly introduce himself while he was changing the flat," he mutters.

I stare as he runs his fingers through his hair.

His lack of honesty is suddenly so plain. Not just this incident I didn't know about until now, but also how he spoke ill of the gnomes at Larkspur Inn to me in private, but complimented them to Mrs. Christiansen's face. How he's treated Ben with disrespect and rudeness but did he best to flatter everyone else.

How did I not see it?

He's not the perfect romance hero he appears to be. Look once, even twice, and you might believe it. But the more I think about it, the more I see him for who he really is.

He's a good writer. He's a good storyteller. He's a good talker.

But he isn't honest. Or genuine. Or kind.

He's nothing like the Mr. Right I talked about with Caitlin.

"Why did you lie?"

Garrett glares at me, his eyes slits. "You're kidding, right? *That's* what you're upset about?"

Like coming out of a dream, I finally see him clearly. And I don't like what I see at all.

He would be a safe choice, but it would be the *wrong* choice.

The Garrett road gets boarded up right then.

My shoulders, which have been tight around my ears all evening, finally lower. The knots in my stomach unravel, and I let out a long, slow breath.

"I don't think this is going to work," I tell him.

He steps closer, his face going scarlet. "Is that so? Why? Because I lied about *Lee*? Hmm? *That's* your deal breaker?"

I know what he's trying to insinuate, but I don't address it.

"Because you're good at pretending to be a great guy. And I didn't see it until just now."

His head jerks back.

I don't wait for him to retort. I turn and hurry back across the street.

"You're making the biggest mistake of your life!" he shouts as I get into my car and shut the door.

I take off, not bothering to look back.

When I get home, I find Mom in the living room. Her wheelchair is parked in the usual spot beside the couch, a previous season of *The Bachelorette* playing on the TV.

I let out a sigh. Just the sight of her is comforting.

"Hey, Mom," I say, moving around her to sit on the couch.

She narrows her eyes slightly. "Hey, what are you doing home? I didn't think you'd be back till late."

I clamp my arms around myself, avoiding eye contact. When I don't answer, Mom grabs the remote and turns the TV off. My heart beats faster as she moves her wheelchair toward me.

"Emma, what's going on?"

Biting my lip, I resign myself to having this conversation.

"I'm not dating Garrett."

Mom blinks. "Oh." She watches me, her eyebrows pinched. "I hope it isn't because of Dad, because we talked about that, remember?"

My heart beats even faster.

"He would've hated Garrett," I say, my voice coming out quiet. "Maybe not at first, but over time he would've figured out the same thing I did."

"And what's that?"

I look over at her, frowning. "Garrett is nothing he says he is."

"What do you mean? I thought everything was going super well."

I lean my head back against the couch and sigh at the ceiling. "He seems like the perfect guy, but he's just good at acting like one."

Her eyebrows go straight up to her hairline in shock.

"His charm and friendliness and everything..." I take a deep breath. "It's just an act. He's dishonest underneath and kind of mean."

Mom sits quietly for a moment, processing.

"You know," she says gently, "I thought maybe he was just trying really hard to make a good impression. It may not have been devious."

I shake my head. "Trust me, it's not that."

I explain everything about Lee fixing his flat tire and the twenty-dollar bill, how he said one thing to me and another to Mrs. Christiansen about her gnomes, and his treatment of Ben. Now she's scowling in disgust, and instead of being comforted that my judgment of Garrett is finally right, it just makes me feel worse.

How could I be so blind?

"I feel like an idiot, Mom."

"You're not an idiot. You're the kind of person a jerk like Garrett seeks out—because you're inherently good and want to believe everyone else is too."

I smile softly, eating up her loyalty and love. My body relaxes a little into the couch.

"I wish I had seen it sooner. My friends certainly did."

Mom pats my knee, smiling at me supportively. "Better late than never, right?"

I nod.

That's the thing about choices. You never really know what you're choosing in the end. What I thought I was saying yes to in dating Garrett wasn't at all what I thought it was.

But at least I proved I *can* take action. I can be proud of myself for the *right* choices I've already made. I thought I was refusing to act, but I was really just doing whatever I could to feel close to my loved ones.

Maybe I've sat back and been mostly content with playing things safe, but that doesn't mean I'm wrong about the important things.

And now I can say I'm not a background character in my own life anymore. If anything, I can be proud of myself for that.

The next morning, I hand Mom the reusable water bottle I packed. Somehow Main Street feels hotter than the night of the 5k, and that puts me a little on edge. Because of the injury to her spine, she's prone to overheating.

"Thank you," she says, and takes a long drink of the ice water.

"If you get too hot, we can go, Mom," Caitlin says, watching our mother closely from where she's sitting in a lawn chair on the other side of her.

"I'll let you know if I do," she answers lightly.

The parade is about to start, and thankfully we found a mostly shaded place about halfway down Main Street. I reach into my bag and pull out my Elinor Riverside book. I start fanning Mom with it.

She chuckles, but doesn't tell me to stop.

Though I typically wear a lot of sundresses in the summer, today I opted for jeans shorts and a tank top, my black hair French braided back into a low bun. None of it seems to have made much of a difference, but not a lot would in this kind of heat.

Waving from across the street catches my attention. I recognize Lacey and the Christiansen siblings, minus Lee. I smile and wave back. There's two empty camp chairs next to them that I assume are for their parents. I take just a moment to find them—down about twenty feet talking to the Gustafsons.

I'm going to need to talk with my friends later. I owe them a huge thank you for trying to have my back. It would've taken me longer to see Garrett's true colors if it hadn't been for them.

I woke up this morning feeling lighter, like a weight had been lifted off my shoulders. Even the thought of running into him today doesn't spoil the relief I feel, because it's over, and I know I've made the right choice in breaking things off with him.

"Lee must be in the parade," Mom notes, waving too.

My eyes drift to the right, to where the parade floats will come into view. I expect the usual handful from local banks and churches. My favorite float is always Vicky's Dance class, where little kids perform classic routines to their parents' favorite songs. Janssen Auto drives a handful of antique cars or hot rods, while the grocery store's giant shopping cart on a go-kart is always a big hit.

Smiling to myself, I realize what I said to Garrett last night was absolutely true. I love it here. Larkspur is my little corner of the world, and I wouldn't want to live anywhere else.

A few minutes later, the police chief's cruiser sets the crawling parade pace, sirens blaring. His wife sits in the passenger seat, tossing candy and silicone bracelets out the window. Another cruiser, the K-9 vehicle follows, but Lee isn't driving. Then, the fire truck rolls through, spraying everyone with squirt guns, and the ambulance. It goes by slowly, two EMTs throwing candy and blowing bubbles from the open back doors.

My eyes follow the ambulance.

Where's Lee?

I look further down the block to where the police vehicles are turning off at the road barrier. A familiar figure is standing there, and my heart leaps a little.

I'm going to need to talk to him about Garrett, too. I want to know more about that twenty-dollar bill and flat tire.

Lee takes a few steps and I frown. I know the way Lee walks. His stride is long and sure and purposeful. But he's sort of...*staggering?* I squint, watching him closely as he takes a couple more of those staggering steps away from the road barrier.

To my horror, he stumbles to his knees.

Before I realize it, I'm on my feet.

He isn't getting up.

Someone sitting near the end of the street quickly goes over to check on him, and everything slows down and speeds up simultaneously. The man runs over to the ambulance, thankfully parked just down the side street, and comes back a moment later with an EMT.

"What's going on?" Mom asks, but I don't hear her.

The two of them help Lee back to his feet. They slowly get him to the side of the street, moving him between the First Century Bank float and the Evangelical Free Church float.

My heart pounds hard in my chest as he disappears from view. The second he's gone, I'm weaving my way through the crowded sidewalk, leaving my family without a thought of giving an explanation.

I have to know if he's okay.

I get to the end of the parade route and look down the side street. The ambulance is still parked, with one of the back doors open. I dart across after the Alma's Diner float goes by, and I don't stop running until I'm climbing into the back of the ambulance.

Lee is sitting on the edge of the gurney, his shirt, socks, and shoes taken off. He's leaning over with his elbows resting on his knees, a bottle of water in one hand. His face is flushed. His hands are shaking.

The EMT is applying a disposable ice pack to the back of his neck. Lee shivers just slightly, his head dropping forward a bit.

And maybe it's the ambulance or the fact that I've never seen strong, able-bodied Lee looking so weak, but something inside of me crumbles. The urgency of the moment gives me some kind of permission to rush close, getting on my knees in front of him.

"Hey—hey, it's okay," I tell him, not even knowing what I'm saying. "I'm here—it's okay." I adjust the ice pack and glance up at the EMT. "What happened?" I choke out.

The EMT—the nameplate on his shirt reads Danny—frowns at me, almost in disapproval of Lee's condition. "Heat exhaustion. He's too stubborn and won't let me take him in. If we can't cool him down in the next twenty minutes, I'm taking him in anyway."

I realize the only reason Danny's holding off is because he probably knows Lee. The EMTs work closely with the police department.

Lee's head lifts slightly, and he blinks at me, eyelids heavy and eyebrows scrunched up in confusion.

"Emma?" he says, like he doesn't trust what his eyes are seeing.

"Hey, yeah. It's me," I tell him, reaching for his free hand. His skin is hot and clammy.

He still looks at me in confusion, "What...are you...doing here?" he says slowly between his shallow breaths.

"Have some more water," I instruct, ignoring him, and he does.

"Not too much too fast," Danny adds, and moves around me to close the ambulance door. Then he comes back, scooting to the front where he cranks the air conditioning.

I've never felt so helpless. I just want to hug him, but he doesn't need my body heat. I reach down and roll up the pant legs of his jeans to expose more skin to the air conditioning. That's something I've done for Mom when she's gotten overheated in the past.

When I look up at him again, his eyes are squeezed closed and his breathing speeds up.

"No," orders Danny, pushing a blue plastic vomit bag into his hand. "Don't you throw up. You need the fluids, dummy."

Oh, they definitely know each other. That comforts me a little.

I take the water bottle from Lee and pour some over his head. He makes a little gasp of surprise, but it seems to help.

"You're okay," I tell him, mostly for my benefit, because I know the second he's in the clear I'm going to burst into tears.

Danny says something into the radio on his shoulder about his condition, turning away slightly as he does.

I move closer to Lee, flipping the ice pack over as he drinks a little more water. After a few minutes he looks up, finally seeing me, and I meet his gaze. I smooth my hand over his bare bicep. A part of me wishes this wasn't such a serious situation, so I could appreciate his shirtless upper body.

Something eases on his face. He leans forward and rests his forehead on my shoulder.

It's a small intimacy, but it tilts my whole world. My heart melts, and it takes almost all of my restraint to keep from kissing his temple. I don't know how it can feel so familiar to be close to him when it's happened so rarely.

This is what it would be like with him. Small, simple affections that have the impact of a meteor strike.

Oh.

Tears sting my eyes.

This isn't anything like Garrett, where every affectionate action and word just felt *nice*.

I was using Garrett to avoid *this*. There isn't anything *safe* about this, because it's all consuming. Because there's no protecting myself from it. Lee goes to the depths of me, and I can't keep him out.

This...this is the kind of thing you don't heal from. This is the raw, gritty, real thing that makes life worth living while you have it, and takes everything away with it when it's gone.

I love him.

Really love him. Like my parents loved each other...

And I'm terrified.

This is the thing I've watched my mother struggle without for the last twelve years.

This is how it would feel to lose him—the fear and the panic is a tangible reminder of it. Losing him would be like the sun going dark. A curtain dropping between us that can never be lifted. The love gone...the grief the only proof it was ever there at all.

Of course, I would be afraid of the kind of love where every little thing has a big meaning. Because the absence of it would be the same way—devastating and unmendable.

How can I bear to love him when I know it's going to ruin me?

Chapter Twenty-Three

Lee

S he smells like sugar.

It's heavenly and comforting. It's all I'm focusing on as I get my wits about me.

Finally, the electric shocks subside from my hands, and my nausea is easing away little by little.

After sitting there with Emma in the back of the ambulance for another ten minutes, my heartbeat strengthens, and my breathing deepens and slows.

That's better.

She was the last person I expected in the back of this ambulance. I thought I was hallucinating, if I'm honest. Like I was on death's door, and my brain conjured her up for me to see one last time.

But she's still here, sitting next to me on the gurney now, holding my hand.

I know her hand belongs right where it is, but I can't help questioning why it's there.

"Chief's pissed," Danny says from my left. He aims an infrared thermometer at my forehead for about the fiftieth time. My body temperature is finally back in a safe range.

"I'm pissed too, if it helps anything," I mutter.

I know better. Chief explicitly told us to drink a lot of water today, and I had exactly zero water. I had nothing to eat or drink this morning before I left for the parade, too anxious about the Hail Mary plan we all came up with last night. This is my fault, and I'm just as angry with myself as he is.

"The important thing is you're okay," Emma reminds us, looking at me intently. I squeeze her hand three times.

I don't even know how she knew something had happened to me. Did she see it? Maybe it went through the crowd like a giant game of telephone.

"I'm sorry for all this," I murmur.

She shakes her head before I've even finished speaking. There's a sweet little pinch to her eyebrows that hits me right in the chest.

"He said you have to go straight home," Danny continues irritably. "Someone else will direct traffic."

"Alright, alright," I groan.

"Are you okay to drive?" Emma asks with concern. "I can take you home, if you need me to."

I almost tell her she should stay and watch the rest of the parade with her family, but I know her offer is genuine. She isn't trying to be polite. And I know how important it is to her that people drive safely and responsibly.

"How will you get home?"

"My mom and Caitlin can pick me up on their way back."

Not *Garrett*?

But I know better than to bring him up.

"You sure?"

She nods quickly. "I—um, left my purse and everything though. I'll go grab it and tell them what's going on." She gets to her feet but doesn't release my hand. "I'll be right back."

I nod, but she lingers for another moment, her face a mixture of anxiety and concern. It hits me hard. She doesn't want to leave me, even though I'm doing better. I realize I scared her.

She clears her throat, glancing at our hands before she reluctantly lets go. Emma steps back, her eyes still on mine, and then she turns and exits the ambulance.

Before I get even a second to think, my phone rings in my pocket.

I get it out and curse under my breath. Apparently, the telephone game finally reached Mamma.

"Hello?"

"Lee Fredrik Christiansen, what in the world happened?" She's out of breath, huffing and puffing, and I can only imagine she's bustling through the crowds on the sidewalk, headed this way.

"I'm fine," I sigh out. "I just got dehydrated. I'm fine."

Mamma gasps like I've slapped her. "You collapsed, they say! Are you trying to give me a heart attack?"

I massage my forehead. "Everything's fine," I repeat. "Danny fixed me up and I'm about to go home."

"*Gud välsigne dig*, Danny!" she exclaims, meaning *God bless you, Danny*. "Tell him I'm going to make him *kanelbullar* as a thank you for saving your life."

I shake my head. Swedish cinnamon rolls are a specialty of hers, and I know Danny will eat the entire plate in one sitting.

"I'll tell him, Mamma."

"Dehydrated," she mutters to herself, scoffing.

"Go back and enjoy the rest of the parade, okay? I'm leaving now. We'll talk later."

"Oh, we'll definitely be talking about this later," she fires back. "It's been too long since you touched the *tomte*."

I barely hold in my groan. That damn *tomte*. "Fine, Mamma. Bring it by later."

We hang up, and I'm just as annoyed with my mother as I am amused. Her anger with me is really love, even if it doesn't sound like it. When she calms down, she'll be softer with me.

I put my shirt back on and get a fluttery feeling in my chest when I roll my pant legs back down, because Emma was the one who rolled them up.

She returns a few minutes later, and I give her my keys. I don't bother with my socks and shoes, opting to carry them instead as we walk down the side street to where I parked my truck.

After the cool interior of the ambulance, the summer heat just feels that much warmer. I want to walk fast, but I decide better of it and Emma matches my pace.

"I've never driven a truck," she says as we come upon it.

"I don't live too far," I assure her.

We get into the truck and buckle up. The last time we were in this truck, I broke myself wide open and let all my walls down. This time I feel like she's seen me in another vulnerable situation, this one physical. Both times, her reactions have surprised me.

She starts up the truck and sits up as tall as she can. She reaches over, taking a second to find the right knob, and then cranks up the air conditioning.

From my pocket, my phone buzzes with notifications, and I'm sure it's my siblings in the group chat. I don't bother checking it.

I direct Emma to my house, a little amused by how carefully she drives. More than anything, I'm smitten. This is the kind of thing I would do—it's an action with a lot of meaning underneath it.

She takes the last turn onto my street, and I indicate which driveway is mine. She pulls in and puts the truck in Park. Letting out a tense breath, she finally relaxes in the driver's seat.

I smile. "You did great, Älskling."

The endearment slips out accidentally, but before she can ask what it means—darling—I open the door and get out.

The engine turns off, and she gets out too. She meets me as I round the hood and hands me the keys.

"It's too hot to wait out here," I tell her, referring to her family coming to pick her up. "Come in."

She follows me to the front door, my heart beating harder as I unlock it. I'm suddenly really glad I'm generally a clean person. Hopefully, Will picked up after himself before he left for the parade earlier.

My heart keeps pounding as we go inside. This is just another vulnerable thing, isn't it? It's surreal that she's standing in my house right now. A part of me wonders if I slipped into a coma and none of this is really happening.

In the kitchen, I watch her look around. Her attention stays a bit on the bookshelf in the living room before she turns back to me.

"Drink some more water," she says. "Please."

I smile softly. "Yes, ma'am."

She blushes just a little, and it floods my chest with warmth.

I go to the cabinet and grab two glasses, filling them at the sink. "Sorry you missed most of the parade," I say over my shoulder.

Emma moves closer, resting one hip against the counter, watching.

"I'm not." Her voice is so small, I barely hear it.

The only evidence she's spoken is her shy expression. She adjusts her glasses, glancing away.

I smile as I hand her a glass of water, and we both drink. The house is silent, and for all I care, the outside world could be too.

"How are you feeling?" she asks with a searching sweep of my face.

"Better." I was tired from not sleeping last night, but now I'm drained from all the heat exhaustion nonsense on top of it.

Emma swallows and nods. Her expression is serious and almost introspective. It makes me want to know what's going through her head.

"Are *you* okay?"

She clutches the glass with both hands, shifting her weight back and forth on each foot.

"That was really scary," she whispers finally.

My chest squeezes like it's in a vice.

She blinks a few times. "My mom overheats really easily because of her spinal injury. There have been a few times over the years where we've almost called an ambulance or had to take her in to cool down," she explains slowly, like every word is hard for her to pronounce. "So seeing *you* like that..." Emma shakes her head slightly. "I never want to see you like that again."

Her eyes go glassy.

Goosebumps rise all over my body as a rush of protectiveness and guilt hit me like a train. I set down my glass and reach for her instinctively, cradling her elbows in my shaky hands.

Her sweet face flushes pink as my thumbs stroke back and forth on her arms, but she doesn't look away or step back.

"I'm sorry," I murmur, my tone coming out even more growly than usual. I want to apologize for it. I want to apologize for how my stupidity is making her feel right now.

Emma stares at me for a beat, and then her eyes go soft. She sets her free hand on one of mine, sending electricity up my arm. "It's okay," she whispers back, sniffing while trying to smile at me reassuringly.

She cares about me.

She came running to my side to make sure I was okay, held my hand, drove me home, was *scared* for me...

I've never wanted to kiss her more.

"Just take a cold shower, drink more water, and rest a lot today, okay?"

I nod and take one more second to relish in the perfect feeling of her skin against mine before I begrudgingly release her.

"Oh, I should text Caitlin your address," she says, setting her glass on the counter and digging into her purse. She clears her throat. "What was your house number?"

I give it, watching as she messages her sister. My mind clunks around, trying to figure out how to cheer her up—how to get her to forget the scary situation I put myself in.

When she puts her phone away and she looks up at me again, I nod toward the living room. "You want to see what books I have?"

Two little giggles escape her. "I thought you'd never ask."

I lead her over so she can check out the titles on my shelves.

It's really something to watch her pointer finger move over the spines. She might as well be moving that finger along my spine. I can't help the shiver that zips through my body.

"No Elinor Riverside," I admit, side-eyeing her. "Not yet, anyway."

She grins. "I haven't converted you to romance yet?"

"Not publicly."

Emma laughs, and I huff out a small laugh too. Her smile lingers as she turns her focus back to the books.

What will she think of the book I'm going to give her tonight? Will it end up on her own bookshelf, or will she give it back to me? Will it mean something to her, or will it be too much?

I clear my throat. "You going to the Street Dance tonight?"

Her finger pauses on my copy of Emily Dickinson poems, glancing suspiciously at me before going on. Probably because she knows I've checked it out at the library recently.

"Yeah, I'm planning on going."

I nod, nerves filling up my stomach. "Save me a dance?"

Emma's eyes widen in surprise, then she immediately blushes. "Oh—I—uh—yes. Okay," she stammers.

I smile even as I wonder if Garrett will pitch a fit about me dancing with her.

Too bad, I guess.

I fight back the urge to ask about him. The less I bring him up, the better, I think. The less I think about him, the less likely I am to talk myself out of the plan for tonight.

A honk from outside startles Emma slightly. "That must be them," she says.

I follow her as she goes into the kitchen to look out the window, confirming her sister and Mom are waiting outside. She turns to me, shyness taking over for just a second before she lets out a slightly nervous sigh.

"Do you—do you mind if I leave my number with you? So you can text me in a couple of hours and tell me how you're feeling?" she says in a rush, as if she's afraid she won't get all the words out if she doesn't say them quickly.

I can't keep my eyebrows from lifting in surprise and she blushes.

"Uh, yeah. Sure." I unlock my phone and hand it to her, vibrating from the inside out with excitement and...*hope.*

She inputs her information into a new contact, and I do everything I can to play it cool when she hands my phone back.

I have her phone number.

How many times have I tried to get myself to ask her for it over the years?

"Thanks," she whispers.

"I'll see you tonight."

Emma nods. "Only if you're feeling well enough to go," she stipulates quickly. "If you're still not feeling right, then—"

"I'll stay home," I finish, even though I fully intend on doing everything I possibly can to be there. I'll drown myself in water and sleep all afternoon. I can't blow this—I wouldn't miss dancing with her tonight for anything.

She smiles a little. "Promise?"

Feeling silly but trying to keep my guard down as much as possible, I raise my pinky finger.

She smiles bigger and holds out her pinky too. We link them and shake, swearing on it.

I walk her to the door and stand there as she walks down the driveway. She pauses before she gets into the car, looking back at me. I give her my friendliest smile, which I'm well aware doesn't actually come out that warm or friendly, and then she slides into the back seat.

I stand there smiling to myself for a long moment after the car pulls away.

Maybe I have a chance...

Maybe.

Chapter Twenty-Four

Emma

As soon as we get back to the house, Mom parks herself in the living room in front of the fan while I get her a glass of ice water.

"You have a lot of explaining to do," Caitlin says as I fill up the glass from the faucet.

I say nothing, because I know I do. I went running down the sidewalk to make sure Lee was okay. They were completely confused when I went back to get my purse and told them to pick me up from Lee's house because I was going to take him home. There wasn't enough time to have a drawn-out conversation, so Caitlin is wasting zero time getting to the bottom of things now that we're home.

She's hot on my heels as I bring the glass into the living room and hand it to Mom.

"Emma, come on," Caitlin barks. "What the hell is going on with Lee Christiansen? Why are were freaking out over him? Last I checked, *Garrett* was the guy you're—"

"No, he's not," I interrupt. I love my sister, but I have never appreciated her confrontational personality.

Caitlin gasps so loud I'm surprised she doesn't choke.

"I know, I know," I mutter, moving between Mom and the fan to sit on the couch. I don't really feel like getting into everything. I'm still reeling from Lee's heat exhaustion and how he asked me to save him a dance tonight. How I somehow found the courage to give him my phone number.

Caitlin fists her hands on her hips, leveling an impatient, expectant expression.

Mom wedges her glass of water between her legs so she can use both hands to turn her wheelchair and face us.

"What happened with Garrett?" Caitlin urges. "I thought he was your dream guy."

I glance at Mom, who gives me an encouraging smile. "Fill her in on Garrett, then I want to hear about Lee."

I nod and blow out a tense breath, looking up at the ceiling. "Garrett *seemed* perfect, Cait. He's everything I said I wanted on paper, but he isn't really anything like that."

She stares at me and I sigh. I collect my thoughts, trying to figure out how to explain.

"Everything about Garrett was...*nice*. Just nice. And it's what I liked about him the most, actually, because...because he didn't make me feel anything big enough to hurt me if he—"

I gulp, my eyes stinging as the truth comes to the surface. Mom's features soften in that motherly, understanding way.

"I would survive just fine if I lost Garrett how you lost Dad," I whisper. "But with Lee—" I stop, unable to get past just saying his name. Because am I really going to say it all—put it all out there and address this? It feels too deep to excavate...too much a part of my body for me to pick apart and bring up into the light.

"Wait, *Lee*?" Caitlin blurts out. "Are you saying you're in love with *Lee*? Not Garrett?"

My lips press together. I can't get myself to say it out loud.

Mom wheels closer and lays her hand on my knee. "That's why you ran to him when you saw him fall," she confirms, as if she thinks I need someone else to spell it out for me.

Tears blur my vision as I look at her. "I wouldn't survive losing him, Mom," I whisper with a trembling voice.

Caitlin stills, finally hearing what I'm saying.

"Who says you're going to lose him, hmm?" she asks, her voice just as quiet. "You shouldn't be letting what happened to me dictate your happiness."

"But I've seen how losing Dad has hurt you so much. *Love* is what makes death hurt so much."

She frowns, her eyebrows knit together. "No. No, that's not it at all, Emma." She squeezes my knee. "It's a waste of your life to grieve something before you've even lost it."

My skin tingles with goosebumps from her words.

That's exactly what I'm doing—wasting my life grieving something I haven't even lost.

Caitlin comes and sits next to me. Her mascara is running down both of her cheeks, and I feel a rush of affection for her.

"You can't pass this up, Emma," she says, her voice wobbling. "We thought Garrett walking into your life was this big sign from the universe that he was Mr. Right, but you know what? Soulmates exist, and it sounds to me like you've known all along who he is."

I squeeze her hand, smiling softly at her.

"It's okay to be scared," Mom encourages me. "But you can't let being scared keep you from experiencing the best thing that will ever happen to you."

Tears spill over, and I swipe at my cheeks.

"I promise you, even if tragedy strikes and you lose him like I lost your dad, loving him wouldn't be the thing you'd regret. You would regret looking back on your life and *not* loving him. I think that's a far more painful thing to handle."

I go back to being in the ambulance with Lee. What if that had been it—what if things had gone even worse and he had died from heatstroke? What if I had to live the rest of my life having never told him how I felt? It would've been the biggest regret of my life.

I would still love him...I just would never have shown him. That would be the real tragedy, I realize.

Mom's right.

She squeezes my knee one more time. "Grief is just love going by a different name," Mom tells me gently.

I nod, my face scrunching up with emotion. Caitlin grips my hand tightly.

We three sit there for a few minutes, dealing with our feelings.

I think about Dad. I think about what he would say at this moment. If Mom had been the one who died and he was the one who lived, he would say the same thing.

Love without holding back.

And I realize even if I knew Lee would die in five years, it wouldn't change the way I feel. It wouldn't change how deeply he's touched my life. It wouldn't stop me from loving him. It would just make me pay attention to every moment—make every single second with him count. I would pour out as much love as I could while I had him.

But that's really no different if I were guaranteed we would have a lifetime together. I learned this lesson from Dad. Take nothing for granted. Love with everything you have.

The truth is...

"I love Lee," I whisper. I look up at Mom with tears in my eyes. "He became a police officer because of what happened to Dad."

Mom's eyes widen and immediately fill with tears.

I love his gruff way of speaking and the way he side-eyes his siblings when they're being ridiculous. I love his appreciation for a good book and that he's secretly a poet. I love how he puts his life on the line at his job day after day to protect our community, and chose his career because of my dad. I love the quiet way he exists wherever he is. I love his kindness and the tender spot he has for kids.

I love him like a really good book that I don't ever want to end. The kind of book that becomes a part of who I am and stays with me for the rest of my life."

I love him unendingly, regardless of circumstance. Whether he's dead or alive.

"So love him, Emma," Mom murmurs.

"Yeah, Emmy," says Caitlin.

I cover my cheeks with my hands and sigh. "That means I'd have to tell him how I feel," I whine.

Caitlin snorts. "Yes. It does."

My stomach rolls with nerves, but beneath it is a quiet assurance. Lee hasn't said how he feels with words, but he's shown me with actions. And I know firsthand how difficult taking action can be.

This time, my choice is the right one. Not made because I want to prove something, but because of love.

Chapter Twenty-Five

Lee

A fter Emma leaves, I finally address the group chat and explain that I'm fine. I text Mamma and tell her I'm going to rest, so maybe hold off on stopping over with the *tomte* for a while.

Then I take a cold shower, throw myself into bed, and crash. When I wake up and realize a couple of hours have passed, I quickly text Emma to let her know I'm feeling a lot better and I will definitely see her tonight at the Street Dance. She texts back saying she's happy to hear I'm doing better and won't have to bail on our dance.

I'm anxious all afternoon about tonight's plan, but I'm holding onto hope because she agreed to save me a dance and gave me her number. Even if she was being polite or just kind, it's still a good sign. *Maybe Garrett hasn't completely won her over yet.*

The Street Dance starts at 8pm, but Main Street closes at 5pm. Restaurants stay open with picnic tables outside for dining and games set up along the street. The Drunken Mallard runs a table with beer and wine. At 10pm the night sky lights up with fireworks.

My chest buzzes with nerves as I drive over to Main Street at 7:30pm. I wander around, running into people I know from work who give me a hard time about my antics at the parade earlier, and others who still have teasing words for me about my poem. Thankfully, I don't run into Chief, though I'm sure I'll get an earful tomorrow when I see him at work.

I'm hyper-aware of the flower book shoved into my back pocket. I looked through it before I left the house, reminding myself of all the words I wrote in it and all the flowers I picked and taped onto the pages.

This little book doesn't feel good enough. It's the epitome of imperfect and raw and mediocre. It falls so short when compared to all of Garrett Waterstone's great works. But it's the best way for me to show her how I've felt about her all this time.

I find my siblings and Lacey hanging out near Cozy Roast. The girls must've convinced Will to take a break from the restaurant for the night, and I'm glad. He's been working hard and deserves a night just to have fun.

Svea spots me first. "Hey, there he is," she says to the others as I weave my way closer.

Lacey bounds forward and hugs me. "Ahhh, this is it!"

I roll my eyes and pat her back twice.

When she pulls away, all the excitement is gone from her face. "Are you nervous? Do you need a pep talk? A drink?"

"No," I growl. "I'm fine."

Well, as fine as I can be.

"I haven't seen her yet, but I've been keeping an eye out," Svea says.

I gulp, nerves prickling my stomach.

"You know who we *haven't* seen?" Will asks, raising his eyebrows. "Ferrett."

"I'm sure he'll be here," I grumble. "It's not like him to miss an opportunity to talk about himself in front of people."

Svea snorts.

We all decided it would be too difficult to try to keep him away from Emma. If he's with her tonight, which I don't doubt, it won't really matter. Because Emma promised to save me a dance. It's my opening to put my heart on the line and give her the book.

"You're nervous," Will comments unnecessarily.

I say nothing, my stomach in knots.

"It'll be fine," Lacey assures me, even though she looks just as nervous as I do. "If she breaks your heart, then...you know, it'll suck and nothing will ever be the same, but we'll be here to help you pick up the pieces and life will go on."

Svea elbows her. "Lace, that's the worst pep talk I've ever heard."

"I'm trying!" she wails, throwing back her head. I just shake my head.

"It's alright, Lacey," I tell her, and take a second to look at each of them. They really have tried their best to help me this week. And even though some of it went sideways, they've had my back in a way I've never let them before, because I've never allowed myself to be this open with them. "I wanted to say thanks. I would've given up if it hadn't been for you guys."

Lacey sniffs, instantly teary-eyed. Will kisses the side of her head.

"We've got your back, bro," Svea says with a genuine smile. "No matter what."

The music starts promptly at 8. John Lofton is playing with a small band, set up on the sidewalk by the four-way stop. The intersection is the area designated for dancing. John's going to play for an hour, and then I think he'll just be playing DJ until the fireworks start.

I hang around on the edge of the dance area, trying to keep my eyes peeled without looking too obvious about it. People are dancing and having fun, and all of it is just background noise because the book in my back pocket is all I can think about.

The sun is on its way down and the sky is slowly darkening, which makes the glow of the streetlights feel more magical as the minutes tick by.

I make my siblings and Lacey go dance so I don't have to feel them staring while I wait for Emma. I think of texting her, but then I see a familiar bespectacled face along the far side of the throng.

My heart jackhammers against my ribcage.

She's here.

She's changed out of her jeans shorts and tank top into a floral-patterned sundress, her hair no longer up in a braided bun, but down and straight like she usually wears it.

Beautiful.

She smiles softly as she watches the people dancing, just like she usually does at the Holly Ball every year.

And like every single Holly Ball, I've watched her like this, trying to gain the courage to ask her to dance. This time, I have her express interest in dancing with me. It should relax my nerves, but it doesn't.

Thankfully, Garrett isn't by her side. I don't see him anywhere, actually, and I'll take it as the good sign it absolutely is.

I stay put through all the upbeat songs until John Lofton plays an acoustic, slowed-down version of "Everything Little Thing She Does Is Magic" by The Police.

My adrenaline kicks in.

It's *now or never, man.*

Sucking in a deep breath and letting it out slowly, I move around the edge of the dance area. The music gets drowned out by my heart beating in my ears. I get about halfway to her, and she spots me coming. My chest squeezes tight, but then she smiles her sweet smile, and I can breathe again.

I pause in front of her, knowing she can see my nerves all over my face.

"Hey," I grit out, through a froggy throat.

She smiles a little more, with an easiness I've never seen before. "Here to cash in already, huh?"

My eyebrows raise at her unexpected teasing, but it's welcome. I quickly huff out a laugh. "Yes. Shall we?" I hold out my hand, hoping she doesn't notice how it shakes.

Emma lifts her little hand and puts it in mine. She squeezes it once as she smiles up at me, scrambling my brain a little.

On unsteady legs, I lead her out to where all the other couples are slow dancing. I have a moment in which I feel like an eighth-grade boy who doesn't know what he's doing, but she just steps a little closer and puts her hand on my shoulder. It tingles beneath her touch. I take her other hand in mine, and then we slowly sway in circles.

I memorize every single thing about this moment. The warmth of her skin against mine. The softness of her cotton dress where my hand is resting at her waist. Her gasoline and honey eyes looking up at me with an openness I'm not sure what to do with. The beginning of a blush creeping onto her cheeks. The sweetness of her perfume.

"You look nice," I manage to say and clear my throat. "Beautiful, I mean. You always do."

"Thank you," she answers softly. "You look—" She pauses, squinting at me just slightly behind her glasses. "A little nervous."

I snort. She's being gracious and we both know it.

"Just trying not to step on your toes," I joke weakly.

She snickers, her gaze flicking to different features on my face. "You're feeling okay, then? After this morning?"

I nod. "I feel fine."

Besides the nerves, that is.

"Good."

We turn in a full circle without speaking as I try to collect my thoughts. The song is probably half over already, so I need to get on with it. I clear my throat again and do everything I can to push through the nerves.

"Lee?" her little voice asks before I can speak.

"Yeah?"

Her gaze moves over my face thoughtfully. "I—I just wanted to say that I'm...sorry."

I blink in confusion. "Sorry for what?"

She sighs and shakes her head. I swear she closes the distance between us just slightly, her eyes focusing on where her hand rests on my shoulder.

"I'm sorry you had to watch me moon over someone who didn't deserve it."

I nearly trip but just barely catch myself. I'm so surprised I can't think of anything coherent to say.

"To be fair, he was very convincing," she mutters begrudgingly, just above the music. "But that doesn't matter now."

What?

My heart beats so loudly in my ear I can barely hear the song ending.

Wait—the song is ending. I didn't say what I wanted to say. My brain clunks through several feelings, mostly panic, confusion, and hope.

The band rejoins John, playing something loud and fast-paced.

She sighs at being interrupted, her hand slipping away from my shoulder. "Come on," she says, tugging me by the hand away from the dancing area to the sidewalk.

I follow her, thoroughly thrown off.

Emma doesn't stop at the sidewalk but takes me further down the side street, away from the music and the crowd. At the corner, she finally stops and turns to me.

I'm grateful for the privacy and the quiet. It will make it easier for me to get the words out. As soon as I figure out what she was talking about.

"You have nothing to apologize for," I tell her, realizing when I finish my sentence she hasn't let go of my hand.

Emma gives me a sympathetic, bittersweet smile. "He was unkind to you."

I stare down at her, the breeze teasing her black hair and flowery skirt of her dress. What she didn't say was—Garrett was unkind and *it wasn't okay with her*. Hope blooms in my chest and some of the tension in my body evaporates.

"That had nothing to do with you and everything to do with him being a jerk," I explain gently.

"Yeah, it's the jerk part I couldn't get past, really," she agrees, her eyes flashing a little facetiously behind her black frames.

She's speaking in the past tense.

Does that mean...?

It sure sounds like she broke things off.

Emma looks down at our hands, and I stare at her, wishing I could read her mind.

But I can't. I've never been able to, which is why I have to say what I need to say.

"I—I want to say something too," I start, and she looks up at me, curious. "I'm not very good at this, so just bear with me, okay?"

Emma nods, even more curious.

I hold her hand a little tighter in mine. Everything around us goes away as I look down at her and do my best to just say it like it is.

"I know how I am, Emma. I'm not charming or warm or overly friendly. I'm...grumpy and growly and not even close to being the life of the party. I'm always going to be rough around the edges and come off more intimidating than I mean to." I swallow, watching the curiosity on her face fade into something serious.

"I'll never have the kind of success Garrett does." Her eyes widen at the mention of Garrett, but I keep going. "I won't ever be rich enough to whisk you away on romantic vacations or buy you diamonds." I shake my head slightly. "But I..."

I hesitate, my breathing picking up. "But there's no one else on this earth who could love you better than me."

She gasps quietly, staring.

"On paper, I don't sound good. All of my redeeming qualities are quiet, humble things, but they're the important ones." I reach into my back pocket and take out the book, my hand shaky. "I can't give moving speeches or write bestselling novels... This is the best I can do. And I hope it's enough for you to even give me a second thought."

Emma lets go of my hand as I give her the book. She holds it in both of her little hands, curiously taking in its warped state before looking back up at me.

"The thing is, Emma—" I stop, my whole body feverish and shaking and terrified. But unlike all those times before, I finally tell her the truth. "I've...I've loved you for a long time. And I never thought you would want someone like me—still don't, actually—but Garrett made me realize I'm much more worthy of you than I thought. I'm much more capable of loving you well than I give myself credit for."

A soft smile moves across her mouth. Her expression is open and kind. At least I can hang my hopes on the fact she isn't disgusted. If she doesn't feel the same, I'm sure she'll do me the kindness of letting me down easy.

I swallow hard, nodding at the book. "So I—I want you to look through this and…"

My pulse ramps up, but I push past my fears. "And if you feel anything even remotely for me in return, then come meet me at the gazebo. If you haven't shown up by the time the fireworks start, then I'll assume you aren't interested and we can forget I ever said all this."

Before Emma can respond, I turn and walk away.

I can't get myself to look back as I go straight to Larkspur Park to await her decision.

Chapter Twenty-Six

Emma

I stand stock-still for a long time, staring after Lee as he walks away into the night.

Every word out of his mouth was beautiful. Perfectly imperfect and everything humble and kind.

And he...*loves* me?

Me?

I almost can't handle it. I almost can't believe it.

But when I really think about it...I can see it. I understand his decision to become a police officer. And that poem? Now there's no doubt in my mind he wrote it about me.

Me!

Here I was thinking I'd be the one to tell Lee how I feel, but he beat me to it. The only other time I've seen him so vulnerable and nervous was when he told me why he became a police officer. I can confidently say there's nothing sweeter in this entire world than watching Lee work so hard to say something important. Maybe the fact that Garrett was so good with his words and spoke so easily, makes Lee's speech seem so much more beautiful to me. Obviously, I know which one I prefer. There's no competition, even if Garrett still had a foot in the race.

Relief spreads through my chest. There's no more Garrett. And Lee *loves me.*

I grin and just barely hold back my squeal of excitement.

I lift the book Lee gave me and take a couple of steps so I'm standing directly beneath the streetlight. There's no title or anything on the navy-blue cover to indicate what it is. When I turn it to the side and look at the edges, I notice how warped and wrinkled they are, like maybe the book got dropped into a puddle at some point.

A journal full of poems? A sketchbook full of drawings?

With my heart beating fast, I open the cover. The first couple of pages are blank and water stained. The next page is heavy and more difficult to turn over, but as soon as I do, I see why.

There's a dried flower taped onto it. It's a slightly faded red zinnia.

I gasp, tracing my fingertip gently over the pressed flower. Lee picked this flower. He preserved it in this book. Why?

Turning the page, I find another flower. This one is a yellow pansy, with a small bit of handwriting. I bring the book closer so I can make it out. His penmanship is neat and a bit cramped, but it clearly says, "the ribbon in your hair."

What?

I turn another page. A sprig of lilac. The next page has a pink honeysuckle. Then a stem of fern with the words "like the green dress you wore today."

My heart goes crazy, my head spinning.

I flip through more pages, becoming more and more overwhelmed by the purpose of this book.

About one-third of the way through, he starts dating the entries, and my eyes get teary. The dates began three summers ago.

It's when I see the first little snippets of poetry that I have to sit down on the curb.

Next to a white gardenia, he's written just five words, but they completely confirm everything I thought I knew about him.

Midnight hair and sunrise smile

I cover my mouth with one hand as tears leak out of my eyes.

He's been writing poetry here...drying flowers he picked because they reminded him of me.

I look at every single page, vibrating with love for this sweet man.

These are all the flowers he's picked for me.

This is a book he's written for me, using more than just words to illustrate his love. And he was drying flowers in this book, not knowing that he's always been so, so much more than just the dirt on these pages to me.

I close the book gently and hug it to my chest, about to burst with happiness.

This is better than any other book I've ever read, romance or not.

Imagining big, strong, stoic Lee picking flowers as he comes across them is almost too much.

He was pretty accurate in his description of himself. Growly, rough around the edges, quiet. But what he didn't say is that beneath all of it there's potent vulnerability and sweetness. Simple gestures with the power to level every single wall around my heart.

There's such depth to him almost no one would believe it if I showed them this book and told him it was his.

And I realize the nameless force I've felt in his presence this week is *love*—the very kind I've been afraid of since my dad died. A love I know without a doubt, I feel for him too and always will, whether he dies tomorrow or in fifty years.

He loves me.

And I love him.

An incredulous, joyous laugh escapes me, and then I get to my feet.

With his book tucked into the crook of my arm, I hurry to meet him at the gazebo.

Chapter
Twenty-Seven
Lee

I feel sicker than I did this morning at the parade as I pace around the gazebo.

I thought saying it would make me feel *better*. Like getting something off my chest and being relieved. But it's nothing like that. It's just sheer helplessness...because I said it and now I have to wait to find out if it was worth the risk. I don't get any say in the outcome.

Emma choosing Garrett would've been my worst nightmare. But a close second would be her not choosing Garrett and then not choosing me either.

I put it all out there—showed her love and let myself be vulnerable with her. I said the words and gave her the book. I did everything I could...and it still might not be enough to deserve her love in return.

There's no getting my breathing under control, I've already figured out, but I keep trying to take deep breaths.

She apologized for Garrett being a jerk. She was scared when my health was in danger this morning. And she hugged me when I told her why I became a police officer.

I keep running those things through my mind as I wait, and it helps a little.

I glance at my phone to check the time. It's been about twenty minutes. Long enough for her to have flipped through the book. Long enough for her to know everything now.

I'm glad that part of my plan was to let her look through the flower book alone. I wanted to make sure whatever opinion she formed wasn't influenced by me standing over her. Also, I couldn't have handled watching her perusing it. Though it isn't much better even just imagining her turning those sacred pages.

I pause at the gazebo entrance, nerves crawling up my neck. With most of the town at the Street Dance or saving spots for the fireworks, this end of Larkspur is hushed, as if the world itself is holding its breath with me.

The sun is gone, leaving only a pale wash of blue. A few stars break through, and when one streaks across the sky, I have no shame in the desperate way I wish on it.

My breath catches and my heart stops when I see the shape of Emma approaching.

It's her...

I blink two or three times, convincing myself that I'm not imagining it.

She's there—walking through the park straight toward the gazebo. And the longer I stare at her, the more I realize she's walking *very* fast.

Some self-preserving part of me kicks in.

Don't believe it just yet. Make sure before you let yourself feel relieved or excited or happy.

Because I couldn't handle it if my joy was ripped away from me if I'm wrong.

When she gets close enough for me to see her face clearly in the darkness, my stomach drops. Her cheeks are shiny. *She's crying.*

I hold my breath as she keeps speed walking toward me. Fireflies billow up from the grass as she walks through it and time seems to slow down. She's clutching my book in her hand.

This is it.

I take a step back as she reaches the few steps up to the gazebo. She moves into the glow of the light perched up at the crux of the vaulted ceiling, pausing at the entrance.

A beat of silence stretches out between us, and I wait, terrified to believe she's really here because she feels the same way I do.

Emma holds up the book.

"I've read hundreds and hundreds of books in my life, Lee. Some of them multiple times because I love them so much." Her voice is quiet and trembling just slightly. "But this...this is my favorite book, and it always will be."

Breath rushes into my lungs.

Hope cloaked in terror morphs into relief washed in bliss.

She smiles. Just a little sweet thing I'll remember for the rest of my life.

"Really?" I gasp out.

Emma nods. "You're not getting it back, I hope you know that."

I chuckle, and she laughs softly too. "You can have it, Älskling."

She comes closer, keeping her happy eyes on mine. "What does that mean?"

I've never seen her look at me like this. Tenderly. Openly. No shyness. No customer service politeness.

I wait until she's standing in front of me to answer. I twine my fingers through hers, lightning zipping up my arm. "It means darling," I explain quietly. "It's what my parents call each other."

Emma beams up at me, even as her eyes get a little teary again. "Say it again?" she requests, and I do. She nods and then does her best to repeat it back to me. I smile at that word coming from her mouth, directed at me.

Before, I could've only dreamed of her calling me that. Now it's reality.

She lifts my hand and holds it against the side of her face. I trace her cheek with my thumb, and she closes her eyes against my touch for just a second before connecting her gaze with mine again. My poor heart can't stop racing, this time for the best possible reason.

"I know how I am too, Lee. I know I'm shy and quiet, and I put up too many walls. I really didn't think I existed to you outside of the library all these years, but still, I've only ever been yours." She sniffs, and her voice drops to a whisper. "I love you, too." Her dark eyebrows scrunch together. "So much it scares me."

I shake my head and move closer, releasing her face and bringing both of my arms around her. She leans into me, her free hand resting on my chest and the book in her other hand lying right there against my heart. Holding her is perfection. Bliss. It's everything.

"There's nothing to be afraid of," I assure her. "There's nothing that could shake this."

"Just one thing could," she whispers up to me. "And all I can do is hope that it doesn't happen until we're both old and gray, and have lived a full life together."

I study her face, finding helplessness and fear written all over her features.

"No. Not even that, Emma," I promise.

She blinks mournfully, those eyebrows still scrunched above the frames of her glasses. "The only way I could bear losing you is if I loved you less...and I don't know how to do that."

My eyes sting. I swear I've read a line like that somewhere. I couldn't tell you who wrote it or what the book looks like, but Emma's version is infinitely better.

"I've tried to love you less for years," I rasp out. "And I—" I shake my head slowly, heart thumping against the book. "I just...failed and failed and failed."

She smiles just slightly through the pain and fear, and I smile too.

"Death changes nothing," I tell her softly. "The flowers in this book are dead, but they still have the same colors and even still smell like they did when they were living—because I preserved them. We'll both die one day, but love will preserve the life we made together."

Emma blinks away a few tears. Her hand curls into my shirt. "How do you say I love you in Swedish?"

My smile cracks wider.

"*Jag älskar dig.*"

She gives it a try. Her pronunciation is imperfect, but I don't care.

I say it for her again, moving closer so my face is hovering near hers. My breathing quickens from our close proximity. *How many times have I wished I could kiss her?*

She smiles up at me and tries again.

Better that time.

I move closer, bringing my lips just inches from hers. My whole body tenses with the sweetest anticipation.

"*Jag älskar dig,*" I say slowly.

"*Jag—*"

I cut her off with my mouth.

A quiet giggle comes from the back of her throat when our lips meet. Hers are soft and warm against mine, tasting like every dream about us I've ever had. Her hand winds around my shoulder as we kiss slowly and thoroughly. Goosebumps rise all over my body, every inch of me alive and on fire.

The future sorts itself out in my mind. Where before, the nightmare was watching her walk down the aisle away from me, toward someone else, now I see her walking *toward me*. I see her smiling at me on that day, and every other day—the normal, boring days and the big, important days too.

When we pull away, I smile at how her glasses are just slightly askew from my nose bumping them. Her face has never been redder, and I have never loved it more. I kiss each crimson cheek.

"I love when you blush," I murmur.

"I love when you grumble," she murmurs back and kisses my chin.

The loud *boom* of a firework startles both of us. "Oh—they're starting," Emma says brightly, and pulls away, grabbing my hand.

We make our way back toward downtown where I parked my truck, grinning at each other as we walk hand in hand.

And when we pull up to where the fireworks are shooting off, there's only peace and excitement in my heart. This is just the beginning for us and I never thought I would get a beginning with her. Just an ending without her.

Emma leaves the book in my truck, and we jog toward where the crowd is gathered, *oohing* and *ahhing* as the night sky explodes with colors above. We stand toward the back, and I don't waste any time stepping behind her and pulling her against my chest. I wrap my arms around her and sigh when she leans her head back against my shoulder.

And just before the finale begins, I catch sight of three familiar people standing about twenty feet away. They're cheering and jumping up and down, but they aren't looking up. Will, Lacey, and Svea are looking at us. Cheering for us.

I let out a contented sigh.

We did it.

A cacophony of colors and sound take over the sky as the finale crescendos. The crowd cheers, barely heard. Once everything is silent and dark, applause breaks out.

I lean down and kiss Emma's cheek. Because I *can.*

She smiles over her shoulder and pecks me on the mouth, making my knees weak.

I know right then that the Fourth of July will always be special to us. Fireworks will be a celebration of the anniversary of this night, when she finally became mine.

The crowd begin to disperse, and I don't notice, too caught up in this sweet moment with the woman I love.

But then someone stops five feet in front of us.

My spine goes rigid.

Garrett stands there, fists clenched and held away from his sides like he's about to enter a cage fight. His face, even in the dim lighting, is screwed up into a scowl that rivals mine. His nostrils flare as his gaze moves back and forth between my face and Emma.

She follows my gaze and tenses in my arms.

"I *knew* it!" Garrett shouts, his voice strangled. "I *knew* you were trying to steal her from me!"

My siblings and Lacey head this way, picking up their pace when they hear Garrett yelling. Some of the people milling around stop too, unable to pass up on something to gossip about.

"Garrett, please. Just calm down," Emma says, stepping out of my arms, but still staying close to me.

He glares at Emma, his teeth clenching so hard a muscle pops in his cheek. "Calm down?" he spits and points at me. "This jerk takes everything I want and I'm supposed to be *calm?*"

I step forward in warning, my blood pressure rising.

There's the man I met on the side of the road.

His charming façade is gone. This isn't the smiling, composed, friendly Garrett Waterstone, who's fooled so many people. This is all Todd—arrogant, selfish, whiny Todd Weiner, who didn't get what he wanted.

Will, Svea, and Lacey push through the small crowd to my side. Their faces are grave, indicating they overheard what Garrett said, even from a distance.

"Shut it, Ferrett," Svea barks protectively.

Todd startles, blinking in surprise at the name she called him.

A couple of people chuckle. His eyebrows slam down behind his glasses, fists shaking now.

"*What* did you just call me?" he seethes.

"You heard me," Svea answers back, fearless. She folds her arms. "And Lee didn't steal anything from you. Lee and Emma have been in love with each other for years, but neither of them knew the other one felt the same."

Emma's stricken expression melts away for a second as she looks at me.

The crowd starts muttering. Todd notices this, and his face goes red. His eyes turn to slits as he looks at Emma.

"So you strung me along? What the hell is wrong with you?"

I move slightly in front of Emma, anger sparking in my veins. "Don't talk to her like that."

Emma's hand touches my lower back, soothing me slightly.

"No, *you* strung *me* along," Emma says fiercely. "You made me believe you're someone you're not. You did this to yourself."

A slow grin spreads across my face, pride welling up in my chest. I smooth my hand up her spine and wrap my arm around her shoulders. She leans into my side, still glaring at Garrett.

Someone jogs through the crowd as Todd's mouth stretches into a sneer, his nose scrunching up. "You—"

"Damn it, Todd," Ben exclaims, pushing his boss's shoulder. "I told you not to do this!"

"Wait—*Todd*?" Emma says.

The name echoes through the crowd around us, and Todd himself deflates slightly.

"Yeah, his name is Todd," Ben confirms, and then slides me a determined glance. "The great, charming author Garrett Waterstone is really just some arrogant, entitled jerk named Todd Weiner."

Svea bursts out laughing, and the crowd follows suit.

Emma stares at Todd's beet red face, her eyebrows knit together in shock. Safe to assume Todd never told her his real name.

"I prefer Ferrett," Will says with a shrug, grinning at me.

"Ben, what the hell?" Todd hisses, throwing one hand out to the side.

Either Ben has a death wish or he's trying to get fired. Maybe both.

Ben sighs as the laughter quiets down. "Listen, I said I'd work for you because you're my brother."

Emma gasps against my side.

What? Brothers?

He treats his *brother* like this? I didn't think my opinion of Todd could get any worse, but it just did.

Svea and I make eye contact, sharing our surprise, but then she grins like she's watching the conclusion of her favorite movie. The crowd, probably twenty people by now, hushes as Ben continues.

"There's a reason you can't keep an assistant, man. And it doesn't have anything to do with qualifications or dedication or loyalty. It comes down to *you*, and how you treat people."

Todd steels himself, standing tall. "You don't care how I treat *you* though, as long I keep giving you raises, right? What does that say about *you*?"

Svea cups her mouth and lets out a long, loud "Booooo!"

Todd whirls around, shooting her a murderous look.

"What does it say about *you*, Todd, that those glasses aren't prescription?" Ben fires back. "And your eyes are only that blue because you wear colored contacts?"

"Ben!" he spits, indignant.

Laughter breaks out as a few others start booing too.

"There isn't one honest thing about you, Todd. And I'm glad she figured it out before I had to tell her."

Emma stills as the booing picks up even more.

I smile to myself, because Todd never had a chance. Every one of us, even his own brother, has been working against him.

Todd's anger morphs into shock, slackening his features. His chest heaves, glancing around at everyone and their judgment of him. He blinks wide eyes, humiliation hunching his shoulders and back.

He looks at me, anger flickering across his eyebrows, but he knows he's lost. Not just Emma, but his reputation in this small town.

And like the true coward he is, Todd Weiner ducks his head and runs, disappearing through the crowd.

Ben calls after him, "Oh, and I *quit!*"

The boos erupt into cheers.

I turn to Emma, grinning down at her. "I didn't think tonight could get any better, but damn was I wrong."

She snickers, and casts one last look over her shoulder in the direction Todd went. When she looks back at me, she sighs like she's glad the spectacle is over.

The crowd finally leaves, a few staying behind to pat Ben on the back. It really was a spectacle. Larkspur will be talking about this for weeks.

Svea skips over to us, beaming. She throws her arms around Emma, who laughs. Lacey and Will follow, hand in hand.

"Think they'll have a matinee of that show tomorrow?" Will asks. "I'd pay to see it again."

"Ben," I call out, and he steps away from Carly Gustafson. When he reaches us, I thrust out my hand.

He smiles, his eyes crinkling, as he shakes my hand.

"That was amazing," Lacey gushes, hopping on the balls of her feet.

"Thanks," Ben says with a chuckle. He takes in a deep breath and lets it out. "Felt good."

Emma links her fingers with mine. "I'm sure it did. Good for you, Ben."

"It was overdue, believe me." Ben's smile goes tight. "I'm sorry he made such a mess."

Emma looks up at me, smiling softly. "It's alright."

"You're not the first woman he's tried to bamboozle," he says, his brows pinched together with contrition. "But you're the first one I didn't think deserved it."

Emma pats him on the shoulder. "Thank you."

"So what are you going to do now, Ben?" Will asks. "Go back to Minneapolis?"

He shrugs. "Yeah, I think so. And if I had to guess, my brother will too." He glances around at all of us with a chuckle. "My work here is done."

Everything inside and out relaxes as peace rushes through me.

It's *over*.

I let out a deep breath, allowing myself to feel the joy of Emma's love, and the gratitude for my family who had my back while I got up the courage to tell her everything.

I kiss Emma's hand.

All is as it should be.

Chapter
Twenty-Eight

Emma

T hree days later, I'm standing in Lee's kitchen as we make dinner.

He worked on Sunday and yesterday, and because it was his turn for overnight shifts, I only saw him once when he came into the library to return his book before work. He caught up on his sleep today, but he still looks a little tired.

Even though I haven't gotten to see him much the last couple of days, we've been texting quite a bit. He explained his work schedule rotates and changes, and has apologized for it at least twice because it isn't something he can control.

He's also warned me he isn't as good a cook as Will is, but he seemed to know what he was doing when he threw the steaks on the grill a few minutes ago.

"I promise we'll go on a real date soon," Lee grumbles, glancing at me apologetically from where he's chopping up a head of lettuce at the kitchen island. "I have to work all weekend, so maybe next weekend, if you're not busy?"

I smile at him gently. "This could count as a real first date. It doesn't have to be some formal thing."

He sets the knife down and moves the chopped lettuce into a bowl with his hands.

"You deserve something special." Even when he says something sweet, it comes out growly. I love it.

"Any time with you feels special. And for some reason—I really like doing low-key things like this," I explain. Mostly because it doesn't quite feel real. Being with him in his house, kissing him, holding his hand, all of it has this sweet, fuzzy, dream-like quality. And as much as I love it now, I know I'll still love those simple things with him even when the novelty of it has worn off.

Lee tips his head slightly to the side. "I do too. But I've waited years to love you outside of my head, so if you don't mind, I'll be spoiling the hell out of you whenever I can."

My eyebrows rise a little before I giggle. His serious expression softens.

"I'm just sorry about my work schedule. It's not ideal but—"

"I know, Lee," I interrupt, laughing. "You don't have to keep apologizing. It's fine."

The intensity of his brown eyes doesn't fade. "I just want to see you every night, and I hate that I can't."

I lean over and kiss him on the cheek. It puts a little of the sparkle back in his eyes. "You know, I had a thought today when I was talking to Henry. We were trying to decide which books we should do for when you lead storytime."

Lee steps closer, abandoning the salad he was making. He takes my hand and kisses it quickly. "What's that?"

"Does the school have a resource officer?"

My question catches him off guard, his thick eyebrows lifting.

"It would be the perfect job for you—you'd still be a police officer, but you'd also get to work with kids. It would be both of your passions in one job."

Lee blinks and says nothing for a long moment. I smile softly up at him as he processes what I said.

I love him so much.

The way he takes his time to figure out what he wants to say. The way his mind works through it all before his mouth says the smallest, bite-sized version of whatever he was thinking about.

"Hmm," he hums, and my smile cracks a little wider. "The department already has a resource officer, but...he's close to retirement."

"Hmm," I echo, letting him pull me closer. His arms move around me, and I twine mine around his neck.

"Maybe I'll talk to Chief about it." The corner of Lee's mouth pulls back in the tiniest little smirk and then he shakes his head, almost in disbelief. "How do you know me better than I know myself?" he mutters as he leans down and kisses me.

My heartbeat skyrockets, making my fingertips tingle.

Lee has no idea how powerful his kisses are. Even the small, quick ones reach all the way to the depths of me. Even those have me blushing like my face is made of lava. Kissing him is everything I was scared it would be. There isn't one *nice* thing about being with him. It's all big, raw, intense. Enough to level all of my defenses.

He pulls away and then ducks back down for one more peck before going out to the deck to check on the steaks.

I take over making the salad, grinning to myself as I cut up cucumbers and cherry tomatoes.

I've looked through the flower book three more times since he gave it to me on Saturday. Every time it calms my fears about losing him the way my mom lost my dad.

Death changes nothing.

And he's right. Death doesn't stop love from existing. Love just ends up wearing a heavy coat of grief, and though that's definitely not ideal, it would be far worse to never let myself be with the man I love. I'd just wear a heavy coat of regret my entire life instead. That coat sounds much heavier to me.

There's nothing I could do for him that would have the same impact and meaning as the book he gave me. I've been wracking my brain for something romantic, and the only thing I come back to again and again is just...loving him well for the rest of my life.

Even the best romance novel in the world couldn't have prepared me for what it's like to be loved by Lee Christiansen. Not even seeing the love my parents had prepared me. I won't take one single day with him for granted. I won't let the fear of losing him steal my happiness now.

I can't believe I ever even seriously considered not taking the Lee road. Especially when the Garrett road turned out to be a sketchy back road and not one that led to the happily ever after Garrett was trying to convince me was at the end.

Lee comes back in with two plates, one bearing the steaks and the other with baked potatoes. My eyes linger on him as he covers the meat with aluminum foil.

I can't imagine how horrible it must've felt for him to watch me with someone else. Knowing what I know now—how he feels about me—it must've been torture to see me hold Garrett's hand and show interest in him.

Lee catches me looking at him, and his brows pinch in concern when he sees my guilty expression. "What's wrong?"

I let out a sigh and step away from the cutting board. "I want to explain about Garrett."

Lee's face goes flat. "I'd be happy if we never talked about him ever again."

"I know. But I...I want to clear up something."

He watches me a little warily, but nods.

"The only reason I was interested in him was because he—"

I pause when his face goes so sour I wouldn't be surprised if he was about to vomit. I snicker and reach for his hand. "Garrett was *nice*. Nothing about him made me feel deeply. I would've had a nice, safe life with him, and if he died young like my dad did, I would've been fine."

Lee's nauseous expression fades.

"Being with him was less about *him* and more about me trying to protect myself from how much I loved you." I swallow hard. "I had to figure out that the risk of losing you wouldn't be as painful as regretting it if I never let myself love you at all." I shake my head up at him, tears stinging my eyes. "So I'm sorry if—if I hurt you because I considered Garrett for a bit."

He lifts his hand and strokes my cheek. "It did hurt to see you with him," he admits, his growly voice low. "But I know you weren't doing it to hurt me on purpose, Em."

My heart flutters as he lets go of my cheek and takes my hand, looking at me with love in his eyes.

"I didn't need you to explain, but I appreciate understanding where your head was at." He kisses my forehead, and I feel it in my soul.

"It took me too long to realize what he was really like."

"I'm sure he fools a lot of people," he assures me and then squeezes my hand three times.

I nod.

"Let's eat," Lee says, pressing one more kiss to my forehead.

I sit next to him at the kitchen island and we eat quietly. Not uncomfortably. Just...quietly. Each of us in our own heads, and it makes me want to sigh with contentment. Despite what he said about going on a "real first date," I really do love this. I remember what he said about not being able to whisk me away on vacations or buy me jewelry. He was apologetic about that, but I couldn't care less.

All I need is this. Just us. Just him.

Two weeks later, the library is full of kids. Storytime is usually a hit, but today there's an even bigger crowd on the rug than usual. I recognize the little boy Lee pretended to pull over weeks ago, sitting at the front with his big eyes glued to the love of my life.

Lee's sitting in the velvet green chair, where I usually sit for story-time, holding *Police Officers on Patrol* by Kersten Hamilton. His voice is low and quiet, but his eyes are bright as he reads to the kids.

I haven't seen him in uniform very often, but I can confirm the man looks *good*. His stocky frame fills out the dark blue material in all the best ways—ways I have every right to appreciate because I love him and he loves me. Because he's *mine*.

My heart might burst with happiness. There's nothing better than seeing Lee interacting with kids in my favorite place in the world.

"Lee's doing good," Regina whispers, joining me where I'm standing in front of the counter.

I smile at her, filled with pride.

"Way better than what's his face would've done."

It's safe to say Larkspur was quick to turn on Garrett Waterstone. By the next morning, everyone was talking about his horrible behavior, helped along by his awful treatment of his own brother.

Henry was the most upset, and still refuses to participate in conversations involving him. A close second was Lee's dad, who gave his signed Garrett Waterstone books to Lee and told him to sell them.

I loop my arm through Regina's. "Absolutely," I whisper back.

She squeezes my arm, keeping her voice down. "It's a shame he turned out to be such a snake. Guess that's why they say to never meet your heroes."

I squeeze her arm too as Lee finishes the book and closes it.

He smiles wide as the kids clap for him, flashing me a pleased glance before Regina and I jump in to hand out coloring sheets. Most kids get right to coloring, finding spots at the tables or on the rug, but some crowd around Lee to ask him questions. These questions vary from "have you ever shot your gun?" to "what's your favorite color?" But he rolls with it, and I can see from the relaxed smile on his face that he's enjoying this.

My heart swells for him, and I hope he can step into the resource officer position in the Spring. Lee talked to Chief about it last week and said he seemed in favor of it.

As if he can feel my gaze, his eyes meet mine. My blush is all love and no shyness.

It hits me that only a month ago, I thought he didn't know I existed. He's shown me over and over again just how wrong I was. And I'm determined to show him every day how easy it is to love him.

Lee excuses himself from the small group of kids, and comes over to me.

Me.

I still can't quite believe it.

My phone buzzes in the pocket of my cardigan. A twin buzzing comes from Lee's pocket as he reaches me.

We frown at each other curiously and check our phones.

There's a message from Svea in the group text chain. She very sweetly added me a few days ago. I don't think they realized that by adding me, I was able to scroll up and see all of their conversations the last couple of weeks. Knowing what I know now about Garrett, I'm glad they were conspiring to keep me away from him.

Svea: *He left!*

Lee looks up, staring for a second, before he smiles.

My heart skips a beat, and I smile back.

Will: *Who?*
Svea: *Ferrett!! Clay said he left last week!*

"Well, that's good news," Lee says. "Now we won't run into him around town."

I nod, sticking my phone back in my pocket. He does the same and takes both of my hands.

"It's for the best," I say with a sigh of relief.

"Yes."

The Garrett road no longer exists now. I can leave that chapter in the past where it belongs. I'd much rather focus on this chapter and the ones yet to come.

I go up on my tiptoes and peck Lee on the lips. He looks down at me with all the affection I never believed he felt for me before this.

"Love you," he says, all gruff and grumbly. "Always."

"Always have and always will," I whisper back.

Chapter Twenty-Nine

Lee

T he fire crackles from the fire pit in my parents' backyard, sending little pops of glowing embers up into the night air. Emma's curled up sideways on my lap, our combined weight possibly exceeding the limit of the camp chair we're sharing. Fireflies hover in the grass beyond the fire pit, their blinking light casting a bit of magic on the scene.

It's been three incredible weeks since I told her I loved her. I brought her to *fika* for the first time this afternoon, and we stayed so long that it turned into dinner. I wasn't sure if Emma would be overwhelmed by my family, but when I gave her an out once dinnertime came, she said she wanted to stay. My siblings and Lacey are here too, and I expected them to tease me whenever I touched Emma, but they just smiled to themselves.

My family is inside, cleaning up after dinner. I can hear Mamma's voice drifting through the open kitchen window as she sings "Så *rider jag mig*" which is a Swedish folk song. It's a haunting tune I've heard her sing many times before, but tonight it hits me hard.

"What is she singing?" Emma asks me quietly, her head tucked beneath my chin. Her fingers are moving lightly down my forearm and across the hand I have resting on her knee.

I hesitate because it isn't a happy song, even if Mamma enjoys singing it.

"It's a song about a man who doesn't know his love has died."

Emma stills against me.

"He's going to see her, making his way through town. He asks the bell-ringers who they're ringing their bells for, and they say it's for a young woman who's going to be laid to rest. Then he comes upon the gravediggers and he asks them who the grave is for. They answer the same, and then he gets to her house to find she's dead and being prepared for burial." I stroke my other hand up and down her back. "Everyone says he'll find someone else quickly, but he says there isn't a woman like her in all the kingdoms."

"That's so sad," she whispers.

Pappa joins Mamma on the last line about there not being a woman like her anywhere else.

I kiss the top of her head. "It's a song about love surviving death," I whisper back.

She lifts her head so she can look at me. There's a bittersweet sort of expression on her face. "*Jag älskar dig.*" One side of her mouth curves up. "I've been practicing."

I smile at her and lift my hand from her knee so I can sink my fingers through her glossy black hair. When I get to the nape of her neck, I leave it there as I move in to kiss her.

She sighs into me, kissing me back languidly. I forget where we are. Everything around us disappears, and it's just my mouth moving with hers, speaking all the words I can't find to explain how deeply I love her.

"Oh my god, they're making out!" shouts Svea from behind us.

Emma startles as we break apart. She tries to get up, but I clamp my arm around her waist tightly, grinning at the way her face has gone perfectly crimson. My face is hot too, but I couldn't care less.

Lacey squeals in excitement as they join us around the fire pit. Will and my parents appear too, taking their chairs.

Emma keeps her face turned in my direction, embarrassed but smiling too. I kiss the tip of her nose, and she just shakes her head with a soft laugh.

SWEDE ON YOU   249

As everyone settles in, Mamma narrows her eyes at me. "How is Lars?"

I give her a tight smile. "I haven't seen him much, Mamma. Think he's trying to lie low for a while."

All the faces around the fire turn somber.

"You'd think he'd be relieved to be free of her," Lacey comments.

"It's more complicated than that," I say, and hesitate for a moment while I decide to give them a little information. These are people who care about Lars, who wouldn't repeat his business to anyone.

"Things between him and Amber didn't end well. Their last fight resulted in her trashing his house."

Svea's mouth drops open.

Lacey gasps.

Mamma mutters something angry in Swedish that I can't make out.

Emma smooths her hand over mine, her dark eyebrows pinched in concern behind her glasses.

"Oh, that's terrible," Pappa says. "Mark said he's pretty down in the dumps, but I didn't know she did all of that."

I nod. "Yeah...she broke most of Grandma Janssen's antique plates and everything."

Svea literally growls. I blink at her, but I shouldn't be surprised by her protectiveness. It's definitely something I understand. She's just as fierce as I am when it comes to the people she loves.

"Well," Will says quietly, "the most important thing is that it's over. Hopefully he can heal and move on."

"Is she still around?" Svea asks through slightly clenched teeth. "Like, did she leave town, or...?"

"I don't know," I answer, and slide her a smirk. "If I see her, I'll let you know."

She smiles but there's an evil glint to it that I recognize. If Amber ever does come back, Svea will be the first in line to make her regret it.

"He might not want to hang out as much," Emma says gently, "but you should keep trying."

I nod. "Yeah, I won't give up on him."

Emma nods too.

It took me a long time to tell her how I feel. It took a long time for me to believe Emma could want me, and believe I was worthy of her. Soon, when he comes out of hiding, I hope Lars can look at me as an example. I hope he'll recognize I'm happy because I'm with the right person, and believe he can find the right person for him. There has to be someone in Larkspur...*someone* who would love him the way I love Emma.

I don't follow the conversation from there as my family talks. Their voices are distant, like they're still coming from inside the house. My parents are sitting to my left, and Emma's attention stays on them as they chat. I imagine she's seeing something she misses—her own parents together, flirting, teasing, talking over each other as they try to tell the same story.

I squeeze her hand three times, and she looks up at me. "Does that mean something?" she whispers, returning my three squeezes with three of her own.

A zing of nerves hits my stomach, but it doesn't hang around. The truth will be sweet to her.

"As a teenager, I stopped saying I love you back when Mamma said it to me," I explain quietly. "I was just being a dumb kid who was embarrassed to say it back, especially in front of Lars or whatever. So she took me aside and said I could say I love you by squeezing her hand three times, one squeeze for each word."

Emma's eyes widen.

I smile at her softly. "Sometimes it's squeezes. Sometimes it's knocks or taps."

Her mouth falls open.

"But—but you've been doing that for years..." she whisper-shouts. "When you leave the library...you knock on the counter three times."

I smile as her shock melts into something softer, sweeter. "You've been telling me for *years*, and I had no idea."

I just shrug.

"*Själsfrände*," Mamma says to us, smiling.

She holds my gaze meaningfully, and I smile back at her. Then she turns to Pappa, saying something to him in a low voice.

My chest goes warm.

"What did she say?" Emma asks.

"*Själsfrände*," I repeat gently, taking in every beautiful feature of her face. "It means..."

I pause, letting my head fall back against the headrest. Peace like I've never known wraps me up. I tuck her hair behind one ear. "It means *soulmates*."

Emma's smile is slow, growing into a beaming beacon. "Teach me how to say it."

I repeat it for her, breaking the word into parts, but she struggles to get it right. I grin through the entire thing, loving that she wants to learn what she can of Mamma's first language.

After several tries, she giggles at her attempts. "I'm not good with my mouth," she explains in both frustration and good humor.

"I beg to differ."

Her eyes go wide at my innuendo, and then we both descend into laughter. Without a doubt, my family thinks I've lost my mind, but I don't know for sure because I bury my face in the space between her neck and shoulder, gasping and huffing and laughing like I've never laughed before. Happier than I've ever been before.

Epilogue

Lee

I push through the front door, taking care not to stomp inside the house. Quietly, I take off my shoes and move down the hall to the kitchen, shaking my head at the light spilling across the floor from the living room.

Overnights have never been my favorite shift, but they're by far my least favorite now that Will moved out and Emma moved in. She doesn't like falling asleep without me, so she usually stays up reading on the couch.

I smile at her, sprawled out against the armrest with one leg peeking out from beneath her favorite navy-blue cable knit blanket. The book she was reading is open, lying across her chest. Her glasses are askew on her sleeping face.

Sneaking closer, I carefully take the book. I take a second to find her bookmark where it landed on the floor. I put it into the book and set it on the coffee table. Then I move the blanket aside and bend down, slipping one arm beneath her legs and the other behind her back. I lift her into my arms and carry her toward the bedroom.

This isn't the first time I've carried her to bed after an overnight shift, and it won't be the last. I don't mind one bit.

She yawns, one hand moving over my shoulder.

"Hi, *Älskling*," I murmur.

She hums contentedly, but then her eyes spring open. "Wait! My book—" she exclaims, half-awake and reaching with one hand toward the couch behind us.

"I marked your page," I assure her with a chuckle, and she relaxes again.

I bring her into the dark bedroom and lay her down on her side of the bed. She takes off her glasses and sets them on the nightstand while I cover her up.

"Be right back," I whisper, kissing her temple.

I make quick work of changing and brushing my teeth in the bathroom and then I'm back, sliding into bed. She scoots back against me and I wrap an arm around her.

She'll have to be up in an hour to get ready for work, but we both would rather have the hour together like this.

It's a dream, coming home to her.

Over the last four months, we've spent a lot of our time here. Cooking, reading, and talking about anything and everything. She has dinner at her mom's twice a week, and I try to join them at least one of those times. We go to *fika* or dinner at my parent's house at least once a week too. Sometimes we go to The Swedish Chef to eat, or sometimes we order in. Once or twice, Emma has gone over to Svea's apartment and had a girls' night with her and Lacey.

The number of bookshelves in the house has tripled since she moved in. This Spring I plan on building some built-in bookshelves in the living room, which will basically cover one entire wall. I'd like to surprise her with it, but I haven't figured out how to get her out of the house long enough for me to pull it off.

Christmas is next month, and she's already excited to experience some of the Swedish Christmas traditions I grew up with. I'm excited because I want to ask her to marry me on Christmas Eve. Not in front of my family, at my parents' house, but here at home, when it's just us.

The more time passes, the more I'm sure that even if Emma and I don't get to spend the rest of our lives together, whatever time we have will be enough.

Sometimes she still gets a worried, pinched look on her face—the one meaning she's feeling scared. I don't think that fear will ever totally go away for her. Losing her dad so suddenly will always bleed over into what we have.

When it does, I remind her that love is the strongest thing and not even death could stop it. I don't care if I have to say it and show it a thousand more times in the years ahead, because I know at the root of her fear is love. And I'll gladly take her love, even if she gives it to me shaking and trembling.

I'll never take for granted that she's chosen to love me. I know full well what she could have chosen instead—what she was tempted to choose instead of me.

Speaking of Todd Weiner, he hasn't set foot in Larkspur since he left. I wouldn't be surprised if his new novel depicts a corrupt, police officer. I don't care what he does or where he is. But sometimes I almost feel like thanking him. If he hadn't shown up here, I might have wasted even more time not going after the girl of my dreams.

Emma sighs in my arms and squeezes my hand three times. I squeeze hers back, and everything inside and out relaxes.

I used to dread the future in a way I couldn't explain to other people. But the future is what I have the most excitement about now. I get to make *plans* now. And every one of those plans includes Emma.

Getting married.

Changing to resource officer in April.

Moving into a bigger house. Having kids and raising them together.

There's nothing I'm not looking forward to.

There's a Swedish proverb that goes, "A life without love is like a year without summer." And I'm so glad that my years without summer are behind me. Every day feels like summer because of her, even now as winter encroaches on fall.

I sink slowly into sleep, breathing in her sweet scent. I do the same thing I do every night when I'm falling asleep. I picture her walking toward me in a gorgeous white dress, smiling and reaching for me.

Maybe this time next year, it won't be a daydream I play on loop. Maybe by then it'll be a memory of the best day of my life.

Then again, I know that every day, even a boring, uneventful one, is automatically the best day of my life because she's in it.

Acknowledgements

Phew! What a marathon this book was. Lee and Emma's story was me on a wild goose chase trying to make an idea work that just *did not work*. I wrote this book at least three times over before I stopped, panicked, freaked out, and accepted that my idea was wrong. Once I let go of the wrong idea, I was able to come up with the right one, and this version flew out of my fingers in just six and a half weeks. Boy, did I learn my lesson—if something isn't working, try something else!

The last two years have been absolutely nuts in terms of my health and personal life, and there was definitely a moment about nine months before finishing this book that I seriously considered quitting this author thing. I'm so glad I didn't. Honestly, I impressed myself with how quickly I went from possibly quitting to completing a final manuscript. I couldn't be more pleased that this book is in your hands.

Thank you to everyone who asked when the next book was coming out, and thank you so much for reading this one. I hope you love Lee and Emma as much I do! The Love in Larkspur Series has been such a sweet journey, and I can't wait to tell Svea's story next. I won't make you wait two years for it, I promise.

In the middle of writing this, I had to find a new editor. That was a curveball I didn't see coming, but it ended up working in my favor. Teresa, I was absolutely terrified when I hired you, but I couldn't have made this book into what it is without your incredible (sometimes brutal but never unkind) editing skills. Thank you for laughing at all the right places and hating Garrett even more than I do.

Special thanks to Mike Thull for answering my many questions about law enforcement. Your thoughtful answers were so helpful in rounding out Lee's profession. Thank you for what you do!

Thank you, Emily, for telling me it was okay to start over with a new idea. Thank you for talking it through with me and getting me to see that I had to let go of what wasn't working.

Thank you to Lyndsey, who stayed up until 3am reading my unedited manuscript! Your feedback was so valuable and being able to ask you specific questions about things was so helpful. Thank you for being my biggest fan. You know that I'm yours.

And thank you to Jon, that guy I married. You've never doubted me and never stopped supporting me, even when I thought about quitting. Thank you for going on this ride with me. I love you.

About The Author

Katie Stearns is a contemporary romance author from Southwestern MN. She lives in a 125 year old farmhouse with her husband, two amazing little girls, and their German Shorthair Pointer, Porkchop. In what little spare time she has, she enjoys baking, photography, reading and rereading romance novels by her favorite authors, traveling with her husband, and watching *The Office*. She's always daydreaming about the next story.

Also By Katie Stearns

On The Dotted Line

Bridges Duet
Water Under The Bridge
Burning Bridges

Love in Larkspur Series
There's No Place Like Gnome

www.ingramcontent.com/pod-product-compliance
Lightning Source LLC
Chambersburg PA
CBHW020130120726
47903CB00007B/2182